# The Other Side Of *Someday*

### A New Romantic Comedy

USA Today Bestselling Author

# T.K. LEIGH

The Other Side Of Someday

Published by Carpe Per Diem, Inc. / Tracy Kellam, 25852 McBean Parkway # 806, Santa Clarita, CA 91355

Edited by: Kim Young, Kim's Editing Services

Cover Design: Cat Head Biscuit, Inc., Santa Clarita, CA

Front Cover Image Copyright Masson 2014
Back Cover Image Copyright aradaphotography 2014
Used under license from Shutterstock.com

To my own Other Side Of Somedays…
Stan and Miss Harper Leigh…

# CHAPTER ONE

"Mmm...," I MOANED, BASKING in the luxurious Egyptian cotton sheets caressing my skin. A whisper of breath warmed my mouth, followed by a soft tongue. It had been ages since I had woken up to the feel of a man's mouth on mine, so I didn't want the moment to end. Keeping my eyes blissfully closed, I tried to remember the previous night. Nothing momentous stood out in my mind, and I certainly couldn't recall meeting a handsome young stranger whom I would so willingly invite into my bed.

The mysterious tongue grazed my cheek and I inhaled, only to be assaulted by a vile stench. I flung my eyes open, my dopey beagle-terrier mix smiling his excited smile at me. Wiping my mouth, I turned away from the dog, pulling the duvet over my head.

"Sport, Mommy's sleeping," I groaned, still half asleep. I would give anything to return to the dream I had been having. There was a man... I didn't recall much about what he looked like, but he had the most mesmerizing blue eyes I'd ever seen. Every time he smiled, my heart picked up just a little bit. When he leaned in to kiss me, my leg kicked out slightly, just like the leading lady's did after her first kiss with the object of her desire in all those romance movies I watched...until the funk of Sport's breath ruined my perfectly innocent fantasy.

Sport burrowed beneath the comforter and found me. He incessantly licked my face, his friendly reminder that he needed to go for a walk. He'd never let me fall back to sleep, so I sat up. Wiping my eyes, I stretched, yawning as I adjusted to my surroundings.

"California," I murmured. The past few weeks seemed like a blur as I gazed out the sliding glass doors at the Pacific Ocean from fourteen floors up. The sunlight rising behind the building made the water sparkle and dance.

A month ago, I was living in the same town I had spent the past twenty-eight years of my life. I was still married to my high school sweetheart. I was happy to maintain the same life I had since birth...until something inside of me snapped, probably the result of walking in on my former husband balls deep in my former best friend on the kitchen island of the house I had paid for with my inheritance.

Despite Will's begging and pleading, I filed for divorce, hired movers to pack my belongings, and left North Carolina with his dog. I knew it was immature and spiteful, but I couldn't let Sport grow up in a house with a revolving door of women. Will was pissed and rightfully so, but I knew him. He would simply replace the dog, just as he would replace me with the flavor of the day.

A wet tongue met my cheek, bringing me back to the present. "Okay, boy," I said to Sport. "Want to go explore your new home?"

The thirty pound dog barked excitedly and darted off the bed, running circles through my legs. I padded across the hardwood floor and rummaged through my suitcase, pulling on a pair of yoga pants and a long-sleeved t-shirt over my tank top. Sliding on my flip-flops, I made my way into the hallway and down a set of stairs, entering the open living area.

I hadn't had a chance to take in my new home since arriving late last night. Still, I couldn't really get a feel for the place, nearly every corner filled with boxes the movers had arranged in the condo while I took my time driving across the country. The lower level was flooded with natural light from the floor-to-ceiling windows adorning most of the walls. The architecture had an almost industrial feel to it. The kitchen was any chef's dream and I couldn't wait to finally settle in and put it to use, despite my relatively mediocre cooking skills.

Sport's paws clicked on the hardwood floors as he ran around the living room, exploring. "Come on, buddy! Let's go for a walk," I called out. He ran toward me, sliding across the travertine tile in the kitchen area and practically slamming into the wall. I laughed to myself. "It's going to take a bit to get used to not having carpeting, isn't it, pal?" He sat on his hind legs and raised his liver-spotted paw.

Finding his collar on the kitchen island, I clipped it around his neck and hooked him up to his leash. He jumped, grabbing part of the leash in his mouth, and we left my new penthouse condo.

After the elevator whisked me down fourteen floors, I sauntered through the lobby and emerged onto Ocean Avenue in Santa Monica, smiling at the doorman and inhaling the late September air. It was a comfortable day. There was a slight chill, but the sun was already beaming, even at eight in the morning.

"Smog," I snorted. "Better than horse shit, I guess." I glanced over my shoulder, hoping no one had heard me talking to myself. The doorman tipped his hat at me and I cringed. "You heard that?" I asked.

"Heard what?" he responded slyly.

"Okay then."

I turned back around and waited for the WALK signal at the crosswalk.

"For the record, ma'am, you'll get used to the smog."

I couldn't help but laugh as I crossed the street to Palisades Park, a grin on my face. For the first time, I actually felt grateful Will couldn't keep his willy in his pants. If he hadn't been stupid enough to bang my best friend at the precise time he knew I would be home every night, I would still be stuck in North Carolina, miserable and waiting for my life to truly begin. Now, I finally had the opportunity to make my dreams a reality, and what better place to do that than somewhere with sun, sand, and surfers?

"What do you think, Sport?" I glimpsed at the amused expression on his furry face as he set his eyes on the ocean for the first time in his life. "Happy to be out of Carolina?" He looked back at me, his tongue hanging out of his mouth as he sniffed every tree and bench we passed, and I knew he was thrilled with his new zip code.

"And the best part? It doesn't snow here, bud! No more having to go out in nasty weather!" I surveyed his reaction, which remained the same. It didn't take much to make a dog happy. Give him a place to shit while looking at the crashing waves of the ocean and he's as happy as can be.

Allowing Sport's leash a little more slack, I stared at the water, tuning out the sound of horns and cars as they drove along the coast of Santa Monica. The waves were peaceful and serene, and I felt a renewed energy.

When I pulled away from the small town in North Carolina I had grown up in, I almost turned my car around at least a dozen times. The thought of leaving the only life I had ever known petrified me. Most women my age probably went through that when they were eighteen and headed off to college for the first time. I never had that experience. Now, as I stared at the Pacific Ocean, sailboats and surfers bobbing up and down in the water, I started to think I was finally where I belonged.

"Why would anyone want to live anywhere else?" I mused out loud.

A sudden and unexpected strong yank on Sport's leash woke me from my thoughts, startling me. Unable to react quickly enough, his leash slipped out of my hand and I watched in horror as he darted down the paved path, apparently on a mission.

"Sport! Heal! Stop! Slow down!" I shouted, trying to get him to obey my lackluster command. It was completely useless. I was never the dog's master. This was just another reminder of that fact.

Chasing him through the park, I was relieved when he finally slowed his pace. However, that relief was short-lived once I saw what had captured his attention so suddenly.

"Sport! No!" My eyes growing wide, my face turned red in embarrassment when he attempted to mount a light-haired dog that easily outweighed him by twenty pounds.

Struggling to catch my breath, I grabbed Sport's chest, doing my best to pry him off the other dog, who didn't seem to mind the affection. "I'm so sorry," I said to the owner of Sport's new girlfriend, keeping my eyes cast downward. For a small dog, Sport was freakishly strong, especially when he was about to get some. "He's fixed, but he has a tendency to take after his daddy."

"Don't worry about it," the stranger replied, both of us attempting to separate our dogs. "Enjoying the love, are ya, girl?"

Just when I couldn't be any more horrified, things took a turn for the worse. "Oh, my god, Sport! Lipstick in! There are people around, buddy! If you were human, your ass would be on the sexual offender registry!"

He ignored me and continued to hump the other dog's leg, his size prohibiting him from getting any higher.

"This may just be the most embarrassing thing ever," I remarked, my breathing labored.

"I'd say more amusing than embarrassing."

"All right, buddy. That's enough."

I leaned in with the intention of using every ounce of strength I possessed to pry my dog off his girl, my motions fast and quick... Too fast and quick. Giving one final tug, my head slammed into the stranger's nose, a faint crack echoing.

"Shit! I'm so sorry," I apologized, no longer worried about my dog's sexual promiscuity. Embarrassment turned into absolute humiliation as I looked up to see this complete stranger holding his nose, blood streaming down his face and into his hands.

"Okay. *Now* you can probably call this the most embarrassing thing ever." He laughed, remaining composed, despite my reaction.

"Here." I rummaged through my bag, pulling out a

messy pile of tissues. "Use this to stop the flow of blood." I held the tissues out to him. "We need to get you to the hospital." I frantically scanned the park, unsure of how far I was from my condo building.

"Thanks, but it's not a big deal."

"But your nose… It's got to be broken." I observed his blood seeping through the tissues.

"It's not broken," he assured me in a nasal tone. "I'd know if it were. You know that kid in elementary school who always suffered from bloody noses? Well, that was me. And it never goes away. All I have to do is bump it and the flood gates open, but it stops pretty quickly." He winked as a warm smile crossed his full lips. In the midst of trying to pry my dog off his, I hadn't taken a second to even look at him. Now that I was, I wanted to rewind the clock so I could perhaps brush my teeth and run a comb through my hair before leaving my condo. He had to be in his thirties and was at least six feet tall. As he lifted his arm to keep the tissues pressed to his nose, he revealed a slight sliver of skin between his t-shirt and shorts.

"See," he said, snapping me back to reality and away from mentally undressing him in my mind. I had read my fair share of romance novels. All the leading men seemed to have a six-pack and a V that disappeared below their shorts. I imagined this man was endowed with such a physique. That was how I pictured him in my mind, anyway.

Removing the tissues from his face, he continued, "It stops as soon as it starts."

I studied his nose. Just moments ago, a gush of blood was running down his face. Now there was nothing, other than a few streaks of dried blood. My gaze roamed from his nose to his gray-blue eyes that seemed to dance with amusement. My uncle always said you could tell a lot about a person from their eyes. I didn't know if that were true or not, but I got the feeling this was a man who didn't take anything in life too seriously, who was just along for the ride, letting the journey take him where it should.

"This was certainly an unexpected way to wake me up before I've even had my morning coffee," he added when I remained silent. If I were him, I would have questioned my ability to form a basic sentence. Raising his eyebrows, he crossed his arms in front of his chest.

Tearing my eyes from his, my face burned with embarrassment. "I don't know which is worse," I began, trying to act like the twenty-eight-year-old woman I was, and not the thirteen-year-old schoolgirl who was drooling all over Logan Benson, the new kid who had just moved to our small town from Atlanta. All the girls seemed to lose half their brain cells whenever he was near, myself included. "My dog humping yours, me breaking your nose, or all of this happening before you've even had a chance to have your morning coffee."

A playful smile crossed his face and I couldn't help but stare. Truthfully, it was more like gawking with a hint of drooling. A bit of scruff covered his chin and upper lip. The combination of the cargo shorts and olive-colored t-shirt brought forward all sorts of fantasies of this man having been deployed on a secret mission for the past week, just now returning to civilization. My imagination ran wild with various scenarios involving loaded weapons, zip ties, and rope.

That was what six months without getting laid can do to a girl.

"I think it's the combination of all three that really makes this a day I'll not soon forget," he commented.

"Grenade launcher," I mumbled, still lost in my fantasy world.

"What?"

"Nothing," I answered quickly, cringing that my internal thoughts didn't stay that way. "Why don't you let me buy you a coffee? It's the least I can do for assaulting you."

"You don't have to," he insisted. "Really. It's no big deal."

"Well, if you won't let me buy you a coffee, how about you point me in the direction of the nearest Starbucks? I just moved and all my stuff is still in boxes, coffee maker included."

"I'll do you one better. I'll show you myself. I'm a bit jet-lagged from getting in late last night and could use the caffeine."

I opened my mouth to protest.

"This way," he directed before I could say anything, heading south.

Frozen in place, I was dumbfounded as to why a man I had given a bloody nose to would go out of his way to walk with me to the closest coffee shop. Was he a serial killer? Would he abduct me and take me to his secret lair? He didn't exactly look like a mass murderer. Then again, neither did Ted Bundy.

"Are you coming?" He glanced over his shoulder, winking.

His wink was like pancakes on a Saturday morning.

His wink was like watermelon on a hot summer day.

His wink was like sniffing your dog's paws... Okay,

that one may not sound too enticing, but trust me. If you've ever owned a dog, you know exactly what I'm talking about.

His wink made me forget all about him being a potential serial killer.

"Not yet, but there's still time for that," I muttered as I caught up to him, tugging Sport with me. We walked along the ocean for a while, then the Santa Monica Pier came into view. A lightness ran through my chest at the idea that I was here, that I set out to do something and I actually followed through. No one had talked me out of it. No one had given me a guilt trip about being selfish. I was in charge of my own destiny for the first time since I could remember.

"What kind of dog is she?" I asked, breaking the silence. It seemed awkward to me. Silence always had that effect on me. It made me nervous.

"She's a labrador-boxer mix. She's probably got some other stuff mixed in, but that's what they figured at the shelter when I adopted Gidget."

"Gidget?" I stopped abruptly. "Is that seriously your dog's name?"

He faced me and shrugged, running his fingers through his light brown hair. "What can I say? I'm a sucker for old beach movies and Sandra Dee."

I eyed him suspiciously. Part of me wondered if Will had bribed this guy to spy on me, but I knew he wouldn't care enough to do so. All he cared about after I left was getting his dog back, and I had already put my foot down on that matter. He was an unfit parent.

"What?" he pushed when I remained silent. "Did I say something wrong?"

"Sorry," I responded, continuing down the path

once more. "You just seem too young to like that movie. I remember watching it with my dad when I was a little girl and dreaming of having my own surf shack on the beach, although I doubt I'd have the coordination to surf."

"I may have dressed up as Big Kahuna for Halloween when I was ten."

I laughed. "I wanted to be Gidget one year, but she was blonde," I admitted, gesturing to my red hair. "So I was relegated to being Annie. You seem to be more like Moondoggie, if you ask me."

He stopped walking and stared at me, his lips turned up at the corners, a small, but heartwarming smile drawn on his mouth. "Who *are* you? I didn't think anyone else liked that movie. At least no one our age."

"Hey!" I punched him playfully. "Don't assume we're the same age."

"Fine. How old are you?"

I gasped in faux shock. "Didn't your mother teach you it's rude to ask a lady her age?" I played up my southern accent and bat my eyelashes. "Especially a complete stranger?"

"Oh, she raised me to be a perfect gentleman," he responded as we came to a stop at a crosswalk by the pier. "But there's a time and a place for everything." He took a step closer.

My entire body flamed from the way he was gazing at me, as if I were a meal and he had gone hungry for days. "Don't you think?" He raised his eyebrows and licked his lips, surveying my petite frame. I would have given anything to know what he was thinking at that moment. I was pretty sure it wasn't about the upcoming Presidential election.

"Yes." I swallowed hard, backing against a metal pole. I had nowhere to go as he drew closer and closer. My heart thumped in my chest, and I couldn't help but think that LA was a *very* friendly town. Or maybe my original gut instinct was right and he *was* Ted Bundy's protégé. His breath whispered against my neck as he leaned toward me, his arm reaching for my waist. He pressed the WALK request button on the pole and stepped back.

I took a deep breath, trying to get my raging hormones under control. I had no idea if this guy was flirting with me or if I was so sexually deprived, I was making it all up in my head. I was starting to lean toward the latter.

"So you just moved to town?" he inquired as if nothing had just almost transpired between us. "Where were you living before then?"

"North Carolina," I squeaked out, questioning my sanity.

"Why the change of scenery? New job?"

"New life."

He smiled. "Nice. I like that."

The crosswalk signal changed and we walked across the street, the background noise of cars honking and crashing ocean waves filling in the silence. Approaching our destination, he turned to me. "Why don't you wait out here with the dogs while I run in to clean up and grab our coffees?" He handed me Gidget's leash and led me toward a small table on the sidewalk.

"I offered to buy *you* a coffee and now you're getting *me* one?" I placed my hand on my hip and gave him an incredulous, albeit playful look. "Doesn't seem fair, if you ask me."

"I *didn't* ask you," he responded slyly, turning from me and heading into the small shop.

I lowered myself to the chair, fighting back my smile, and turned my eyes to the street, soaking in everything about my new hometown. The Santa Monica Pier was visible just a block or so away, tourists already beginning their day as they strolled along the boardwalk. Men and women in business attire entered and exited the coffee shop like a revolving door, obviously needing their caffeine fix to start their day. Sport and Gidget simply curled up at my feet, sniffing each other. Dogs were such basic creatures. A simple butt sniff was all it took.

"Hope you like Americanos," a voice interrupted. "That's what I got."

"I'm not picky when it comes to caffeine." I turned my attention to see my new friend take the seat opposite me. "And after driving across the country, I've sworn to never take a good, strong cup of coffee for granted again."

Taking a sip, he then placed his cup on the table between us and leaned back into the chair, crossing his arms over his chest. His muscles stretched the fabric of his shirt slightly. It wasn't in such a way that I thought he was about to rip his shirt off and announce to the world that he was the Incredible Hulk. It was just enough so I knew he cared about his body.

"You drove across the country?" he asked, cutting through my thoughts about whether the Hulk was green all over...including you know where.

"I've always wanted to do it, and I knew I may never get the opportunity again. Since I'm all about having a new adventure, I figured starting with a cross-country drive was perfect. Sure, I could have just as easily flown and had my car shipped, but that sounded boring. I even spray-painted my name on a car at the Cadillac Ranch in Texas."

"You're definitely not like a lot of people I know, Dixie," he commented, taking another sip of his coffee.

"Dixie?"

"Yeah. That accent of yours... It's cute." He beamed the most amazing smile at me, his lips full, his eyes brimming with amusement.

Heat flamed my face and my heart fluttered uncontrollably, all because of a knee-weakening look from an attractive man. Taking a deep breath, I once more tried to calm the hormones raging inside me from my lack of intimacy over the past six months. Of course, it had been at least five years since I really felt fulfilled from sex. I had relied on myself to take the edge off when needed. Life with Will was all about Will...in his job and in the bedroom. Now that I was completely unattached and in a brand new place, I was like a lioness in heat, ready to pounce on the first attractive man who so much as looked at me in any way that might indicate a modicum of interest.

"So what's your deal?" I asked, focusing the conversation on him instead. "You mentioned you were jet-lagged from flying in late last night. Work or pleasure?"

"I was out of town on a shoot."

"You're, like, an actor or something, aren't you? You're too pretty not to be."

He laughed, the sound warm and comforting. "No, I'm not an actor, but thanks for the vote of confidence."

"Then what do you do?"

14

"I'm a producer."

I put my hands up. "Please don't say you're an associate producer because I've seen *State and Main* and I know all about how an associate producer credit is something you give to someone instead of a raise."

He scrunched his eyebrows. "You've seen *State and Main*?"

"Of course! One of my favorite last lines of any movie."

He laughed even louder. "We are oddly similar." Our eyes met, an awkward silence stretching between us.

Out of nowhere, my phone began ringing, the sound of Kenny Loggins' "Mr. Night" blaring.

"Big fan of *Caddyshack*?" He raised his eyebrows.

I smiled. "A little." I grabbed my phone out of my bag, scowling when Will's face appeared on the screen. I knew he was only calling to convince me to bring Sport back to him once again. One thing was certain. He was a persistent bastard.

"Don't let me keep you."

"You're not keeping—"

"I need to get my day started anyway." He got up from the chair and grabbed his dog's leash. Holding his free hand out to me, I placed mine in his. I held my breath when his skin met mine. "It was great having you 'bump' into me, Dixie. It's truly a meeting I'll never forget." His gentle touch was everything I imagined it would be. Soft. Comforting. Warm. Inviting. Then he winked and walked away.

"Goodbye, Moondoggie," I mumbled, slumping into my chair, enjoying the view of his breathtaking backside. It was better than any glimmering ocean view I'd ever seen.

I bolted upright. "Shit! I never even found out his name!" Sport cocked his head at me. "I guess you don't have those kinds of problems, do you, buddy? As long as her butt smells good, you couldn't care less about whether she has a name or not, do you?"

He leaned his head on my leg, allowing me to pet him. Part of me was upset I didn't find out more information about my mystery man. For the briefest of moments, I felt a connection to this complete stranger…one stronger than I thought possible after a fleeting encounter. Or maybe I simply imagined it. Even before my marriage ended, I had been alone. It was entirely reasonable that my mind was playing tricks on me, wasn't it?

Alone at my table, an emptiness seeped in. I glanced around, envious of couples and friends laughing over their morning cups of coffee. I knew absolutely no one in this town, aside from a stranger with gray-blue eyes whom I assaulted and then never found out his name. The doubt I had kept at bay over the past month was returning and I needed to hear some encouraging words about how to start a brand new life.

Picking up my phone, I called my uncle, the only family I really had left, desperate to hear him tell me how proud he was of me, how he knew it was time for me to finally spread my wings and fly. Instead, all I got was his secretary telling me he was in court all day. Sighing, I threw my phone into my bag, stopping when my eyes fell on a leather-bound journal. I was reminded of the day I left North Carolina and the conversation I had with my uncle.

"*I knew you'd be the one to leave the nest, Baylee.*" *His voice wavered, obviously torn about my impending departure.* "*You have your mother's adventurous spirit. Do you know that?*"

"*I don't feel that way. Hell, I've never lived anywhere but here.*"

"*Either did your mom, but that didn't stop her from doing what she wanted.*"

"*I wish I could remember her.*"

*It was quiet for a moment as we stared at each other. He always thought of my mother whenever he saw me. I inherited her vibrant red hair, fair skin, and short and slender frame. From what I knew, my uncle and mother were nearly inseparable growing up, always getting into trouble together, always holding the other one up when they needed it. The stories he told me about their childhood made me feel as if I actually knew her.*

"*Listen…*" *He cleared his throat.* "*I've thought a lot about this, and I think you should have this.*" *He reached into his messenger bag and produced a small, leather-bound journal, the pages yellowing and torn.*

"*What is it?*" *I asked, examining the cover just as my eyes settled on the gold monogram etched in the corner.*

"*It was your mama's journal. I gave it to her the day after she got her diagnosis, thinking it might be therapeutic for her to write down her feelings. She hated when people worried about her and had a bad habit of lying to everyone about how she was truly feeling. She always wrote in a journal as a kid, so I thought this would be a good way for her to process everything.*"

"*I don't understand. How do you have this? Did Dad know about it?*"

*He nodded.* "*I felt bad keeping it, but he insisted I hold onto it. You see, when I finally went home to Charlotte after you were born and your mama died, a package was waiting for me. This journal was in it. Your mama knew her time was up, Baylee. She held on as long as she could to make sure you arrived. You became her sole purpose for living. And this journal…" He caressed the weathered cover as it lay in my lap. "This is what she did the last several months of her life. I just figured since you're starting out on your first big adventure, you might want some inspiration from the woman whose last big adventure was having you."*

Throughout my drive across the country, I had kept the journal close to me, not wanting to let it out of my sight for a minute. I was curious about what the pages contained, but I was also apprehensive about reading her words. When I turned that final page, I knew the only piece of her I had would be gone. I wasn't sure I was ready to say goodbye to the woman I never even met. But maybe my uncle was right. Maybe I needed to read my mother's words. Maybe they would give me the encouragement I needed now that I was on my own for the first time in my life.

Removing the journal from my bag, I stared at the cover, inhaling the aged papers. "I love that smell," I said softly, opening to the first page.

*April 20*

*What am I? Fifteen? That's how I feel…like I'm writing in a diary. So here goes…*

*Dear Diary,*

*I have cancer.*

*Fucking cancer.*

*I'm not quite sure it's sunk in yet. I don't know if it ever will. The doctor said I had a thirty percent chance of surviving if I began intensive chemotherapy immediately, but that would kill the little life growing inside of me. I love Perry with all my heart. He says we'll try again when I beat this thing, but I only have a thirty percent chance of that happening. I am one hundred percent pregnant, due on November 25th. So I choose life, but not mine. Perry will understand.*

*Now I must begin the daunting task of living my life in the little time I have left. You know how people always say "Someday, I will"? Well, I've hit my someday. Someday begins today, and the first thing I'm going to do is see the Pacific Ocean. You may ask why the Pacific Ocean. Well, on my first date with Perry, we went to the old drive-in, which was more like a cow pasture with a shitty screen. The feature movie was Gidget.*

I gasped. No wonder Dad loved that movie, I thought, then returned my eyes to my mother's flowing script.

*It's a silly beach movie, but it brings back memories of the butterflies. And the butterflies never left. To this day, when I gaze at Perry, I still feel like the giddy sixteen-year-old at the annual church cookout who was asked out by a boy from another town. Now, I'm a twenty-nine-year-old wife and soon-to-be mother who has cancer.*

*When I got my diagnosis last week, you want to know the first thing I did? I made a list of all the things I've always wanted to do. I've had to redo the list in order of importance because I fear I won't be able to do everything. I have to pick and choose my battles while I fight the battle that has begun raging its own war against me... Time.*

I closed the journal and returned it to my bag. Pushing the chair back, I got up, grabbing Sport's leash. I headed back toward my condo, staring out over the ocean that the mother I never knew yearned to see as her first step in beginning to live her life.

"Someday begins today," I murmured with conviction, repeating my mother's words.

# CHAPTER TWO

THE REMAINDER OF MY day passed in a blur as I did my best to put a dent in the mountain of boxes filling most of the free space in my condo. In a rush to get out of North Carolina, I had thrown everything I owned into boxes. As I unpacked them, I was faced with reminders of what I wanted to forget. I thought by packing up and moving somewhere new, I'd be able to leave my past, and Will, behind. As I unboxed my books and organized them on the built-in shelves in what would be my office, I came to the realization that was easier said than done.

Brushing the dust off the cover of my senior yearbook, I flipped through the pages, although I knew it wasn't a good idea. Our pictures adorned nearly every page. Homecoming queen and the starting quarterback… We were the couple everyone wanted to be.

As my eyes scanned the photo collage from the homecoming dance, I stopped when I saw the expression on the face of the seventeen-year-old version of myself. Will and I were standing there, he in his crown, me in my tiara. He was beaming as he held me in his arms. I was smiling, too, but it almost seemed forced, as if I already knew our entire relationship was a farce. I wished I could remember what was going through my mind at that moment. Maybe that there was more to life than being known as someone's girlfriend, then wife. I was never just Baylee. First, I was Perry's daughter, the sole heir to one of the most lucrative lumber companies in the country. Then I was known as Will's girl. I didn't think too much of it then, but as the years passed, I wanted people to know me for me, not for whom I was dating or married to.

I turned the page, my eyes falling on a collage of baby photos of the graduating class. Right in the center was one of Will and me together as infants. We had known each other practically our entire lives. Hell, our first kiss was the result of a game of Spin the Bottle gone horribly wrong during the summer between my sophomore and junior year of high school. I had never thought of him in a romantic sense before. I actually cringed when the bottle fell on me. I couldn't remember finding any of the boys I went to high school with attractive. All that mattered was graduating at the top of my class and having my choice of colleges to choose from.

It's amazing how one moment can change everything.

I often wondered what my life would have been like had that bottle landed on Julie Williams sitting beside me. I still remembered the look of excitement on her face when the bottle began to slow and nearly landed on her before moving just a little bit more, pointing at me. If it had landed on her, maybe I wouldn't have wasted the past decade of my life. Hell, Will was screwing Julie the duration of our relationship anyway.

Instead, that one moment changed the trajectory my life had been on. The following week, my father died of a heart attack. Will came to the funeral and Camille, my lovely step-monster... I'm sorry... step-mother commented about what a nice young man he was before insinuating she had heard we swapped spit. And that was what kissing Will was. Simply an exchange of bodily fluids. I assumed that was all it was supposed to be, considering he was the first and only boy I had ever kissed. But I knew there had to be more to it. I had always imagined a kiss should feel electric, exhilarating, breathtaking, magical. Will's kisses were, for lack of a better word, mechanical, like he was reading an instruction manual and simply followed the steps. There was no spark. There was no breathlessness. There was no magic.

Will was calculated. He knew enough that if he charmed Camille, she would do her best to convince me to give him a chance. He came to see me nearly every day that summer, plastering a fake compassionate expression on his face, asking how I was coping with the loss of my father. I should have known he was only interested in my father's multi-million dollar lumber company I had inherited.

Our first date was like anyone would expect their first date to be when sixteen…going to see a movie with a bunch of friends. He slung his arm around my shoulders and kept it there the duration of whatever crappy action movie he selected. He had bathed in aftershave, and I thought I was suffering from an allergic reaction from the constant sneezing. He simply asked, and I quote, "What the hell is wrong with you? You don't have some sort of contagious disease, do you?" Just when I didn't think things could get any worse, he leaned over and whispered, "I'll be Burger King and you be McDonalds. I'll have it my way and you'll be loving it."

I had stared at him, questioning whether he really did just say that or if my ears were playing tricks on me.

I expected to see a smile crack his lips, but I was met with a smug expression instead, as if he considered himself to be Einstein's protégé for coming up with that little gem.

I didn't know why I continued to date him. I kept telling myself it wouldn't last, that it was just a fun way to spend my last few years of high school. Somehow, it all spiraled into marriage when the ink on our diplomas had barely dried. Hell, his proposal had even made the local news when he got down on one knee after the football team won the division championship and asked me to marry him. I must have said "yes", but couldn't remember doing it.

We became the town's own fairytale. I was thrilled for a minute. I was so busy planning a wedding it hadn't really set in that I was about to make a lifelong commitment to Will. The closer it got to our wedding date, the more I began to second-guess my decision. Every time I considered backing out, Camille insisted, in her condescending voice, that it was just nerves. Part of me kept telling myself it would get better once we were married, that we were just in a strange transition phase between high school and starting the rest of our lives. I even agreed to put my dreams on hold. Instead of going to NYU as I had planned, I enrolled in a local college and stayed in the same town where I had grown up.

When I walked in on Will banging Julie, it felt like a burden had been lifted off my shoulders, despite how hurt I was. I had always been suspicious regarding his fidelity. In my mind, our marriage fell apart the second he refused to support my dreams. Camille blamed his infidelity on my refusal to have a child with him. Children never solved marital problems. They only added to it.

A glow filtered into the room, tearing my attention from the yearbook, and I glanced out the window to see the sun beginning its descent beyond the horizon, casting a beautiful combination of pink and orange hue on the ocean. Soaking in the magnificent view of my first West Coast sunset, I realized I'd never get the fresh start I needed surrounded by the reminders of my former life.

Everything had to go.

# CHAPTER THREE

THE SUN STREAMED INTO my bedroom what seemed like just minutes after I had finally crawled under the covers. After hours of swearing at my possessions, as well as drinking several tumblers of whiskey, I was satisfied with my decision to start from scratch and rid my life of all memories of Will. The only one that remained was Sport, but with each passing minute, the less I thought of Will when I looked at the dog. Instead, I saw my cross-country partner. I saw my foul-breathed bed companion.

As if on cue, Sport jumped on me, tail wagging, and licked my face. "Enough, buddy. Mama was up late so let's calm down on the tongue action for a minute." A cheesy grin crossed my face when a pair of blue-gray eyes flashed before me. "Now *that's* some tongue action I wouldn't mind," I commented.

A rush of adrenaline coursing through my tired body, I pulled the duvet closer to me, giddy from the memory of my chance encounter the previous day with Mr. Blue Eyes. Moondoggie. Nosebleeder. I knew the likelihood of running into him again in a city the size of LA was slim to none, but that didn't matter. The encounter stood for more than a random meeting in the park. It gave me hope.

Sport yipped, bringing me back down to earth, his wagging tail becoming a weapon. It was useless to try to go back to sleep. I reluctantly got out of my comfortable bed and shuffled down the stairs, the dog on my heels. He ran around in circles at my feet before darting for the foyer, pulling his collar off the entryway hook.

"Okay. Let's go for a walk. Please don't hump any strange dogs today. Okay, buddy?"

He yipped once more, and I couldn't be sure if he was saying "Okay, Mom", or "This thing has a mind of its own".

Taking the leash from Sport, who was reluctant to relinquish control to me, I locked the door behind me and proceeded toward the elevator. When I came out in the lobby and walked to the door, I smiled a warm greeting at the same doorman I had met the previous morning.

"Enjoy your walk, Miss Morgan." He tipped his hat and I nodded, crossing over to Palisades Park.

The weather in LA was unlike anything I had ever experienced. It could be barely fifty degrees in the morning, but by noon, the temperatures would be close to eighty. A slight breeze blew my hair, and the vibrant sunshine, combined with the smell of the salty sea air, infected me with a thrilling sense of adventure. I wanted to experience everything my new town had to offer and I couldn't wait to explore, starting with the shopping in LA to replace the items I decided had no place in my new life, which was pretty much everything I owned. Goodwill was going to love me.

As I made my way south, retracing the same path I took yesterday, I would have been lying if I said I wasn't searching for my nameless acquaintance. I wondered where he lived, what his day was like, whether he was thinking about me just as I was thinking of him.

"We don't even know his name, Sport," I commented as he marked his territory on a palm tree. He looked up at me, squinting while he relieved himself. "So we should probably stop thinking about him, although if you ever experienced shivers just from the proximity of a complete stranger, I'm sure it would be just as difficult for you."

"I kind of like it that way, don't you? Not knowing each other's names?" a familiar voice said. I refused to believe he was actually near me, overhearing the conversation I was having with my dog. I was clearly delirious.

"Great. Now I'm hearing voices," I mumbled, resisting the urge to turn around.

A sexy chuckle echoed behind me as I felt a tug on Sport's leash.

"You're really behind me, aren't you?" I cringed.

"It would appear so." His voice was light and amused. I could just picture him standing there, his arms crossed in front of his body, emphasizing what I could only imagine was a rather sculpted chest.

"And you overheard me say…"

"Something about a shiver, Dixie."

I turned around slowly, my face growing red when I saw him standing behind me wearing a t-shirt and cargo shorts, Gidget at his side. It was almost exactly as I had pictured in my mind. Almost. The real thing was infinitely better.

"You should get your ears checked, Nosebleeder," I retorted dismissively, avoiding his eyes.

"Nosebleeder?" He barked out a laugh.

"Since I don't know your name, I need to call you

*something.*" I tossed my hair over my shoulder. God, I hated this. I was trying to flirt with this gift to all females and gay men, but I had absolutely no idea how to even go about doing so. I was fairly certain all my inane attempts at flirting were just making him question my sanity.

"Well, if that's what you're going to call me, I should probably tell you my real name. I'm not sure I want to be known around town as Nosebleeder."

"Suit yourself." I shrugged. "I actually don't mind being called Dixie. Your move, Nosebleeder." I winked at him. Winking was good flirting, right? I had no idea. I just prayed my attempt at a wink came off as sexy and not as if I had an uncontrollable twitch.

"Sebby," he announced, holding his hand out toward me. "Technically, it's Sebastian, but everyone calls me Sebby."

"Baylee," I replied, taking his hand. It was strong and warm, his fingers wrapping around mine surprisingly pleasant. "Everyone just calls me Baylee." A nervous laugh escaped, followed by an unexpected snort. *I can't believe I just snorted*, I thought, cringing.

"It's nice to put a name with the face," he said, keeping my hand enclosed in his, ignoring my goofy snort. To make matters worse, a slight fluttering in my stomach caused me to giggle like a pre-teen at a boy band concert, obviously too dumbstruck to string two words together.

"Likewise." Finally finding my voice, I tore my hand from his before I could no longer let go. All I could think about as I stared at him were his lips and how perfect they would feel pressed against mine. Our kiss would be simple, but more fulfilling than any kiss

I'd ever experienced. There would be some sort of emotion behind it. His kiss would make me feel something…something I hadn't felt before but had fantasized about more than I cared to admit.

His kiss would be magic.

"I was hoping I'd run into you again," Sebby admitted, lowering himself onto a nearby bench. I followed his lead. Our dogs curled up in front of us, happy to watch the morning joggers pass by. I was just happy to be close to Sebby. Screw watching the morning joggers. "I walk Gidget in this area the same time every morning when I'm in town."

"I wanted to stay in bed, but Sport would not let that happen. I don't think he's adjusted to California time just yet."

Sebby nodded as he stared out at the ocean in the distance.

"So…," I said, breaking the stiff silence. "You must live around here then."

"I do," he replied. "Although, lately, I feel like I've been living everywhere but here."

"Lots of traveling for work?"

"More or less."

"Does it get tiring always being gone?"

When I was living in North Carolina, I barely ever left my hometown. I couldn't imagine what it would be like to have a job that took me across the country, maybe even around the world, on a regular basis.

"You're just full of questions this morning, aren't you?" he replied with a smirk. "Any reason for that?"

"I'm a naturally curious person…and we'll just leave it at that," I retorted, trying to exude a certain level of confidence. I couldn't tell him the truth. That he intrigued me. That the way he smiled made my insides knot and tingle. That I barely knew him, but I wanted to.

"Well, then, to answer your question... Yes, it does get tiring. When I'm on the road for a long period of time, I start to miss home. But when I'm home for more than a month or so, I get restless and want to go. Work on a new project. Film in a new city. Expand my horizons."

I met his eyes to see a refreshing level of excitement and enthusiasm. Passion exuded from every pore as he spoke of his travels. I couldn't help but feel jealous that I never had that kind of reaction with regard to what I did. Yes, I loved running the local newspaper back home, but it wasn't fulfilling for me. Ever since I was a little girl, I had dreamt of writing a book, but I never had the audacity or encouragement to follow that dream. Will's voice was always in the back of my mind, putting down anything to do with writing.

"*Nobody wants to waste their time reading a book when the movie's always better.*"

"What's your story, Baylee?" Sebby asked, breaking me out of my memories. "Why did you leave North Carolina?"

"I told you yesterday. I wanted a new life."

"You don't want to talk about why you *really* left home, do you?" His voice was almost quiet and hesitant.

I sighed. "It's not that. I'm sure it's nothing you haven't heard before. Girl marries her high school sweetheart a few months after graduation, giving up her dreams to support him with his. Girl is happy for a while, then she realizes where the term 'honeymoon phase' comes from. Girl feels guilty when guy pushes to have a baby, but she isn't ready for that. Girl actually begins to hate herself for depriving him of having a baby…until she walks in on him screwing her former friend on the kitchen island, slapping her with the truth that they had been sleeping together off and on for the past twelve years." I glanced at Sebby to gauge his reaction.

Pity formed in his eyes. "Baylee, I'm—"

"It's okay," I interrupted. I didn't want anyone's sympathy. I just wanted to move on with my life. "At least I got a dog out of it."

He studied me for a minute before breaking into a throaty laugh. "I'll have to save my question about that for another day, I'm afraid." He glanced at his watch. "Do you think maybe you'll be available for me to run into tomorrow around the same time?" When he raised his eyebrows, my pulse raced at the prospect of seeing him again.

I wanted to shout "yes" at the top of my lungs, but I didn't want to seem too eager. I had seen enough movies to know that playing hard to get made you seem more desirable. I probably shouldn't have been taking dating advice from John Hughes' films, but I was otherwise clueless about how to act. At least I'd never given my panties to a geek… Yet.

"I'll have to check my calendar, but I think I'm free. I'll pencil you in."

"Great." He beamed, that devilish smile of his widening to reveal a set of perfect teeth. "Looking forward to it, Baylee." He retreated from me at a comfortable jog, Gidget keeping pace, and I gawked at the well-defined leg muscles as they disappeared from view.

"As am I, Nosebleeder," I whimpered.

I fucking whimpered.

# CHAPTER FOUR

"YOU MUST BE THE new girl," a voice with a subtle Midwestern accent said as I fumbled through my purse for my keys later that morning.

I snapped my head up and smiled warmly at a tall brunette who appeared to be in her mid-twenties. "That's me," I responded. "I'm Baylee." I held my hand out to her and she shook it.

"Nice to meet you, Baylee. I'm Sophia." Her nearly waist-length hair was a dark shade of brown, lightening in color toward the ends. She had a fair complexion with dark eyes that stood out on her face. She was dressed casually in a pair of skinny jeans and an oversized cowl-neck sweater, but still looked remarkably put together. Everyone in this city did.

"I've been wondering who lives across from me."

"Oh," she exhaled, her smile growing wider. "This isn't my condo. I do live in the building, but house-sit for the person who lives here. Clean up the place, cook, run any errands he needs."

"Wow. He sounds kind of high maintenance and lazy," I joked

"Nah," she replied, laughing. "I don't mind. It's an easy job and pays more than what I was making as an assistant to some big studio exec downtown. Plus, it gives me the flexibility to go on auditions."

"Are you trying to land a role, too?"

"Yeah. You?"

"No. It just seems like everyone I've met so far is connected to the entertainment industry in one way or another."

"You get a lot of that here."

"Duly noted." Turning from her, I unlocked my door and glanced over my shoulder. "It was nice to meet you, Sophia." I smiled politely. "I'm sure I'll be seeing you around." Opening the door, I started into my condo.

"Hey, Baylee!" she called out just as I was about to shut the door.

"Yes?" I popped back into the hallway.

"I know we just met and you barely know me, but if you don't have any plans tonight, I'm having a few people over. Nothing big, just a few friends I've made in the building. Most everyone here is older. There's not a lot of people our age. We do game nights once a week. It'll be a good chance for you to meet more people who live here."

"I wouldn't want to intrude."

"You wouldn't," she answered, her eyes bright. "I moved out here on a whim and didn't know another soul. I know how it can be."

"How did you know I'm new to town?" I asked.

She smiled a genuine smile. "That accent. If you're not new to LA, I'll eat my hat. Come over tonight," she pushed. "It'll be fun. Promise."

"I don't know…" It wasn't that I didn't want to meet new people. I had just spent the last ten years of my life catering to someone else's needs. I wanted some "me" time. Time I could curl up on the couch, eat pizza, and do whatever I wanted…including fantasize about Sebby and our planned meeting the following morning.

Sophia narrowed her gaze at me, scowling in a light-hearted manner.

"Fine," I huffed, then smiled. "I'll think about it." I winked.

"Good!" She beamed. "Seven o'clock. Unit 6B. Be there, or I'll drag you out. I *do* know where you live."

~~~~~~~~~~

A LITTLE AFTER SEVEN, I did a final check of my makeup in the full-length mirror, then set out for Sophia's condo on the sixth floor. I had no idea what I was in for or if I'd even have anything in common with her and her friends. Sure, she seemed nice enough when I met her earlier today, but she didn't appear to be the type of person with whom I would typically spend time. She was beautiful and confident, and I could only imagine her group of friends consisted of more beautiful and confident women who were all hoping to make a name for themselves in the movie industry. I couldn't let that dissuade me, though. It wouldn't have gotten in my mother's way. This was the start of a new life, a new adventure. This was my chance to discover who I really was. So, with a bottle of Pinot Noir in hand, which the clerk at a wine store down the street assured me was rather tasty, I casually knocked on her door.

"Baylee!" Sophia exclaimed in a rambunctious voice as she pulled the door open. "You made it! I wasn't sure if you were going to come or not, but I'm so glad you did!" She wrapped her arms around me, hugging me as if we were old friends seeing each other for the first time in years.

"Thanks for inviting me." I weakly returned her embrace. The faint scent of alcohol made its way to my nose, and I had a feeling her warm greeting was most likely due to the booze, not my presence.

"Anytime!" She released me, pulling me through the foyer and into her condo. "It's always fun to have fresh meat join in. Spices things up a bit." She winked.

"Umm, what exactly did you mean by 'game night'?" I raised my eyebrows.

She inhaled quickly. "Gosh, not *that*, although I'm pretty sure the way it came out, it could be taken the wrong way. Come. I want you to meet everyone."

She dragged me toward the living area overlooking the darkened Pacific Ocean. It was a smaller floor plan than my condo, probably about a quarter of the size. It still boasted floor-to-ceiling windows on the focus wall, but the kitchen and living room were substantially smaller. What it lacked in space, though, it made up for in comfort. The condo appeared cozy, framed photos of Sophia and people I assumed to be her friends and family covering nearly every surface. It made me feel homesick, but not for North Carolina. I was homesick for the life I wished I had. The life I was now looking for.

"Everyone," Sophia said, bringing me back from my thoughts. I snapped my head up to see a group of men and women who were probably in their late twenties or early thirties. It was not what I had expected at all. I had assumed her friends would all be gorgeous, as if they just finished their latest shoot. Instead, it was quite the mix of all different walks of life.

"This is Baylee," Sophia continued. "She just moved here. She's the new owner of the penthouse condo."

An impressed whistle sounded and I looked in its direction at a tall, thin black man with a shaved head who had impeccable style. "Nice, girlfriend," he commented in an effeminate voice. "I'm Marcel, 10A, and I may just be a tad jealous knowing you get to share a hallway with Eddie." Fanning himself, he swooned like a damsel in distress, which was met with eye rolls and polite chuckles.

"Eddie?" I asked.

"Your neighbor. I've been hounding Miss Sophia for years to set me up with him but, alas, he's straight." He pouted, winking at Sophia.

"Well, we all can't be perfect, can we?" I joked.

Marcel laughed heartily and pulled out a chair next to him, patting it for me to sit down. "I like you, Miss Dixie." I paused, reminded of Sebby. I thought it peculiar that in less than forty-eight hours, two people called me the same nickname. I shrugged it off, though. I supposed with an accent like mine, I shouldn't have been too surprised.

Smiling, I sat next to Marcel. He poured some wine into a glass that had miraculously appeared in front of me.

"And no," he continued, "we certainly all can't be perfect, but that neighbor of yours is damn near close. Isn't he, ladies?" He looked around the table at the few females there.

"I'm staying out of this," Sophia answered quickly. "He's my boss."

"Oh, please," a tall woman said in a scratchy voice. She had wild, dark curly hair, bold glasses, bright red lips, and arms covered in tattoos. "Like you've never fantasized about him ordering you to strip down so he could have his way with you." She rolled her eyes and turned to me. "Hi. I'm Lacey. Sophia's roommate."

"Hi, Lacey," I responded. "Sounds like the start of a romance novel, although I'm pretty sure the whole boss seducing the employee trope is overused at this point."

"You've got that right," Marcel mumbled under his breath.

"That's the thing about fantasies," a man who appeared to be all muscles said. "They lose their appeal if it becomes real life. Most of the time, the fantasy in your head is probably nothing like the reality anyway. Plus, doesn't he have a girlfriend?"

"Way to ruin *my* fantasy," Marcel sneered playfully.

Listening to everyone talk about my new neighbor sparked my interest. I had yet to meet him, but the way my new group of acquaintances made him sound, I could only imagine he was devastatingly handsome. He was probably tall with dark hair and brooding eyes that seemed to change color with his mood. He always dressed remarkably well. Only the best designer suits for him. Men wanted to be him, and women wanted to be with him. I could have been way off in my fantasy, but my imagination was on overdrive. That was the thing about being a writer who had her voice suppressed for years. Now that I was free to do whatever I wanted, I couldn't help but see a story in every situation I encountered.

"To finish the introductions so we can get game night underway," Marcel added, "this hunk of muscle is

Darren." He squeezed the biceps of the blond man sitting next to him. I was pretty sure he had to have his t-shirts custom-made to fit his enormous arms and chest. "He lives in 8D, and this is Cora." He gestured to a petite woman with soft features and pixie cut strawberry blond hair. She had emerald green eyes, milky-white skin, and a distinctively pointed nose that contrasted with the rest of her soft features.

"Hi," I said.

She returned my smile. "I'm down in 4C."

"I'm never going to remember this," I joked.

"You'll get there," Marcel encouraged.

"Now that the introductions are over..." Sophia carried a few trays of hors d'oeuvres from her kitchen and set them on the table in front of us. "Let's get the games started. Baylee, hope you like Pictionary."

"Pictionary? I haven't played that in a coon's age."

Marcel spit out his wine. "Coon's age?" he choked, barely able to contain his laughter. "What exactly is a coon's age?"

"It's a unit of measure in the south," I deadpanned.

The room grew quiet for a protracted moment as I waited for everyone's reaction. Now that I heard it out loud, I hoped I hadn't offended anyone. As if on cue, everyone burst out laughing, the raucous noise filling the space.

"Unit of measure in the south," Marcel repeated, chuckling through his teeth. "I like your style, Miss Dixie." He wiped his eyes and filled his glass with more wine.

"Fair warning for all of you..." I reached for my wine glass and took a sip, swirling the red liquid in my mouth. I half expected it to taste sweet with a hint of effervescence, like so many of the wines my friends back home drank. The top-shelf wines at our local Walmart in North Carolina left much to be desired. This was nothing like that. It had a spicy, smoky flavor, but wasn't heavy. It was the kind of wine my uncle drank. Mature. Cultured. Sophisticated. Not some alcoholic liquid poured into a bottle with a wine label slapped on it. "Drawing is certainly not my strong suit, so I feel bad for anyone who is unlucky enough to be on my team."

"After a few drinks, it's *nobody's* strong suit," Sophia assured me. "And don't worry about that. We don't play to win. We just play for fun."

"Boy, do we." Marcel nudged me. The way he was grinning made me think there was more to this game of Pictionary than Sophia had originally let on.

"What does he mean by that?" I asked.

"Nothing, just that this isn't your traditional game of Pictionary," Sophia explained. "We play by different rules than what you're used to."

"This is Karaoke Pictionary," Lacey announced.

I raised my eyebrows. "Karaoke Pictionary?" I had only gone to Karaoke once in my life and that was enough. I wasn't sure I was ready to make an absolute fool out of myself in front of a room of people who were complete strangers just minutes ago.

"We came up with it a few years back after way too much alcohol," Darren added. "Actually, it was mostly Cora's idea."

I turned my attention to her. She shrugged. "What can I say? I was a complete band geek in high school, and sang in a band in college. I've always loved music and I think these guys were sick of me ignoring them in favor of the microphone whenever we got together. Hence, Karaoke Pictionary was born. And it's become a staple ever since."

"It's a nice release after a long week of work," Lacey explained.

"Well then…" I swallowed a large gulp of my wine, the effects starting to take hold. It made me feel lightheaded, a subtle tingling running through me. A warmth began to spread from my ears to my cheeks and I relaxed into my chair. "Let's play."

"The rules are pretty simple, Baylee." Sophia grabbed an easel from the hallway closet and propped a whiteboard on it. "We have six people, so we'll split into two random teams. We don't use the traditional Pictionary board or any of that. Over the years, we've written down items on notecards." She pulled out a large keepsake box and flipped it open, revealing what had to be nearly five hundred notecards. "On the bottom of each card is the category and number of points. That's the only thing you can tell your teammates when it's your turn to draw. Mixed in are some notecards that are in the music category, along with the number of points awarded. It's up to the person drawing whether to attempt to sketch the song title or to perform it. If you draw it, your team has to guess the song title correctly to be awarded the points. If you choose to perform, you're automatically awarded the points."

I looked around the table at the giddy expressions staring back at me. I had a feeling they all chose to sing instead of draw. Hell, it was a sure way of scoring points for your team.

"Don't look so scared, Dixie," Marcel said, getting up from his chair and heading toward the large television in the living area. "It's all set up." He grabbed the remote and flipped through what appeared to be a database of hundreds of songs. "Just find the song on the card and press play." He stopped on "Like a Virgin" and, within seconds, the familiar strains of the Madonna song boomed through the condo.

I expected him to stop the music once he had shown me how it worked, but that wasn't the case. Instead, he picked up a microphone that fed into the surround sound and belted out the lyrics to the Material Girl's hit song, dancing around the living room as if he didn't have a care in the world. Everyone else cheered him on, clapping and grooving along to the tune. I got lost in the mood, mouthing the words to the song as they appeared on the television screen, although Marcel didn't seem to need them at all.

It seemed like such a mishmash of people. There was the jock (Darren), the gay one (Marcel), the beauty queen (Sophia), the eccentric (Lacey), and the band geek (Cora). I wasn't sure where I fit in just yet, but it didn't seem to matter. We were our own little *Breakfast Club* (cue "Don't You (Forget About Me)" by Simple Minds). However, in our case, it was more along the lines of being a Wine Drinking Karaoke Pictionary Playing Club.

"You know, Marcel," Darren's deep voice cut through when the music died down and Marcel returned to the table after taking a dramatic bow, "something makes me think that there is absolutely nothing virgin about you."

"The song is '*Like* a Virgin'," Marcel replied, winking. "And you're right, sweetheart. There *is* nothing virgin about me. How about you?" he flirted, wiggling his eyebrows.

43

"Okay. Teams!" Sophia interrupted, anxious to start the game. She passed around a small bowl containing several pieces of folded up paper, a number one or two scratched on each of them. I drew a two, as did Marcel and Cora, leaving Sophia, Darren, and Lacey to form the other team. Taking the lead, Sophia decided to draw first, pulling a notecard out of the box. I watched with amusement as she sauntered up to the whiteboard and furrowed her brows, trying to figure out how to draw whatever was on the card.

Hours flew by, more wine was consumed, and a large amount of generally indecipherable masterpieces were sketched on the whiteboard as I got to know this unassuming group of people. I told them all about my recent divorce and Will's infidelity that led to me packing up everything I owned and heading west until I hit the Pacific Ocean.

I discovered that Marcel was one hell of an interior designer. He even offered to work his magic on my place, speaking in an excited voice about a multitude of ideas he had for the enormous space I now lived in. With all the right touches, he was certain this job could land him in one of the top design magazines. I seriously considered taking him up on his offer. I had only been here two days, but I was more than aware that my new condo lacked any sense of personality. I wasn't sure what my style was, but I was certain Marcel would do an amazing job redesigning my place into something that felt more like a home to me.

Darren, as I suspected, worked in the security field. He had gone into the Marines after high school and now worked in the private security business. Based on the fact he could afford a condo in this building, I assumed business was very good. Lacey was a Harvard graduate who was now a tax attorney, much to my surprise. I had trouble picturing her wearing a suit and going to court.

"That's the good thing about being a tax attorney," she explained once she saw the bewildered expression I had trouble hiding. "We don't really go to court that much. Plus, I find my clients are much more comfortable with me when they see I'm wearing jeans, as opposed to some stuffy suit."

Out of everyone there, Cora had the juiciest story to tell. She was left a large sum of money when her husband of seven years, Steven, was killed in a car accident. Now, she devoted all her time, and his money, to charity work. Apparently, Steven was speeding down Pacific Coast Highway...or as the Angelenos surrounding me lovingly referred to it as "PCH"...in his sports car, his mistress in the passenger seat. The truth was, Cora had just found out about the affair and was getting ready to serve him with divorce papers. While she was saddened to hear of his passing, she was still his wife and inherited his enormous fortune.

"Bless his heart," I said, shaking my head.

Cora looked at me, her brows furrowed. To her, I was sure it sounded like I was sympathizing with her now deceased husband.

Smiling, I explained, "That's another southern phrase. It's a polite way of saying poor, sad fucker."

Everyone at the table roared in response, a few repeating "Bless his heart".

"I'll drink to that." Sophia raised her glass, and we all followed suit.

"And the kicker? His little slice on the side tried to contest his will on the grounds that Steven had set up a bank account in her name and was paying the mortgage on a house he bought for her in Beverly Hills," Cora added. "Steven was about fifteen years older than I when we met. He had a great job and only grew more and more successful during our marriage, giving me the freedom to do whatever I wanted. You can understand what a shock it was when the lawyers went through his estate and I was told about all these properties he owned, of which I had no knowledge. But it didn't matter. His will left everything to me. I evicted all his pieces of ass and sold the houses. Occasionally, I see one of them when I have an appointment with my money manager."

"Why? Does she work there?" I asked, thinking how awkward that must be. Everyone chuckled.

"Not exactly. She works at the coffee stand in the lobby of the building. It's tragic, really," she mused sarcastically. "Having to go from living in a six thousand square foot luxury home in Beverly Hills, getting a manicure and pedicure nearly every day, and not having to work to barely making minimum wage and living God knows where. I'm usually not one to take pleasure in watching someone's downfall, but like I've always said, karma's a bitch. Yes, Steven cheated, but carrying on with a married man is just as bad in my eyes."

I nodded. I could sympathize with what she went through all too well. I didn't love Will, so ending our marriage didn't completely destroy me, but knowing he had been unfaithful wasn't easy to overcome. I couldn't help but wonder whether I was the problem.

"So, Baylee," Lacey said a short while later as we all took a small break after Darren performed a particularly amusing rendition of "Total Eclipse of the

Heart". "Have you had time to explore LA yet?"

"Not really," I answered, taking a sip of some much needed water. My mouth was incredibly dry from consuming more glasses of wine than I could count. "I've only been here for two days." A small grin crossed my face. "I've just been settling in, taking my dog on walks..." I trailed off, my cheeks flushing red with the memory of bumping into Sebby...literally.

"Hmm," Marcel said. "Is there a reason you're blushing right now? Did you already meet someone?"

Biting my lower lip, I nodded. "But it's not like you think. It was probably one of the most embarrassing moments of my life."

"How do you mean?" Lacey asked as everyone leaned in closer to me.

"I gave him a bloody nose."

"You what?!"

"My first morning here, I was taking my dog for a walk and was in desperate need of coffee. As I was walking Sport—"

"Your dog's name is Sport?" Darren interrupted.

I rolled my eyes. "I didn't name him. If I had, he'd have a good name like Max or something. You know. A dog name."

"So, as you were walking Sport...?" Sophia urged me to continue.

"Right. So I was walking Sport in Palisades Park, enjoying my new surroundings, when he bolted away from me and I lost my grip on his leash. Before I could react, he ran toward another dog and started humping her, even though he's fixed. As I was trying to pry Sport off the other dog, I bumped into her owner's face pretty hard and gave him a bloody nose. God, it was so embarrassing." I buried my face in my hands. "I had been in LA for less than twenty-four hours and I could already be charged with assault."

"But…?" Marcel smirked, able to sense there was more to the story. The truth was, I wasn't sure what else to tell them about Sebby. I wasn't sure what our story was. Was I looking forward to running into him again tomorrow morning? Of course, but I wanted to keep that to myself.

"Nothing really. We had coffee together, then ran into each other again this morning. We have a plan to run into each other again tomorrow."

"Mmm-hmm…," Marcel said, taking a sip of his wine. "And you're sure you don't want to do more than just 'run into' him?"

"I'm not sure, but maybe just being friends is what I need right now. Hell, I've only been divorced a little over a month. I was in that relationship for twelve years. Maybe I just need to know what it's like to be single again."

"You can be single and still have fun," Sophia reminded me.

"And that's exactly what I intend to do."

# CHAPTER FIVE

DURING THE NIGHT, SEVEN little dwarfs had crawled into my skull, mining for diamonds or gold or whatever it was they did before calling it a day and singing "Heigh-Ho" all the way back to their little dwarf cottage. At least, thanks to all the wine I had consumed the previous evening, that's what it felt like when the sun cruelly woke me up the following morning. My mouth was drier than the Mojave Desert in July, and it felt like I had only slept for minutes instead of hours.

Groggily opening my eyes, the first thing I saw was the clock on my nightstand. It was nearly nine. It took a minute for that to register in my brain. When it finally did, I bolted up, grabbing my head to steady the spinning room, then ran into the bathroom. In a great feat of multitasking, I brushed my teeth while trying to diminish the bags under my eyes with concealer. I spit out the toothpaste and wiped the residue from my mouth before pulling my matted hair into a messy bun, securing the few fly-aways with an elastic headband.

Within seconds, Sport and I were dashing through the lobby and out onto Ocean Avenue. The wind was blowing the palm trees around on that Friday morning, but that didn't stop runners and cyclists from getting in their morning exercise. I had only seen winds like this during a storm, but there was barely a cloud to be seen, the sun shining brilliantly in the autumn sky.

"These are what we call Santa Anas," the doorman said as I waited at the crosswalk, obviously noticing the bewilderment on my face. "They typically come around September or October. Makes it a great day for surfing."

I turned toward him. He was tall and lean with tanned skin, and I estimated he was in his forties. Based on his appearance, I got the impression he spent most of his spare time on a surfboard. My assumption could have been wrong, but something about his dark brown hair that grew lighter at the ends, carefree demeanor, and enthusiastic smile reminded me of all those 1960s beach movies I grew up watching.

"I don't think we've been properly introduced." He held his hand out toward me. "I'm Jeffrey."

"Baylee." I smiled, shaking his hand.

"I know." He winked, tipping his hat to me. "Enjoy your walk, Miss Morgan."

I crossed over to Palisades Park, biting my lip to reel in the grin that was bursting to crawl across my face when I thought of my impending meeting with Sebby. I slowed my enthusiastic steps so as not to appear too anxious, although I wanted to run toward our unofficial meeting spot and not waste an instant of our time together.

Approaching the bench where I had assaulted Sebby just a few days ago, a small smile crossed my lips when I saw him sitting there, Gidget at his feet, with two coffees in hand.

"Hey," I said, sitting beside him, trying to remain calm and collected when my senses, and libido, were on high alert. Much like our last two meetings, he was dressed casually in a t-shirt and cargo shorts, even in the chilly temperatures.

"Rough start to the day?" He held out a cup of coffee and I grabbed it, taking a much needed sip. There was nothing like that first slug of coffee in the morning, even more so after a night where you gave Jack Kerouac a run for his money with the amount of alcohol you consumed.

"What makes you say that?" I asked once the effects of the caffeine dulled my throbbing head.

He chuckled softly, a velvety smooth melody. It was as sweet as buttercream frosting. I had always been convinced you could tell a lot about a person by the way they laughed. Some were loud and obnoxious, as if the person wanted everyone to know he was amused. This person needed to be the constant center of attention. Some laughs were forced, quiet, and shaky. This was the type of person who was timid, unsure of whether or not it was socially acceptable to laugh. And then there were those who laughed as Sebby did — a combination of genuine amusement and happiness. It wasn't forced. It wasn't obnoxious. It was perfect. There was no denying it. Sebby gave good laugh.

"Your voice is a little scratchy this morning."

My mouth curved into a smile when I met his amused eyes. "Just had a late night. I met one of my neighbors yesterday and she invited me over to her condo for game night—"

"Game night?" he interrupted, narrowing his gaze at me.

"Yeah. Game night," I repeated. "You know. You get together with friends and play board games. Surely a man as worldly as you would have heard of game night before."

"I know what game night is, Dixie," he replied. "It's just…"

"It's just what?"

"Nothing." His confused expression softened and was instantly replaced with a coy smirk. His dimples popped, causing a warmth to settle in my stomach and limbs, despite the brisk air. Or it could have been the hot coffee, but I prefer to think it was Sebby's smile that forced that reaction.

"So…," I began after several silent moments passed.

"So…," he repeated, eyeing me. He leaned back, relaxing into the park bench. I could feel his eyes studying me once more.

"What?"

"What do you mean 'what'?"

"Why are you staring at me like that?" I demanded with a sly smile.

"You don't want me looking at you?"

"No. I mean yes. I mean…" I took a deep breath. "You're making me feel self-conscious. Do I have something in my teeth?" I showed him my teeth.

He peered at my mouth as if looking for a piece of broccoli I missed, then flashed his beautiful smile once more. "No. You're good. You just intrigue me, Baylee. That's all."

"Oh, do I?" I tilted my head at him, wondering what brought forward such honesty.

Keeping his eyes glued to me, he nodded slowly. "Yes. From what I've learned about you in the few short minutes we've spent with each other this week, I'm pretty certain you're unlike anyone else out here. When I look at you, I see some of myself when I first came out here. God, I was so excited. I felt like I had the world at my fingertips. Now, sometimes I feel as though I've lost that enthusiasm along the way, which shows in my work. So maybe hanging out with you will bring back that excitement. Call it research."

"Research?" I raised my eyebrows. "So you're using me as a test dummy?"

"No. As inspiration."

He glanced down at our two dogs curled up at our feet, happy as clams to be outside and checking out the people walking by. I remained quiet, unsure of how to respond. Something about the way Sebby ended that sentence made me think he wasn't quite done with what he wanted to say and was trying to compose his thoughts. Part of me hoped he was about to ask me out to dinner or something…like a real date. My first real date, since I wasn't too sure you could count going to the movies with all your high school friends a date.

"You like games?" he suddenly asked.

"What?" I furrowed my brow.

"Game night. You like games?"

"I suppose…," I dragged out.

"Then let's play a little game of our own. Every morning, we'll meet for coffee and I get to ask you one question — any question — and you have to answer honestly."

"Why?"

"Like I said, you intrigue me. So what do you say, Dixie? Care to be my muse?"

Biting my lip to hide the grin that wanted to crawl across my face at the thought of being the muse for Mr. Sex On Two Legs, I cocked my head at him. "Sounds a bit one-sided, if you ask me. You get to peek into my head. What do I get out of it?"

"My company?" He smiled, running his hand through his wayward hair.

I scowled.

"And free coffee every morning?" His face lit up with hopefulness.

"Tit for tat, buddy. You ask me a question, I get to ask you one in return."

He pulled back, rubbing his chin as he debated my proposition. "And why do you want that?"

"What can I say?" I shrugged. Leaning toward him, I narrowed my eyes. "*You* intrigue *me*."

He closed the space between us and my lips parted slightly. I didn't know what I expected him to do, but I no longer had any control over my body. This man, a complete stranger just a few days ago, had an inexplicable pull on me. Of course, as my luck would have it, that was the exact moment a seagull decided to perch on a nearby garbage bin, sending both our dogs into a frenzy. The chorus of barking was enough to make anyone think we had an army of dogs, instead of just the two.

"Sport, calm down, buddy," I soothed, running my hand along his short coat.

"Either chase the damn bird or don't, Gidget," Sebby added. "Don't just sit here and growl."

When the seagull got the hint and moved on to a different garbage bin, our dogs calmed down, resuming their security detail.

"Well then," Sebby said. "I suppose fair is fair. Each morning, I ask you a question, and you ask me one in return. Deal?" Raising his eyebrows, he held his hand out to me.

"Deal." We shook on it. Leaning back on the bench, I took a sip of my coffee as the wind picked up. It was a crisp, cool morning, but sitting next to Sebby warmed me, as cliché and cheesy as that sounds. "So, what's your first question?"

Placing a finger over his mouth, he turned to survey me, deep in thought. "Hmm. There are so many different ways I could play this. I could be boring and ask you your favorite color, whether you like pineapples on your pizza..."

I scrunched my nose in disgust.

"I take that as a no, so that's off the table. And I'm sure all of those questions will give me one piece of the puzzle. Or I could delve deeper, but then I run the risk that our game will be over before it even starts."

"And we wouldn't want that to happen, would we?"

"Certainly not," he replied. "I mean, I couldn't do that to Gidget here." He gestured to his dog. "She seems to have taken quite a liking to Sport." He winked.

"So what approach are you taking?"

"An unplanned one." Pinching his lips, he stared at me for several anxious moments before his face brightened. "Do you prefer sunrises or sunsets?"

"That's a random question," I commented.

"Not really. There's a lot you can tell about a person based on the answer to even some seemingly innocuous questions."

Scrunching my nose, I wondered what the answer could possibly reveal about me. "Fine," I exhaled. "I'll answer your question."

I paused to consider. I remembered going to the beach with my dad, watching the sunrise over the Carolina coast. There was always something so powerful about seeing the sun appear over the horizon, as if it brought hope for a new day. Until just a few days ago, I had never really experienced a breathtaking sunset. But as I witnessed my first one over the Pacific Ocean, that orange-red sun disappearing behind the horizon, it was symbolic of wiping the slate clean, which was what I wanted to do with my move out here.

"Both," I said.

"That's not an answer. You can't choose both."

"Why not?" I shot back. "I simply can't choose which I prefer."

"What if you were on death row, about to be executed, and you were given the choice of watching the sunrise or sunset one last time before being put to death. Which would you pick?"

"I'd never be in that situation. I'll never kill someone." I crossed my arms in front of my chest, feigning indignation.

Sebby chuckled. I would do anything to keep hearing that beautiful sound fall from his lips. "You want to know what I just learned about you that has absolutely nothing to do with sunrises or sunsets?"

"Enlighten me."

"That you, Baylee, are stubborn."

I shrugged. "I'm Irish. What do you expect?"

"Just pick one. Don't think too much about it. Say the first thing that pops into your head."

"Fine," I huffed. "Sunrise. A sunset is like wiping

56

the slate clean, but a sunrise is just full of hope. They're both beautiful, but I think I like what a sunrise represents better."

A small smile crossed his face. "Me, too."

"Why?"

"Is that your question for the day?"

Curious about his own reasons, I nodded. "Sure."

Looking away, he stared out over the crashing waves of the Pacific Ocean and toyed with the lid on his coffee. "When I finished film school and was trying to make a name for myself, I worked long days. The thing about this industry is that it's not a typical nine-to-five job. If you just want to punch a time clock, do something else. Even though I had a film degree, I didn't have a lot of experience, so I did everything to make directors and producers want to hire me, even if I was just a runner or something. I eventually hung around different sets long enough that one of the directors allowed me to work as an editorial assistant when the film went to post. I wanted to learn everything about the process. Granted, they teach you some of that in school, but it's mostly theoretical. I was getting hands-on experience on a daily basis, so I didn't want to squander the opportunity.

"Every day before the sun came up, I would go into the post house where the film was being finalized. I would stay there, working until after the sun went down again. The days blurred together as I learned from the best of the best — the best editors, directors, producers, music arrangers. We were getting close to deadline and had to work overnights to make it." A wistful expression crossed his face as he looked up at the sun shining above us.

"I'll never forget that last night when the final cut was approved. We all went up onto the roof of the building to celebrate with some beers, only to see the sun rising over the mountains, shining on downtown LA. I had worked my ass off for months, even forsaking relationships, but as I stood drinking with this group of people who had become like a family to me, I grew homesick for my own family, who I had barely spoken to since starting to work on that set. That sunrise made me realize there are more important things in life than my career. Don't get me wrong. I still vowed to do everything I could to be the best in my profession, but I didn't want to lose sight of who I was as a person anymore."

"So what happened?" I asked. I was enthralled with his story. It was apparent that Sebby was ambitious. I was envious of his motivation and drive to do everything he could to achieve his dreams. He probably had a strong support system in his family, people telling him to reach for the stars. I wondered what that was like.

"Job offers came in," he continued. "I had built a reputation for myself as a hard worker, so I started to get phone calls from studios to help on various projects. I worked my way up from just a production assistant, then editing, then producing. It wasn't too long until I got my first big break. One of the contacts I had made over the years got a project green-lit by one of the studios. Big budget. Huge stars. He asked me to be on his producing team and I agreed, but only on the condition that there would be no overnights. I didn't want to miss another sunrise. He agreed, and that's been my rule ever since. And if it weren't for this rule of mine, I probably never would have run into you, so now I'm even more grateful for it."

He smiled and peered at me. There was an honesty in his gaze I wasn't expecting. He wasn't trying to hide anything from me, wasn't trying to pretend to be someone else. It was refreshing.

"I'm happy you have this rule in place, too."

# CHAPTER SIX

THE NEXT FEW WEEKS seemed to fly by as I attempted to make my new condo into a home. Marcel was over at my place at least several times a week, going over all his big ideas for completely redecorating it. Every Thursday night, I went to Sophia's for her weekly game night. I spent the rest of my free time reading or people-watching around Santa Monica Pier.

As much fun as I was having with everything else going on in my life, one particular person seemed to preoccupy my thoughts nearly every second of every day. I no longer had to drag myself out of bed in the morning to take Sport for his walk. Instead, I jumped up, excited about meeting Sebby for coffee as we continued asking completely random questions.

*What's your favorite movie?*

*What do you wish you could change about yourself?*

*If you could have dinner with one person, either dead or alive, who would it be?*

Coffee together became such a regular part of my routine that when the last week of October arrived and Sebby had to head out of town, I felt lost as I walked Sport. Since I had nothing to look forward to, my pace was a little slower, my feet dragging on the pavement. A creature of habit, I lowered myself onto the park bench that I was certain had a permanent impression of both our asses in it.

As I took a sip of the coffee I had to bring today, my cell phone vibrated in my purse. I half expected it to be Marcel with some new idea for my condo. I was pleasantly surprised to see a text from Sebby, as if he knew I was thinking about him at that precise moment.

*Favorite member of the Rat Pack?*

A smile crossing my face, I contemplated a witty response.

*Dean Martin. Sure, Frank had a fantastic voice, and Sammy was an unparalleled entertainer, but Dino was the whole package. And I'm all about the whole package.*

A reply arrived almost immediately.

*I've heard that about you. Miss me?*

*You've already asked your one question for the day. My turn. Do you like clowns?*

*Clowns, Dixie? That may be the most random question you've ever asked.*

*Perhaps. Just answer me.*

*I've never made it all the way through the movie* It, *if that answers your question.*

I hastily searched the web, grinning when I found a

picture of a vicious-looking Pennywise the Clown and sent it to him.

*That's it, Dixie. This means war.*

*Bring it, Nosebleeder.*

~~~~~~~~~~

WHEN THURSDAY MORNING ROLLED around, I still had no idea what to wear to the Halloween version of game night I would be going to at Sophia's, which I heard was notorious for being pretty epic. Everyone had that one holiday they loved, and Sophia's was Halloween. From the sound of it, everyone else had been planning their costumes for the past few months. I couldn't remember the last time I actually dressed up for Halloween. Will and I had been invited to parties, but he always found some excuse not to go.

As I sat on the park bench that morning, Sport at my feet, I grabbed my phone and typed a quick text to Sebby.

*Halloween Party tonight. What should I dress up as?*

*You're seriously wasting one of your questions on what I think you should get for a Halloween costume?*

*Sounds about right. What do you think?*

I kept my eyes glued to my phone as I waited for his reply, each second that passed seeming like hours. Finally, my phone buzzed and I couldn't open my messages fast enough.

*Ginger from Gilligan's Island. You've already got the red hair going for you. Just get a leopard print bathing suit and a life saver with the S.S. Minnow written on it.*

*Ginger? Really? I thought most guys had a thing for Maryann. Plus, where do you expect me to find a leopard print bathing suit at a moment's notice?*

*You live in LA now. Leopard print bathing suits are a dime a dozen. And what can I say? I'm a sucker for a red-headed woman.*

I hummed Bruce Springsteen's song of the same name for the rest of the day.

~~~~~~~~~~

"WELL, HELLO, MISS DIXIE!" Marcel shouted as I let myself into Sophia's condo that evening. I had taken Sebby's advice and decided to dress up as Ginger. May as well use my red hair to my advantage. However, instead of wearing a leopard print bathing suit, I opted for a glamorous gold sequin gown and white feather boa. I spent hours and too much hairspray recreating Tina Louise's hair, curling it at the ends and teasing it near the roots to give it the volume it needed.

"Hey, Marcel," I said, hugging him, taking in his pirate costume. Sophia's condo looked nothing like it did the previous times I was there. The lights were dimmed and dry ice "smoked" through the living area, giving it a spooky vibe. People I had never met before mingled, trying to avoid bumping into the coffins or headstones she had erected. "Looking good."

"I hope so. Sophia invited this guy she did a

commercial with a few months back and, let's just say, I've been crushing on him ever since I met him."

"Is he…?" I raised my eyebrows, unsure of what the proper etiquette was. I had never met anyone who would openly admit they were gay before. Sure, I had my suspicions about one of my high school friends, especially considering he was probably one of the most attractive guys in town yet I'd never seen him with a woman. I couldn't care less either way, but I knew he'd receive backlash from the entire community, which wasn't something a member of the town council could easily explain away. Still, I always felt bad he had to keep who he was to himself.

"You mean gay?" Marcel joked.

"What? It's an honest question. I don't know how these things work."

"Do you want me to draw a picture, sugar?" He grabbed my hand and pulled me through the party and into the living room where Sophia had set up the whiteboard for tonight's game of Karaoke Pictionary. Based on the already inebriated condition of some of the people in attendance, I had a feeling it would be one game I'd never forget.

"I don't need a picture, Marcel," I insisted, but he refused to listen.

"See what happens is…" He picked up the black marker and started to sketch on the whiteboard. "When one man finds another man attractive…"

I closed my eyes, trying not to peek at what he was drawing.

"…they want to do something to let the other know they're interested."

"I'm not an idiot," I huffed, opening my eyes and

taking the marker from him so he couldn't turn his R-rated sketch into an X-rated one. "I get that. And I certainly don't need you to illustrate it in black and white. I just didn't know how you could tell someone else was gay. That's all."

"The same way you can tell if a guy is straight," he responded quickly. He made it sound so obvious. "You just...know."

"You mean to tell me you've never been wrong?"

"Have you?"

"I've really never had the opportunity to be wrong."

"Well, I have." He placed his hands on his hips. "And, over the past five years, I can remember only one instance of reading a guy wrong. It's a risk you have to take. It usually pays off."

"It doesn't scare you, knowing there's a small chance you might be wrong?"

"Of course it does, Miss Dixie," he admitted, heading toward where Sophia had set up a bar stocked with more bottles of wine and alcohol than I thought we could ever drink. "But that's part of life. Taking risks. I've met some amazing people and have been in some incredible relationships I never would have experienced had I let my fear overtake me. So you should do the same thing, especially with Mr. Nosebleeder you can't stop blushing over." He raised his eyepatch and winked.

"What do you—"

"Oh, please," he said dramatically, rolling his eyes. "Since we met, we've been spending an awful lot of time together. And every time I've asked you how your morning has been, a stupid grin crosses your face because you're thinking of your little Nosebleeder. It's great you're out there and meeting people. Just don't be afraid to make the first move."

"The only way that will ever happen is if he were to spike my coffee with a heaping shot of whiskey." Marcel handed me a glass and I raised it to my lips, savoring the wine. Over the past few weeks, I had become rather spoiled in the wine category. My new group of friends seemed to have quite exceptional taste when it came to that delicious California nectar, and I was more than happy to reap the benefits.

"Why?" Marcel pushed.

"Oh no, you don't. You don't get to put me on the spot."

"Do you like this guy?"

I avoided his eyes. "Maybe," I admitted. Sebby was attractive, funny, and had a personality I couldn't help but be drawn to. But wasn't it too soon? Wasn't it too easy? "But, like I said weeks ago, I'm not sure I'm ready to date. Anyway, he'd just be a rebound, and we all know those never end well."

"Not necessarily. I've had some great long-term rebound relationships. I think you should make the first move. Look at things from his point of view. You're recently divorced and have been pretty vocal about not being ready to jump into a new relationship right now. He may be playing the friend card because he thinks it's the only shot he has at spending time with you. So put your big girl panties on and tell him how you feel. And speaking of big girl panties… Nice dress, Ginger." He held his elbow out to me and I put my arm through his.

"Thanks, Captain Jack."

We made our way across the living room and joined what had become my small little circle of friends, our Wine Drinking Karaoke Pictionary Playing Club, and the hours flew by. There was something about being dressed up as someone else that made everyone's inhibitions disappear. My friends were always a lively bunch. Tonight, they were even more so.

At the height of the frivolity, Sophia, dressed as Magenta from *Rocky Horror Picture Show*, complete with frizzy curly hair and a short maid's dress, ushered everyone into the living room and we all went through the process of being assigned teams for tonight's game of Karaoke Pictionary. I couldn't remember how, but playing Pictionary stopped being important at some point and we all devoted our full attention to Karaoke.

With no rules, Sophia jumped up from the couch and dragged Darren with her. His normally intimidating physique was covered by the realistic costume he wore of Riff Raff from *Rocky Horror*, perfectly complementing Sophia's Magenta. His dark suit was dingy with stuffing around the shoulders to make it appear as if he had a slight hunch. His face was covered with pale makeup, his eyes bloodshot, and the application of his stringy blond wig looked professionally done. That didn't surprise me in this town.

Darren draped his limp arm around her, catching me off guard. "Are they together?" I whispered to Marcel.

He grinned. "Took you long enough to pick up on that."

"This is the first time I've actually seen him touch her."

He shrugged. "It started as a casual thing, but it's recently become more serious, although neither of them will admit it." He rolled his eyes and turned his attention back to Sophia as she searched her catalog of music. I had a pretty good feeling what song she was looking for, and when the opening bars of "Time Warp" sounded through the cramped living room, the crowd, which had blossomed over the past several hours, stood up and danced along with Sophia and Darren, who sang the parts of Magenta and Riff Raff respectively.

"I'm surprised you didn't dress up as Dr. Frank N. Furter," I said to Marcel as we all took a jump to the left.

"I can go back to my condo and change if you want me to," he joked, winking.

"Please don't tell me you have a secret stash of leather, fishnets, and heels in your closet." I laughed, thrusting my pelvis forward in accordance with the instructions in the lyrics.

"Wouldn't you like to find out, Miss Dixie!"

Sophia began to sing the second verse, her voice imitating Magenta's so well, I had to do a double take to make sure it was my neighbor. "Do they do this often?" I asked Marcel as we continued to dance.

"A little-known fact about Miss Sophia... She *loves* this movie. When I was new here, she dragged me to a midnight showing. I had no idea what I was getting myself into. I'll never forget when we walked up and saw almost everyone in full costume. I thought Sophia would be out of place dressed as she was..."

"Which was?" I asked, intrigued.

"You're looking at it, sweetheart. She's gone as Columbia, complete with sequined mini tuxedo, but she rocks the Magenta look. *I* was the one out of place that night, wearing just a t-shirt and jeans. Everyone in our group was in costume. Hell, even her boss dressed up as Eddie."

"Her boss meaning my neighbor?" I pressed, my interest piqued once again about the mysterious man living across the hall from me who seemed to be more of an enigma than anything.

"One and the same. He even rode up on a vintage motorcycle, just like in the movie. Of course, our Eddie is nowhere near as chubby as the Eddie in the movie. Not even close, girlfriend." He raised his eyebrows at me.

"I'm starting to think y'all are just making this guy up. I've been here a month and I've yet to meet him."

Marcel scanned the crowd as the song came to an end. "Well, tonight may be your night, sugar. Sophia mentioned he might make an appearance."

"Well, be sure to point him out to me when he gets here."

"Oh, you'll know. If you see a tall, lean hunk of man with silky hair you just want to run your hands through and two-day-old scruff you want to drag your tongue across, that's your man."

"You're describing half the men in this town, Marcel."

He sighed. "Don't I know it, Dixie. Don't I know it."

Music continued throughout the night, the old adage that you should never give a drunk a microphone proven by the sounds coming from the speakers. Red plastic cups covered nearly every available surface, and I felt bad for the crew Sophia hired to come clean tomorrow morning.

As the clock neared midnight and I was in the corner of the living room, trying to maintain my composure as one of Sophia's drunk friends sang a stirring rendition of Patsy Cline's "Crazy", the lyrics mostly indecipherable through her slurred speech, an excited scream echoed from the kitchen. The entire place went practically silent for a split second before the roar of the party resumed.

"What's going on?" I asked Marcel, craning my neck to see someone walk into the kitchen and nearly get tackled by a very intoxicated Sophia.

"It looks like your neighbor made it." He grabbed my hand, pulling me from my comfortable spot on the couch and into the kitchen. "Allow me to introduce you to him, although you probably won't see him for another month or so after today at the rate that man works."

He navigated the crowd of people circling a man whose appearance fit Marcel's description perfectly…at least from the back. His light brown hair looked remarkably silky, and there *was* a part of me that wanted to run my hands through it to see if it felt like it looked. He was tall with what appeared to be a nice figure. His costume consisted of a brownish robe, open in the front, and loafers. I watched him make his way through the crowd, standing on my tiptoes to try and see what he looked like, but his back was toward me. Still, there was something eerily familiar about his gait.

"Eddie!" Marcel approached him as I stood off to the side.

"Good to see you, man. It's been a while." They shook hands, hugging briefly.

"Keeping yourself busy?"

"More like out of trouble." Both men laughed.

"The Ice Queen isn't in town, is she?" Marcel shivered dramatically.

"No. She refuses to believe there's a world outside the concrete jungle of New York City. And she's not that cold once you get to know her."

I remained fixed in place, feeling as if I were a fly on the wall, observing old friends conversing about people I knew nothing about.

"I'll believe that when I see it," Marcel said, disbelief evident in his voice. "Come here. I want you to meet your new neighbor." He ushered Eddie out of the crowd, his face coming into view.

I wish I could rewind time and remember every precise thought that entered my mind as that tall physique slowly faced me and I took in those familiar gray-blue eyes, full lips, and smile, but it all happened so fast.

"Nosebleeder?" I asked, incredulous. His facial hair had grown out a little over the week he had been gone, but there was no mistaking who it was.

"Baylee? What are you doing here?"

"Wait a second," Marcel interrupted. "You two already know each other?"

"He's Nosebleeder," I said, my voice low.

"Holy shit, Miss Dixie!" Marcel exclaimed, his hand covering his mouth. "This is a twist I certainly wasn't expecting!"

"You and me both," I responded. "I thought you said his name was Eddie."

"We have nicknames for everyone," Marcel explained. "We started calling him that after going to that midnight showing of *Rocky Horror.*"

I nodded, my eyes fixed on Sebby as I ran through the past month in my mind...the morning coffees, the questions, everything I had learned about him from Sophia and Marcel. I never would have imagined the Eddie they all spoke of was the same man with whom I spent my mornings. And who was this "Ice Queen" I heard Marcel mention? The way she was referred to made me believe she was his girlfriend...or worse.

My Irish temper rising, I grabbed Sebby's hand and pulled him out of Sophia's condo into the deserted hallway. I had questions I needed answers to and I didn't want the entire party to overhear.

Spinning around to face him when we reached the vacant bank of elevators, I prodded, "Did you know?" I could feel my cheeks turning red. I wasn't sure if it was due to anger or embarrassment. Or perhaps the wine.

"Know what? That you were my neighbor?" He stepped back, raising his hands in defense. "I'm just as surprised about this as you are!"

Pinching my lips, I studied his face, wishing I could see some sign he was telling the truth. I didn't know what to think anymore.

"But I told you about game night!" I shot back. "You must have put two and two together!"

"Truthfully, it did cross my mind," Sebby admitted. "Then I shook it off. I mean, you have to agree that the chance of us meeting and you being my neighbor is pretty slim."

"Yes, but..." I tried to come up with something to counter his argument, but I knew he was right. There was nothing about me mentioning game night that would make him think I was his new neighbor. If I were in his shoes, I would have done what he did…consider it briefly, then wave it off as a coincidence.

"Baylee, you—"

"And what about this 'Ice Queen', as Marcel called her? Is she your girlfriend?" I crossed my arms in front of my chest.

"Yes, she is," he said. I expected to see the telltale signs of a guilty conscience — shifting from foot to foot, lowering his eyes, stuttering, running his hand through his hair — but none of that happened. His gaze remained unwavering, his stance firm.

"When were you going to tell me about her? Or were you just going to lead me on and hope to have a little something on both coasts?" I fumed.

"Whoa, Baylee," he soothed, his voice softening as his brow furrowed slightly. "I meant what I said. I genuinely enjoy hanging out with you, but I never led you on to think I was interested in you as anything other than a friend who gave me a bloody nose one morning."

I thought he *was* interested and that's why he wanted to spend time getting to know me. Maybe he was just friendly. Maybe I had been out of the dating world for so long, I had no idea what flirting looked like these days. Hell, I wondered if I even knew what flirting was to begin with.

"But men and women can't just be friends!" I exclaimed, losing my patience. "It's impossible!"

"Says who?"

"Me! There will always be that thing between them." I gestured between our bodies, growing more and more exasperated with the entire situation.

Narrowing his gaze, an awkward silence surrounded us. Then his lips curved into that smile I had grown accustomed to seeing nearly every morning. "Really, Dixie? Did you hear what you just said?"

I pinched my lips together, my nostrils flaring. I was pretty sure I looked like a dragon who was about to set fire to her attacker, but as Sebby stared at me, that smile plastered on his face, I couldn't stay mad at him. It all seemed so absurd. Hindsight was always twenty-twenty.

Now that the truth was out, could we really just be friends? I had never had a guy friend before. Sure, I had grown close to Marcel over the past few weeks, but he had absolutely zero interest in dating me. At some point, things were certain to get complicated between Sebby and me, especially considering I had been attracted to him since the moment I laid eyes on his blood-covered face. Was that a good enough reason for me to toss out our "friendship"? One thing was certain… I hated the thought of waking up tomorrow morning and not being able to meet him at our park bench for coffee and a question.

Sighing, I softened my expression. "So you really are my neighbor?"

"It appears so." He shoved his hands into the plaid shorts he wore underneath the robe.

Studying the complete ensemble, an epiphany washed over me. While he was missing the full mustache and beard, he had the rest of the look down perfectly. Dark sunglasses, robe, white t-shirt, dingy plaid shorts, beat-up loafers. "You're the Big Lebowski!"

He flipped the sunglasses over his eyes and took a

small carton of milk from the pocket of his robe. "I'm not Lebowski. I'm the Dude."

"Your costume isn't complete," I added. "You're missing a rug."

Laughing, he placed his hand on the middle of my back and led me toward Sophia's condo. "It really did tie the room together," he joked.

Why did this man have to be so damn perfect?

# CHAPTER SEVEN

MY ALARM WENT OFF the following morning, just as it had every other morning over the previous few weeks, but something was different. The knowledge that Sebby was my elusive neighbor still weighed on my mind. One minute, I was giving myself a pep talk that men and women became friends all the time. The next, I was convinced it was impossible. How could it work when I was attracted to him? Sure, I told myself I had no desire to get into any sort of relationship, being just weeks out of a ten-year marriage, but was that really how I felt? Maybe the connection I had to Sebby sparked something I wasn't anticipating. Maybe I wanted to feel beautiful, something Will never did. And maybe, for these past few weeks, Sebby *did* make me feel that way.

Sport jumped onto my massive bed and nudged me with his wet nose. Dogs are creatures of habit, and mine was no different. He had grown so accustomed to going for a walk at the same time every morning that being thirty minutes past the time we usually left, it was throwing his routine off.

I looked at his eager eyes and wagging tail. I couldn't deprive him of his morning exercise just because I was unsure about whether or not I wanted to face Sebby now that the cloud of alcohol from last night had dissipated. Truthfully, I wasn't even sure he would be at our morning meeting spot now that I knew who he was.

I threw on a pair of yoga pants and a light jacket, then put Sport's collar around his neck and hooked him up to his leash. Pausing briefly as I exited into the hallway, I stared at Sebby's door. I probably looked like a stalker when I held my ear up to it, trying to hear any noise coming from within. I thought I knew who he was, but armed with the knowledge that we shared a hallway, it was almost like he was a completely different person. How was it possible I had never run into him before? Yes, he worked long hours, but surely I would have heard Gidget barking from inside his condo. Then again, based on the price of these places, they probably made sure to install soundproof walls and flooring.

Feeling a tug on the leash, I snapped out of my thoughts and retreated from Sebby's door, allowing Sport to drag me into the elevator, through the lobby, and across the street toward our usual morning destination.

As I navigated down the pathway at a leisurely pace, the closer we got to the park bench, the more clammy my hands became. My heart rate picked up and nausea settled in my stomach. I didn't know if it was from all the liquor I had consumed the night before or if it was the prospect of seeing Sebby. What if he was here but wasn't expecting me to show up? What if he gave some thought to my intoxicated outburst and came to the conclusion that I was right? That men and women couldn't just be friends. I never considered that he would want to end our "friendship". Now, the notion unsettled me.

Instead of being consumed by my thoughts, I should have been paying attention to Sport. He darted away from me and toward our park bench, jumping onto the dog he must have missed while her owner was out of town.

"Reminds me of a certain day a few weeks ago," that familiar deep voice commented. "Apart from the bloody nose, of course."

"That can definitely be rectified if you're into that kind of thing," I joked, biting my lip. Shifting from foot to foot, I remained standing, feeling awkward. Sebby held a cup of coffee toward me, and I eyed it skeptically. He was acting as if nothing had changed. And maybe I was making a bigger deal out of it than it was. Maybe nothing *had* changed.

Relaxing, I took the coffee from him and lowered myself onto the bench. I avoided his eyes, staring out over the ocean at what appeared to be storm clouds in the distance. A heavy silence settled between us and I didn't know if I should be the first one to speak or not.

"So…," I started.

"I didn't…," he said simultaneously. Our eyes met. It was obvious we were both uneasy about where our newfound knowledge left us. "You go first," he prompted, always the gentleman.

"Nah. I'm not sure what I was going to say anyway."

Drawing in a breath, he licked his lips, toying with the beverage sleeve on his coffee cup. "I was just going to say that I didn't expect you to show up today."

"I almost didn't," I confessed.

"Why?"

"Is that your question for today?" I took a sip of my coffee.

A small smile crossed his lips. "No. I have a good one planned and that's not it. Call it me just wanting to clear the air."

"I thought we did that last night," I remarked, although I knew that was the furthest thing from the truth.

"You were pretty tipsy last night, Baylee. I want to see what *sober* Baylee has to say."

"What is there to say, Sebby?" I exhaled. "So what? The guy I unceremoniously gave a bloody nose to just so happens to be my mysterious absentee neighbor. Nothing's changed."

"And what about your argument last night that men and women can never truly be friends?"

"The jury's still out on that one, I suppose," I admitted truthfully.

"Will you at least give me the chance to prove they can? I hate the thought of not being friends with you just because you don't think it's possible."

"You honestly think you can prove that to me?" I raised my eyebrows, unconvinced.

"I sure do. When I'm through with you, the only thing you'll see when you look at me is a eunuch."

I grimaced, a playful look of horror on my face. "But you're *not*, are you?"

"Why?" he asked in a high-pitched voice. "Would that bother you?"

Shaking my head, I punched him lightly in the arm. "Jackass."

"It took you this long to figure that one out? I'm beginning to question your observational skills, Baylee…" He stopped short. "You know what? I have no idea what your last name is."

"Why do you want to know? Plan on stalking me?"

"I don't need your last name to do that. I know where you live." He raised his eyebrows in a sinister way, rubbing his hands together.

"You just gave me a reason to sell my place and move."

"Please don't," he begged. "The last person who lived there was the neighbor from hell. She was older and, I swear, had super hearing. Anytime I came home from work late and made any noise, she would shout at me. It felt like I was living across the hall from my grandma. Finally, her son decided to put her in assisted living. I had a feeling she wasn't all there mentally. She was convinced people were breaking into her condo during the day and stealing her dishes. She also had her wedding dress in some sort of display case. She told me that bandits broke in at night and were cutting off pieces of the vintage lace."

"Really?" It sounded like someone in my family. I was close with my uncle and father, when he was still alive, but my extended family had more branches than a California redwood. I couldn't keep track of who was married to whom, which kids belonged to which parent, not to mention all the kids born to teen moms because of unplanned pregnancies. My extended family had lots of baby daddies. I had come across an article one day about a woman having her tenth child from a tenth man and was almost certain I was related to her in some capacity.

"I asked her son about it when he was clearing out her condo. He said when they were going through her things, they found a big box containing her chinaware. Apparently, she had used it to eat off of but never washed it so it just sat in a box, dirty, for God knows how long."

"And the wedding dress?"

"He discovered a bunch of old and faded doilies around the condo. When he held them up to what remained of her wedding dress, he noticed a striking similarity in the lace patterns. She must have started chopping up her dress and making it into doilies to pass the time."

"I hope I never lose my mind like that," I commented. "I'd rather someone smother me in my sleep than walk around not knowing who I am."

"You and me both. Speaking of which... Are you going to share your last name with me?"

"Morgan. Baylee Morgan..." I trailed off, tearing my gaze from his.

"What?" Sebby asked, eyeing me.

"Nothing. It's just... The last ten years, I was Baylee Cooper. It's been a while since I've been able to call myself Baylee Morgan."

"I like it."

"What about you?" I asked. "What's your last name?"

"Powers." He offered his hand and I took it in mine. We didn't shake. We just sat there in silence, absorbed in each other's touch. When our eyes met, I couldn't help but think this was something extraordinary... Something magical.

"Well..." I pulled my hand from his, the angel on my shoulder sternly reminding me that he had a girlfriend. "Now that we've been formally introduced, we should probably get on with our questions. Don't want to make you late for the rest of your day."

"Right." He cleared his throat, regaining his

composure. "Remember the day we met?"

"How could I forget? I gave you a bloody nose."

He laughed briefly. "Well, after I left the coffee shop that day, I doubled back when I realized I had never gotten your name, but it looked like you were deep in thought, reading a book or something. What was it?"

His question caught me off guard. The past few weeks of asking questions hadn't been too personal, but this one hit deep. I didn't know if I was ready to share this part of my life with him yet...or ever.

"Remember our deal," he added, seeing my hesitation. "I get to ask you any question I want and you have to answer it truthfully."

"Yes, but—"

"But nothing. Judging by your reluctance to answer, I know I've hit on something you probably haven't talked about in years, if ever. Sometimes, we really want to talk about it, but have no one with whom to do so. I'm your guy." He beamed. "I'm more than interested in learning about this side of the intriguing Baylee Morgan."

Drawing in a long breath, I glanced down at my bag where the journal was. I liked keeping it close in case I needed a boost.

"It was my mother's journal." I swallowed hard. "She died a few days after I was born. I never got to know her."

Closing his eyes, Sebby hung his head. "Baylee, I'm sorry."

"Before I headed out here, my uncle gave me her journal in the hopes that I'd have some guidance on this big adventure of mine." I reached into my purse and pulled it out, showing him. Flipping through the worn pages, I continued. "I've only read a few entries, but she definitely had a unique outlook on the world. She…" I stopped abruptly when I noticed a folded up piece of notebook paper shoved in between a few of the pages toward the back of the journal.

"What's that?" Sebby asked, noticing my reaction.

"I'm not sure." Unfolding the piece of paper, my eyes scanned what appeared to be a list, some items scratched out with a date next to each one.

"Looks like a bucket list," he commented.

"An unfinished one." I stared at it, swallowing through the lump in my throat. "She wrote about making a list of things she wanted to do before she died. That's what she documented in this journal, I guess." I ran my fingers along the worn cover, silence engulfing us. Turning to Sebby, I asked, "Do you have a bucket list?"

"Is this your question for today?"

Pausing briefly, I nodded. "Yes. Today's question for you is whether you have a bucket list."

He reached down and scratched between Gidget's ears, considering my question. "Well, I don't really have a bucket list, per se. I have things I've always wanted to do, but I've never written them down and made it my mission to check them off."

"Like what?"

He glared at me in a playful way. "I'm pretty sure you already asked your allotted question for the day."

"It's a necessary follow-up," I quipped. "You can't get off that easily."

A sly grin crawled across his lips and he slowly

turned to face me. Replaying my words in my head and hearing the double entendre, my cheeks turned red.

"Given the right person…" He raised his eyebrows, chuckling.

My mouth curled into a small smile, despite my brain shouting at it not to react. "Just tell me what would be on your bucket list," I demanded, trying to ignore how carefree and comfortable I felt whenever I was around Sebby. "Perv."

"Learn to fly," he replied without missing a beat. "There's something so romantic and nostalgic about flying. I've always been fascinated with air travel, even when I was a little boy. My room was full of model airplanes, and I dreamed of learning to fly one of them."

"So what's holding you back now?"

He stared ahead. "You know how it is," he said after a comfortable silence, the wind whipping around us. I could see rain beginning to fall over the ocean. I knew I should hurry home to avoid getting stuck in a downpour, but I couldn't leave. I didn't want to waste any opportunity to spend time with Sebby. "Life gets in the way. I finished high school, went to college, then became obsessed with making a name for myself in this industry. Everything else in my life was put on the back burner."

"You should do it," I urged. "I mean, if it's something you've always wanted to do, look into it."

"And you should finish what your mother started."

My eyes widened.

"What's stopping you, Baylee?"

I shrugged. "It just doesn't seem right to me. This

was my mother's list, and—"

"A list that was never finished. You said you never knew her. Maybe doing this will make you feel closer to her. I think it would be a wonderful tribute…and maybe you'll find yourself along the way." He raised himself from the park bench and began to walk away.

"What do you mean by that?" I called after him.

"Exactly what I said," he replied over his shoulder. "I've learned a lot about you over the past several weeks, Baylee. From where I'm standing, it looks like you're still trying to figure out who you are as a person. It might be good for you to leave yourself open to new things, new experiences."

I opened my mouth to protest and rattle off a million reasons why completing my mother's bucket list was the worst idea ever, but he cut me off.

"Just think about it."

Then he jogged away from me with Gidget, leaving me to give some serious consideration to his proposition.

*Bastard.*

# CHAPTER EIGHT

*Skydive.*

*Ride on the back of a motorcycle.*

*Fly in a private plane.*

*Watch as many cinematic masterpieces as possible.*

*Learn to ballroom dance.*

*Spend the night in a haunted house (a legitimately haunted one, not just a cheesy house decked out with zombies for Halloween).*

*Break a few rules and don't get caught.*

*Go to a farmer's market and make something with all the fresh produce.*

*Learn how to skateboard.*

*Go wine tasting.*

*Learn how to do yoga (and not just from a workout video. Go to a real yoga class).*

*Put my feet in the Atlantic Ocean, Gulf of Mexico, and Pacific Ocean…all in one day.*

*Learn how to surf.*

*Write a book.*

*Learn how to toss pizza dough.*

*Sleep on the beach under the stars.*

*Have a champagne picnic in Central Park by Bethesda Fountain at midnight on New Year's Eve.*

My eyes ran down the items on my mother's list

that she never got to experience. Her list was quite extensive and my face lit up when I pictured my father and mother doing some of the things she had crossed off...

~~Get a fish pedicure.~~

~~See the Great Barrier Reef.~~

~~Pet a penguin.~~

~~Attend the Kentucky Derby.~~

~~Write something in wet cement.~~

~~Cross the intersection at Abbey Road.~~

~~Watch the sunset from Key West.~~

~~Have a child.~~

Since arriving in town, I was unsure of the direction my life would take. I couldn't just sit around my condo all day and do nothing. I had told myself time and time again that this could be the perfect opportunity for me to do what I had said I would do for years...write a book. Perhaps this list was exactly the inspiration I needed to find my story.

A chiming from my laptop caught my attention, indicating a FaceTime call. I folded my mother's list and placed it back in her journal, then clicked on my laptop. I was greeted by my uncle's comforting eyes that reminded me of pulled pork, cornbread, and sweet tea.

"Uncle Monty," I breathed. "It's good to see you."

"You, too, kiddo." He wore a pressed suit over a crisp, white shirt and designer tie. Based on his wardrobe and the large glass windows behind him, I knew he was at his office. I didn't think he had taken a day off from work since my wedding. Even then, he was constantly on his cell phone "putting out fires", as he called it. "How's everything going out there? I've tried to get in touch with you a few times, but kept missing you."

"Sorry about that. I've been pretty busy."

"Making some friends, I assume?"

"A few," I answered, then proceeded to tell him everything that had happened since leaving North Carolina. I asked if he had heard any news from back home, to which he said he hadn't. I didn't expect him to. He rarely spent time in my hometown, apart from paying me the occasional visit. Now that I was gone, I doubted he had a reason to leave Charlotte. I knew *I* wouldn't.

As I was about to close out our video chat, I remembered the list I had discovered hidden between the pages of my mother's journal. I knew if anyone could tell me about that list, it was my uncle. "Can I ask you something?"

"Of course," Uncle Monty replied.

"Did you know about the list my mother made of all the things she wanted to do before she died?"

His face fell just slightly before his eyes brightened, as if recalling some rather fond memories. "Of course. Hell, I helped her write it."

"I found it in her journal. She never got around to a few of the things, so I was toying with the idea of seeing if I could finish the list for her."

Taking a protracted breath, he closed his eyes briefly before returning them to me. "I think your mother would like that. She'd be happy to know that, regardless of the fact you don't remember her, her legacy can live on through you."

The Other Side Of Someday

A small smile crept across my face and I nodded. I didn't know why I needed my uncle's approval to complete my mother's list, but I felt better knowing he liked the idea. "Thanks, Uncle Monty."

"You bet, kid. What are you going to start with?"

I pulled the sheet of paper out of the journal and scanned it. Nothing shouted out to me. My mother had my father to join her on this journey. Who did I have? My brain went to the first person I could think of — Sebby. I could just envision all the fun we would have checking items off the list, but I didn't think it was right to share such a personal journey with someone who had a girlfriend, despite his assurances that men and women could be friends. Maybe that was the point of this. Maybe I didn't need someone at my side to finish the task my mother set out to complete.

My eyes falling on one item that seemed fairly straightforward, I smiled at my uncle. "I think I'm going to learn yoga."

A laugh bellowed from my laptop. "Now *this* I'd pay to see."

~~~~~~~~~~

LATER THAT AFTERNOON, I pulled up in front of a yoga studio I had found online. Even though it had amazing reviews, I was a bit apprehensive about leaving my condo and driving the few short miles to the studio. Back home, I was never the shy girl. Hell, I knew everyone in my small town. But out here, I only had a handful of friends, being in unfamiliar territory for the first time in my life. I didn't know why, but I was nervous about walking into that yoga studio, everyone turning to stare at the new girl. I had to keep reminding myself that my life wasn't some cheesy, coming-of-age, *Mean Girl*-esque movie.

As I parked my car and fed the meter, I checked my watch, seeing I had time to kill before class was slated to begin. I took in my surroundings, my eyes falling on an adorable little coffee shop right next to the yoga studio. *Kismet*, I said to myself. Perhaps a few shots of caffeine was exactly what I needed at the moment.

The aroma of coffee met me the second I opened the door and walked into the small café. It was fairly busy for a Friday afternoon. There were people set up with laptops, typing away. Some tables were filled with women in workout gear, and I assumed they had just left the yoga studio. I simply rolled my eyes at their perfect makeup and hair with not a strand out of place. That had always been one of my pet peeves — women who viewed going to the gym as a beauty pageant. For me, working out was a release. If my makeup hadn't melted off by the end of my workout (on the off chance I banged my head and was idiotic enough to even put makeup on before heading to the gym), I clearly didn't work out hard enough.

Navigating my way around the tables, I ordered an espresso, found an empty table, and sat down, leaning my yoga bag against the wall. I pulled out my e-reader and got lost in the romance novel of the day. I was so immersed in the book, I hadn't heard anyone sit at the table next to me.

"Coming or going?" a voice asked, which I ignored. "I said, coming or going," the voice repeated, louder. I tilted my head up to see Mr. Tall, Dark, And Handsome smiling at me, taking me by surprise. The last thing I expected was to have a charming, attractive, muscular man strike up a conversation with me. I could tell by the way not one piece of hair was out of place that this was a man who cared about his appearance. It was completely different from the beer-drinking, football-watching guys I had grown up with back home.

"Excuse me?" I asked, checking over my shoulder to make sure he was, in fact, talking to me and not someone else or, God forbid, was on the phone. I could just picture myself holding a conversation with him, only for him to be talking to someone on his hands-free unit.

He gestured to my bag. "Yoga. Did you just finish a class?"

"No. I'm signed up for one at two."

"New to town?"

I nodded. "Is it that obvious?"

"A little bit, but don't worry." He leaned in toward me, lowering his voice. "Your secret is safe with me." He pulled back, his eyes bright. "I'm Dennis." He held his hand out, beaming.

"Baylee," I said, shaking his hand. "Do you do yoga?" I raised my eyebrows as I surveyed his loose tank top, exposing incredibly toned biceps and pectorals.

"Sure do. It's a great release, don't you think?"

"Really?" I tried to hide the disbelief in my voice. You wouldn't catch any of the guys I knew back home doing yoga, even if their life depended on it. Our small town didn't even have a decent gym. Combine that with the abundance of fried food, most people refused to put any effort into maintaining a healthy lifestyle. I was the odd bird out. I had always been pretty healthy and, quite possibly was the only person in my hometown who owned a pair of running shoes. I refused to fall victim to the cycle. Much to Will's dismay, I ate healthy. If he refused to cook for himself, he could eat what I did.

"It's great for flexibility," Dennis explained, winking. I couldn't help but think that there was a double meaning to that. "What class are you signed up for?"

"Mat Pilates."

"Me, too. Come on. I'll walk with you and show you around."

"You don't have to."

He stood up from his table and held his hand out to me. My eyes bulged when I saw how tall and ripped he was as he stood in front of me with his hand extended, his eyes beseeching me to take it. You know those guys you see on covers of romance novels? The ones with the ripped muscles whose veins were visible? Well, that was Dennis. He probably had zero percent body fat.

"Come on, Carolina. Walk with me."

I slowly raised myself from my chair and bent to grab my yoga bag.

"I've got this," he said, taking the bag from me and slinging it over his broad shoulders. If this fine specimen wanted to carry my yoga mat and walk with me to class, I wasn't one to complain.

"How did you know I was from Carolina?"

"Your accent," he started, holding the door of the coffee shop for me. "In a town of struggling actors, I guess we can all pick up on dialects fairly easily."

"I see. Can you do accents?"

"Yes, ma'am. I surely can," he said in a Texas drawl, tipping his imaginary cowboy hat toward me.

"You're really good at that! It sounds so natural."

"Actually, truth be told, it *is* natural for me. I was born and raised in Texas, so I grew up speaking like that. It wasn't until I moved out here that I started to lose the accent."

"I like the Texas drawl." I smirked at him as I sauntered into the yoga studio. I could feel him surveying my body, my hips swaying flirtatiously as I walked through the quaint reception area. The aroma of lavender and honey invaded my senses. I was barely a few feet inside, but I already felt more relaxed than I was just seconds ago.

"Dennis!" the bubbly blonde at the front desk said as we approached. "Who's your new friend? Are you trying to make me jealous?" She pouted, her expression playful.

"Never, Ashley," he crooned. "This is Baylee. We just met next door. It's her first time here, so I thought I'd make your job easier and show her around."

She typed at her computer, then returned her attention to us. "Here you are. Baylee Morgan. You're booked in the two o'clock Mat Pilates class. Dennis is taking that, too, so go ahead with him. We give all our new clients the first class for free, but if you enjoy it, come back and see me afterwards. We'll get you signed up with a bundle. Have fun!"

"Thanks." I smiled politely at her.

"This way." Dennis placed his hand in the middle of my back and led me from the front reception area down a long hallway decorated with miniature water fountains, the sound of soothing meditation music echoing in the corridor. I inhaled deeply, feeling all the craziness and stress of the past few months melt off instantaneously. "It's nice, isn't it?" he whispered.

"I'd come here just to sit in the hallway," I replied.

"They have a meditation room that's even more soothing. No class, just a room you can go into and relax."

"I'd never leave."

"It is kind of hard." He narrowed his gaze at me, as if he were trying to focus his eyes on my face and not the bit of cleavage visible from the tight, yellow yoga tank top I wore.

My uncle always said that when God closed a door, he opened a window. Being here and deciding to check things off my mother's list filled me with the freedom I'd been looking for since leaving North Carolina. I was channeling my mother's spirit, and she would tell me to leave myself open for something new. Maybe Dennis could be my something, or *someone*, new. Marcel kept insisting I needed to get my rebound relationship out of my system. Dennis would do quite nicely.

"Follow me. Class is about to begin." He gestured with his head toward a room and I followed him inside. Several people nodded to him as we entered, and he made polite introductions. I was surprised at how friendly everyone was. I had a preconceived notion about everyone in LA — rude, self-centered, in their own bubble — but I was finding it wasn't true at all. The few people I had met here were welcoming and inviting.

Dennis and I set up our mats side-by-side and I sat down, stretching in preparation for the beating my body was probably about to endure.

"Have you done yoga before?" Dennis asked, his voice low, trying not to disrupt the quiet ambience in the room.

"A few times," I answered, "but only videos. In my small town in North Carolina, they didn't even have a gym, let alone a yoga studio."

"This will be fun then. And this is a great class to start out with. It's more of a mixture of yoga and Pilates, so you're not holding the poses for what can feel like hours on end. It's more motion-based. I think you'll like it."

"Do you come here often?"

A breathtaking smile crossed his face, his teeth bright against his tan skin.

I cringed. "That sounded like a cheesy pick-up line, didn't it?"

"Yeah, but I've heard them all. Believe me. You can't imagine some of the lines I've heard at the clubs out in West Hollywood. Based on experience alone, I could write a book on how *not* to pick up a guy."

"I don't think I want to know." I rolled my eyes.

"You probably don't." He winked just as the instructor stepped up to the front of the room and got our attention.

During the forty-five minute class, a flash of heat spread through me whenever I stole a glance at Dennis and saw his eyes glued to my body, causing sweat to bead on my brow. Or it could have been the intense workout I was getting from the Marquis de Sade of yoga instructors. Regardless, it had been years since anyone gazed at me in such a way that made me feel attractive. If nothing else, that was what Dennis did for me. He made me feel desirable again.

After the class finished, I gathered my things, wiping

the sweat from my face.

"So what do you think, Carolina? Am I going to see you again?" Dennis asked in a seductive voice that nearly took my breath away.

I gave him a flirtatious smile over my shoulder. "You know what? I do believe you will." I sauntered down the hallway and toward the lobby of the studio.

"Baylee, wait!" he shouted, running up to me as I walked out the door. I stopped and turned to face him, a sly grin crossing his face. "Can I get your phone number?" I raised my eyebrows at him, taken aback by how forward he was. "Just in case something comes up and I can't make it to class, or if I want to switch to a different one," he floundered. "That's all."

Biting my lower lip, I entered my phone number into his cell and then retreated from him, swaying my hips more than usual. Once I was settled in my car, I pulled the yellowed piece of paper from my mother's journal and crossed *Learn how to do yoga* off her list.

# CHAPTER NINE

*May 2*

*I saw the Pacific Ocean today. Santa Monica, California, is just as beautiful as I imagined, apart from the homeless people and the fog, which everyone out here calls a "marine layer". It's the most peculiar thing I've ever seen. Perry and I woke up this morning and looked out the window of our hotel. We could barely see ten feet in front of us, the fog so thick and heavy. After a few hours, the sun was shining brightly. When I mentioned the word "fog" to our concierge at the hotel, he just laughed and knew we were from out of town, as if the country accent didn't make it obvious. So that's what I've learned today. In California, fog is called a marine layer.*

*Apparently, so is the smog.*

*I also had abalone. I had no idea what it was, but they said it was a rare type of seafood. I'm certainly enjoying trying things I never thought I would, but hate the fact it was a death sentence that forced me to finally do all the things I always said I wanted.*

*I'm starting to feel tired. I don't know if it's because of the pregnancy or the cancer. It's probably a combination of both. I can see how much my decision is hurting Perry, but he'll have years of new memories to make with our child...the wonderful person we created from a love of pickup trucks, drive-in movies, and dreams of a surf shack on the beach.*

A sudden knocking on my door tore me away from my mom's first impressions of Santa Monica. After getting home from my yoga class, having checked an item off her bucket list, I felt a closeness to her I never did growing up. I had heard stories about her from my uncle, father, and other people who knew her, but it was hard for me to really grasp who she was as a person. Now that I was walking in her footsteps, in a manner of speaking, I felt her. Wanting to strengthen that connection, I spent the past few hours flipping through her journal, reading about her own adventure in checking items off her bucket list. It inspired me and I was already thinking about what I would do next.

Setting the journal on the coffee table, I made my way to the foyer, Sport close on my heels. I opened the door, assuming it was Marcel with more samples for me to approve for his big remodel of my condo.

"Hi," I said, surprised to see Sebby standing there.

"Hi." He stared down at me.

"No work today?" I leaned against the doorjamb, crossing my arms in front of my chest.

"I'm taking a day off. All work and no play makes Sebby a dull boy," he joked.

"What are you working on?" I asked, my interest piqued.

"A movie."

"Oh really, smart ass?"

Shoving his hands into the pockets of his cargo shorts, he shrugged. "You may have seen previews for it. Some psychological thriller starring Matt Damon and Jennifer Lawrence."

I raised my eyebrows. "You're producing *that*?" I couldn't mask the surprise in my tone. Sure, Sebby had shared bits and pieces of what he did for a living, but it never occurred to me that someone as young as he would be producing such big budget films. I almost wanted to ask him if he had ever worked with Kevin Bacon, just so I could tell someone that I went from twenty degrees of separation to just two.

Sebby nodded, not saying a word, smiling his boyish smile at me. I had to remind myself that he was off limits due to his harlot girlfriend, who I was sure was actually quite lovely.

"Umm... Is there a reason you knocked on my door, or...?"

"Right. Want to work on that list of yours?"

"With you?"

"Why not? There were actually quite a few things on it I wouldn't mind doing. And I really think this is something you should do. Maybe it'll help you find some inspiration to write that book."

"What book?"

"The book you mentioned you always wanted to write."

I scowled. *Sebby and his damn questions*, I thought. Weeks ago, he had asked what I was planning on doing now that I was on my own. After joking about collecting unemployment for the rest of my life, I finally told him about my dream to write a book.

"And, need I remind you," he continued, "you have to. It's on that list." He smirked.

"Did you memorize the entire list in the two seconds you looked at it?" I lowered my voice. "Are you, like, *Rain Man*?"

"No. Definitely not. I just have a really good memory. So... Care to come over and watch one of the greatest cinematic masterpieces of the twentieth century?" His eyes lit up, the excitement plastered on his face making it difficult to refuse.

"Which would be…?"

He winked. "You'll see."

My curiosity getting the best of me, I said, "Fine, but I need to shower first. I just got home from yoga."

"Great. Come on by when you're done. The door will be open so just let yourself in. Feel free to bring Sport. Gidget would like that."

"Should I bring anything else? Wine or beer? Something?"

"Nope. Just yourself. See ya soon, Dixie." He turned from me and headed across the hall to his condo, leaving me to question our "friendship" once more.

"What do you think, Sport? Can a man and woman really be friends without complications?" I asked, eyeing my dog as I padded through my home toward the stairs.

The traitor simply yipped in response, his tail wagging.

"Of course you'd think that. You're just looking to get some ass from your new girlfriend."

Stripping out of my yoga clothes, I hopped into the shower.

"I don't see how being friends with a guy could possibly work out," I said to myself as I stood underneath the showerhead, basking in the feel of the water on my skin. "Then again, he seems to think it will. He's definitely off limits, so why am I still thinking about him after meeting Dennis? He should have taken my mind off him. Why didn't he? I guess Sebby and I have a lot in common, which could explain it. Okay. We both like dogs and the movie *Gidget*, so we have two things in common. I wonder if he talks to himself in the shower, too. Hmm… Sebby in the shower…"

I closed my eyes, taking comfort in the hot water, the image in my head causing my breathing to increase and my skin to come alive in anticipation of his phantom touch. "*Baylee Grace!*" I scolded myself. "Okay. Let's rethink that… Dennis in the shower." I closed my eyes once more, trying to imagine what it would feel like to have Dennis' strong arms around me, pinning me up against the wall as water cascaded over both of us. The fantasy was incredible, his rippling body thrusting against me as I threw my head back, lost in the ecstasy enveloping me. Then, instead of Dennis' smoldering dark eyes, Sebby's gray-blue eyes flashed through my mind.

"Dammit!" I screamed, running my hands through my wet hair in frustration. I needed to find something to distract me from the fact I was drawn to Sebby for some inexplicable reason…or at least to release some of this pent-up sexual tension. My hormones were raging like a teenager's. Hell, I was fantasizing about nearly every member of the opposite sex who I found attractive, but I had to stop daydreaming about Sebby. Nothing could ever come of our friendship. I knew how much it hurt to find out your significant other had been unfaithful. I refused to be the other woman, no matter the pull he had on me.

Resolved to stay strong, I finished showering, then dressed in a pair of jeans and a green sweater that brought out the color of my eyes. Finding some gel, I allowed my hair to retain its wave, coercing it into some sort of manageable style. Putting on a bit of liner, I framed my small eyes, making them appear bigger and brighter than they were. I finished the look by applying just a touch of blush to bring out my already rosy cheeks, then ran some pink gloss over my lips.

Surveying my appearance in the full-length mirror, I shrugged. "Well, this is as good as it's going to get."

Heading back downstairs, I grabbed my cell phone and keys, turning to my dog. "Come on, Sport. Let's go see your girlfriend. At least one of us is going to get some."

I locked the door behind me and approached Sebby's condo. I was about to knock when I remembered his instruction to just let myself in.

Turning the knob, I entered his foyer. The floor plan was identical to mine, except in reverse. Sport ran from me like a dog in heat, no pun intended.

"Sebby?" I called out, hesitantly walking through the entryway and into the open living space.

"Holy shit!" I exclaimed when my eyes settled on him standing in front of his refrigerator, but that wasn't what caught me completely off guard. It was the fact he was standing there, holding a towel in his hand, exposing himself in all his glory. I spun around, my entire face turning a shade of red that would put my hair to shame.

"Shit!" he shouted. "Did you take the world's quickest shower or something?!"

"Balls," I muttered, keeping my eyes glued to a large print of a vintage DC-10 hanging in the entryway.

"What?" he countered, his voice turning light and amused. I could almost picture that sexy and adorable smile drawn on those kissable lips of his.

"There were balls…and stuff."

He laughed harder than I had heard him laugh in the few weeks I had known him, the rumble echoing in the open space.

"I'll never be able to look at you again without seeing your balls, Sebby. Just thought you should know that." I drew in a long breath, trying to settle my nerves. Seeing his mouth-watering body completely bare didn't help matters any. "Here's what I'm going to do. I'm going to go back to my condo and have a shot of whiskey. Or tequila. Or gin. Or whatever will make my blood pressure drop. And then I'm going to come back and we'll try this again. Okay?"

"I promise I'll be dressed when you come back."

"Why were you bare ass naked in your kitchen anyway? Did you want me to walk in on you like that? Were you trying to show off?"

"Do you think I have something to show off?"

"I… Well…" I shook it off. "I'm not answering that."

"Okay then."

"Okay."

"Baylee…?"

"Yes?" I turned around, as one often does when their name is called.

"Jesus!" His eyes grew wide as he hastily attempted to hide himself.

"For fuck's sake!" I spun back and faced the door once more. "Did you not think to cover yourself up after the first time I walked in and saw you naked? I'm still standing here. You know, bath towels serve some rather astonishing purposes these days, the most useful of which being something to wrap around your waist to keep your junk covered! I'm leaving and taking *two* shots of whiskey. Be back in five minutes."

I stormed out of his condo and back into mine, rummaging through the cabinets for the bottle of whiskey. Unable to find a shot glass, I simply threw back the bottle, trying with everything to forget what I had just seen.

But I couldn't. You know those guys you see wearing a t-shirt that fits just perfectly, their muscles defined, and you wonder what they look like without it on? Then you have the good fortune of seeing what lies beneath and all you can do is drool because it's just as good as you imagined? Well, that was Sebby.

Will was an attractive guy…in high school. Quarterback of the football team. Then he got a job selling cars, which was when he started to let himself go. Looking at Will now, his appearance was nothing like the athletic guy I knew in high school. He had a nice body back then. And, not to sound too superficial, but I wanted to be around an attractive guy again…just not Sebby, except as friends. Dennis was handsome and well-built. Maybe a little *too* well-built. Sebby was…perfect.

"Dammit!" I screamed, throwing back more whiskey. I wiped my mouth and stashed the bottle in the cabinet. Taking a deep breath to compose myself, I left my condo and walked across the hall.

About to turn the knob to let myself in, I hesitated. I didn't know if I could stand barging in on him naked again. What if he got a phone call and didn't have time to get dressed yet? Shaking my head, I held my fist up to the door and knocked quietly.

"You can come in, Dixie!" I heard from beyond the door.

"Are you decent?"

"Yes."

"Are you sure? I don't want to——"

The door immediately opened and Sebby stood in front of me wearing a pair of loose-fit jeans and a linen button-down shirt, the sleeves rolled up. "Told you. I'm decent."

*Yes. Yes, you are.*

"Good." I pushed past him and into his living area. Surveying his furniture, he had a bit more of a traditional taste in décor than I was used to…everything big and comfortable. I headed toward a large beige sectional in front of the giant television and sat down. Gidget and Sport jumped up to sit next to me.

"Sport! Down, boy. This isn't your home."

"It's okay," Sebby assured me. "Dogs are family members, and family members get to sit on the couch. Want a glass of wine?" He headed toward the kitchen as I snuggled up to the two dogs sitting on either side of me.

"Sure."

"Red or white?"

"I'm easy. Surprise me."

"You got it."

Trying to busy myself, I stood up, scanning all the picture frames adorning the walls. "Is this your girlfriend?" I asked, picking up a photo of Sebby with a stunning blonde, her smile wide.

"No. That's my sister, Laurie."

"Where does she live?"

"Back home," he answered, making his way toward me with a bottle of wine and two large glasses.

"Which is…?"

"Jersey, but not *Jersey Shore* Jersey," he corrected before I could respond. "I lived in New York Jersey."

"Which is…?" I prompted again.

"The part of Jersey that's practically in New York. Birthplace of the great Frank Sinatra, *my* favorite member of the Rat Pack," he emphasized as I recalled our text conversation earlier this week.

"Do you miss it?" I returned to the couch and sat next to Sebby before Gidget and Sport weaseled their way between us.

"I don't miss New Jersey, but I miss my family."

"Are they all still back there?"

"Yeah. I was the first one to leave. For what I wanted to do, I needed to be out here. Sure, New York has great film schools, but I don't know." He let out a sigh. I could sense he had made this argument more times than he could count. "I wanted to get away from home and have some independence, which is kind of hard to do when you go to school just across the river from where you grew up."

"How old were you when you left?"

"Aren't you nosy?" He uncorked the wine and poured it into the glasses in front of him. "I'm pretty sure you asked your allotted question earlier today."

"Well, if we're going to be friends, I figured it would be nice to know what I'm getting myself into."

"Point taken," he teased. "I was seventeen when I came out here for college."

"Where? UCLA?"

"No. USC."

I scrunched my brows. "That's in South Carolina."

He laughed. "No. Out here, USC is the University of Southern California. They have a great film program, so I left Jersey to pursue my dreams and haven't looked back once."

I brought the glass to my mouth, tasting the smoky red wine.

"Do you like it?"

Licking my lips, I nodded. "It's my favorite kind of wine, actually."

"What? Pinot?"

"No. Open." I smirked. "Now, what is this great cinematic masterpiece you want to watch? I'm expecting to be completely blown away."

He grinned, grabbing the remote, and the television screen sprang to life.

"This better be good." I sipped my wine once more, nearly spitting it out when the first few measures of the opening song played, followed by that tell-tale whip. "*Blazing Saddles?*" I looked at him, incredulous. "*This* is the greatest cinematic masterpiece of the twentieth century?"

"I didn't say that," Sebby countered. "I simply argued it was *one* of them."

"I thought we'd be watching *The Godfather* or *Apocalypse Now* or something like that. Hell, maybe even *Titanic*. But *Blazing Saddles?*"

"Come on, Dixie." He nudged me with his elbow. "You love this movie. I know you do. Mel Brooks is a goddamn genius. The man should win the Nobel Peace

Prize. If more people were exposed to his movies, there would be less war."

"That's a bit extreme. His movies do put a smile on my face, though, especially *The Producers*."

"Matthew Broderick or Gene Wilder?"

"That's not a fair comparison. One's Ferris Bueller and the other is Willy Wonka. I refuse to answer as it's comparing apples to chocolate."

It was silent while he seemed to assess my response. Out of nowhere, he laughed an all-consuming, gut-splitting laugh. "I like you, Baylee. I have a feeling I'm really going to like being friends with you."

He leaned back on the couch, settling in to watch what he considered to be one of the greatest cinematic masterpieces of the twentieth century, and I followed. I liked how comfortable his home was. It was what I always imagined a home would be. Will liked everything to have a modern flare, so I decorated our former house in that style. Leather couches, angular tables, everything neat and orderly. It didn't feel lived in. But Sebby's living room was exactly that. It was a room he lived in. Bits and pieces of his life adorned every wall and table, each trinket, photo, and plant giving me another piece of the Sebby Powers puzzle.

As "The Battle of Rock Ridge" played, I turned to steal a glimpse at him, grinning when I saw his lips moving along with the lyrics of the song.

"So," I said, getting his attention, "what made you want to go into film? When did you know this was what you wanted to do?"

"When I was seven. I remember the date. October twentieth."

"Really? You remember the exact date? I know

people who can't remember their spouse's birthdays. That's impressive."

"I guess."

"So what happened on October twentieth?"

"I went to The Meadowlands with my father to watch a Giants game."

"A football game changed your life?"

"It wasn't the game itself. Before kickoff, we were able to go into the control room. He knew someone who worked for the network or something. I don't really remember the connection, but I *do* remember how wide my eyes went when I stepped into that darkened room and saw all the small monitors in front of me. There were dozens of people wearing headsets, and I was mesmerized by the whole process. I always loved watching sports on TV. What seven-year-old little boy doesn't?"

He turned to me, his eyes brimming with enthusiasm, a frenzied quality to his voice. "After that day, I wanted to know everything about how television worked. I wrote my first screenplay when I was eight. It was some story about a mutant alien coming to earth and turning all the school teachers into fellow mutant aliens so they could brainwash all of us."

"So *that* explains it," I teased.

"Well, when you're eight..." He shrugged.

"I think it's cute. So..."

"Right. The Giants game. It was life-changing for me. When you're seven, I guess life-changing experiences have a lower threshold than when you're older, but being able to see the cameras, the monitors, the control room... I was in awe. When we got to watch them call the first part of the game from the control room, I knew where I wanted to be. I wanted to be in that room. I wanted to be the one in charge."

"But I thought you liked making films?"

"Oh, I love it, but I've always said that if I get the chance to produce for the NFL, I'd leave this in a heartbeat. The rush of a live broadcast, the adrenaline pumping, knowing you only have one chance to get it right… There are no words to explain how that would feel. Shooting a film, well… There's no rush there. Yes, we have deadlines and budgets to worry about, but it's not the same. You have as many takes as you want to get it perfect. There are some days you work on one three-minute scene all day long…dressing the set, checking lighting, then finally shooting. You don't have that with live TV. One chance, just one. Some people would hate the pressure, but something about that rush… I don't know. I want that."

"Wow," I muttered in disbelief. "I don't think I've ever heard anyone speak so passionately before."

He shrugged, his ears turning red. "There's nothing *you're* passionate about?"

"I always wanted to be a writer. I studied English and journalism in college. Then I worked as the editor of our town's newspaper for about five years, but my job always came second to Will's joke of a career selling used cars. Sure, our newspaper was small with a dismal circulation, but I loved that paper. It made me feel as if I was doing something with myself. And now…" I let out a breath.

"Yeah?" he pushed.

"I don't know," I said thoughtfully. "I was a bit of a dreamer, too, I suppose. I remember writing my first

110

book when I was in third grade. It even won a statewide award. Throughout middle school and high school, I kept a journal to jot down short stories or ideas for a novel. Then I married Will. He never understood why people would want to read books, so he certainly didn't support me when I said I wanted to write one."

"What's stopping you now?"

"Absolutely nothing." I felt a weight lift off me at the notion that there was no longer a barricade standing in the way of me finally pursuing my dreams. No more trying to make everyone around me happy. No more having to listen to a husband laugh at the thought of me writing a book. No more trying to defend my reluctance to manage my father's lumber company to my step-mother, who was still bitter that she wasn't left a portion of the business. "Although I have no idea what my story even is. And I guess that's partly the reason I decided to take your advice and work on my mom's bucket list. Maybe there's a story there. Or maybe I'll find some inspiration along the way."

He smiled. "Good for you, Dixie."

I took a sip of my wine and refocused my attention on the movie, a fluttering in my stomach. I had only known Sebby a few short weeks, but I felt like we were old friends. His words from this morning rang through my head. The more time I spent with him and got to know him, the more I started to believe we *could* simply remain friends. Since finding out he had a girlfriend, I was more open and forthcoming with him. I didn't feel like I had anything to prove, worried he would judge me. There was a freedom to it that wasn't there yesterday.

Relaxing into the couch, I rubbed Sport's belly, thinking how normal and comfortable watching a movie with Sebby was, our two dogs curled up between us. Sebby's hand roamed from Gidget to Sport, scratching his ears.

"You know what I just realized?" I tilted my head and looked from Sport to Sebby. "Sport normally doesn't like people. It's not that he's not a friendly dog because he is, but only if he's comfortable around you. It usually takes him a while to feel at ease around anyone other than me or Will. Probably because he was found abandoned and fending for himself. He's got a bit of a tramp in him."

"Maybe he knows I'm a dog lover. Dogs are perceptive little critters."

I shook my head. "No. He's been around other people who have owned dogs and was still a little hesitant around them. But with you, well...look at him!" I smiled at Sport rolling around, trying to get Sebby to continue scratching his ears. "He likes you."

"What about you?"

My heart dropped to my stomach. "What do you mean? Do I like you?"

Our eyes met. There was a sparkle in his gaze that made me want to melt into the couch. Or maybe it was simply the reflection of the setting sun on the Pacific Ocean.

"As friends," he added.

"Of course," I said, shaking my head. "I like you...as a friend."

"Good. To new friends." He raised his wine glass and I followed, toasting our new friendship.

Out of nowhere, the sound of Kenny Loggins' voice filled the room, tearing my attention away from Sebby.

"Sorry. I meant to silence that." I grabbed my cell off the coffee table.

"You can answer it if you want. I don't mind."

I looked at the phone. "I don't recognize the number… Some eight-one-eight area code."

"That's the valley. Get it."

"Are you sure?" I asked, my finger hovering over the ANSWER button.

"Of course."

"Thank you." I turned from Sebby and walked toward the windows overlooking the ocean. "Hi. This is Baylee."

"Hey, Carolina," a familiar smooth voice crooned.

"Dennis?" I said, surprised. "Wow. You didn't waste any time calling, did you?"

He laughed. "I like you. You're straightforward and don't beat around the bush. Tell me how you really feel." I could hear the smile in his tone.

"Is something wrong? Are you switching classes?" I asked, remembering the reason he had requested my phone number in the first place.

"Yes and no. My boss scheduled a client meeting for tomorrow, so I can't make class, but I wanted to see if you'd like to get together on Sunday."

"Sure. What class did you have in mind?"

"Not for a class, Baylee. On Sundays, there's this fabulous little farmer's market just down the street from the yoga studio. What do you say? I know how much it sucks being new to town."

"That sounds completely different from anything I've ever done before." Not to mention, it was on my mother's bucket list. I was crossing things off faster than

I expected I would.

"Please say yes. I'm not a freak or serial killer, and I have no ulterior motives. Honest."

I looked at Sebby, feeling awkward about agreeing to a date with another man when he was just a few feet away from me. But why? He had a girlfriend. He had no say in whom I should or shouldn't date. And Dennis seemed like perfect rebound material.

"You know what? I'd love to. Count me in."

"Fantastic!" Dennis responded, his tone animated. "Text me your address. I'll pick you up at eleven on Sunday. See you soon!"

"Bye." I hung up, ambivalent about my impending date.

"Everything okay?" Sebby's husky and endearing voice cut through my thoughts, bringing my attention away from the sunset.

"Actually, yes. Everything's great." I made my way back to the couch and settled next to our two dogs just as Madeline Kahn sang about being tired.

"Why's that?" he asked.

"I have a date Sunday morning." I tried to sound enthusiastic but probably failed miserably.

"Oh really? With whom?"

I shrugged. "A guy I met at yoga earlier. His name's Dennis."

"A date? On a Sunday morning?" He paused, raising his eyebrows as he tilted his head to the side. "Where?"

"The farmer's market. He says it's fabulous."

"Umm... Baylee, were those his exact words?"

114

"Yes. Why?"

A small smile crept across his face. "Let's think about this for a minute. You met him in yoga class. He used the word fabulous. He's taking you to the farmer's market."

I furrowed my brow, not understanding what Sebby was trying to infer.

Sighing, he said, "Sorry. All signs point to him hitting for the other team."

"What do you mean? What other team?"

"His favorite pirate is One-eyed Willy."

"Oh, from *The Goonies*? I love that movie!"

"No, Baylee. Focus. He's as straight as a three-dollar bill." He raised his eyebrows at me as if trying to tell me something with his expression.

"There's no such thing as a three dollar bill, Sebby." I crossed my arms over my chest.

"He's *gay*, Baylee!" he shouted, exasperated. "He likes men! He's more interested in your ex than he is in you."

"You haven't even met him!" I shouted back, jumping off the couch and glaring at him. "There's no way! His voice is very masculine. He has an amazing body. He even mentioned something about awful pick-up lines he's heard at some clubs in West Hollywood!"

Sebby looked at me, his eyes growing wide, before breaking into a laughing fit. I had no idea what was so amusing to him.

"What?! What's so funny? Are you going to let me in on your little joke?"

He held his stomach, barely able to breathe from laughing so hard.

"Maybe I'll just leave. Come on, Sport. Let's go." I spun on my heels, heading toward the door, although I really didn't want to. I wanted to spend more time with Sebby.

Darting off the couch, he grabbed my arm, preventing me from taking another step. "No. Don't leave. I'm sorry, Baylee. You really have no idea, do you?"

"No, I don't! And I'd appreciate it if you didn't laugh at my expense, Sebby."

A thoughtful smile crossed his face. "How much exploring have you done around town?"

I shrugged. "Not much."

"That settles it. Tomorrow, I'm taking you on Sebastian Powers' official Hollywood tour."

"What does that entail?"

"Just showing you the different neighborhoods that make up the wonderful city of Los Angeles." He beamed.

"Fine," I huffed, placing my hands on my hips. I hated that I was more excited about the prospect of spending tomorrow with Sebby than I was about my outing with Dennis on Sunday. "But are you going to tell me what's so funny about West Hollywood?"

"We call it WeHo. It's known for its very large homosexual population and gay bars. Your Dennis is gay."

"There's no way. I don't believe it."

"Suit yourself," Sebby sang. "What does he do for a living?"

"I'm not entirely sure. He mentioned something about being an actor, but I don't know if it's a full-time thing for him."

Sebby grinned.

"Don't even…!" I shoved him playfully.

"Come on, Dixie." He slung his arm over my shoulder and pulled me back to the couch. "Let's finish watching our movie. It's *fabulous*!"

# CHAPTER TEN

"COME ON, BAYLEE!" A voice bellowed the following morning, coupled with an obnoxious knocking. "Let's get going!"

I ran to the front door and flung it open, smiling at Sebby standing in the hallway, a backpack slung over his shoulder. His hair was damp from a shower, a bit of scruff visible on his chin. I normally wasn't a fan of men who didn't shave on a daily basis, but there was something about the bit of facial hair on Sebby that made my mouth water.

"What exactly do you have planned for today? What's in the backpack? We're not going to rob any banks, are we?" I had no idea what we would be doing. All I knew was he had told me to dress comfortably with good walking shoes, so I opted for a loose-fitting yellow tunic-style sweater, dark jeans, and a pair of pink Converse. It was cute but comfortable at the same time.

"No, Baylee." He held his hand out and I took it, allowing him to lead me down the hallway and toward the elevator. "We're not going to rob any banks... Well, I don't think we are." He winked just as we began our descent to the lobby.

"Then where are you taking me?"

"Everywhere." He grinned his devious smile at me. "This town is full of inspiration. Maybe we'll find your story today. And I'm sure we can cross a few more items off that list of yours."

The elevator doors opened and he took long steps through the lobby. I chased after him. "Like what?" I prayed he hadn't done something crazy, like book us a skydiving lesson. Most normal people who had only known each other a few weeks wouldn't do that, but I was beginning to learn there was nothing normal about Sebby.

"I'm not quite sure yet, but I have a few ideas. As your new *fabulous* BFF," he continued, his tone light before turning serious once more, "it's my job to show you around your new city and hope that something you see inspires you to finally pursue your dreams, not to mention get you on the road to crossing that item off your mother's list. There's no better place than LA, a town that was built on people's hopes, aspirations, and dreams. That's what I'm going to show you today."

He turned from me and strode toward the large glass doors, the passion with which he spoke leaving me speechless. In all my twenty-eight years, not one man had ever been able to do that.

"Good morning, Mr. Powers. Miss Morgan," Jeffrey said as I caught up to Sebby and we walked outside together. "Big plans today?"

"Well, yes. I'm hoping to show Baylee what an invigorating city LA can be. She's a writer looking for her story."

"Is that right?" he said. "Have you written anything I may have heard of?"

"No. Unless you've read my eighth grade diary about how dreamy Logan Benson, my secret crush, was."

Jeffrey smirked. "Can't say I have. Good luck. I

hope Mr. Powers is able to show you what you're looking for."

He gestured to the valet attendant who had just pulled up in a stunning black Camaro, the engine rumbling as it idled. Sebby held the door open for me, helping me in like a perfect gentleman.

"Wow. Nice car. Dad would certainly approve," I commented.

"Good to know." He ran around to the other side of the car, getting behind the wheel.

"He loved muscle cars," I explained, trying to make conversation as he pulled onto San Vicente, heading east along the tree-lined boulevard. "My dad, that is. He had a sixty-nine Z28. Is that what this is?"

A boyish grin crossed Sebby's face. "Yeah. Well, not a sixty-nine."

"Obviously." I rolled my eyes.

"I swore I would never spend more than fifty thousand on a car, which goes against the typical mentality out here, but I couldn't resist. The second I test drove this bad boy, I was sold."

"I'm jealous." I caressed the dashboard, feeling the vibrations of the engine on my palm.

"If you want, I'll let you drive it. You *do* know how to drive a stick, right?"

"Of course I do! What kind of question is that?"

"Mercedes doesn't even know how to drive."

I tilted my head at him, pressing my lips together.

"My girlfriend," he explained, answering the question that was readily apparent on my face. I couldn't help but get the feeling he didn't like talking about her around me. If we were going to be the friends he said we could be, I didn't want him to feel uncomfortable sharing parts of himself with me…including stories about his girlfriend. Yes, I had thought there could have been something between Sebby and me, but that was all ancient history now. At least that was what I needed to tell myself every time he smiled and those unruly butterflies danced in my stomach.

"I'm sorry. I never even asked her name."

"It's okay."

"So she doesn't drive?" I inquired. "I couldn't imagine."

"She was born and raised in Manhattan, so she never saw the need to learn. I definitely found it odd, considering I couldn't wait until I got my license."

"And she's still in New York?" I asked, recalling his and Marcel's conversation at Sophia's Halloween party.

"She's one of those lifelong New York residents. According to her, the world begins and ends at the Hudson. Or, better yet, it begins and ends at Fifth Avenue." He let out a barely noticeable sigh before readjusting his expression, smiling once more. "She says there's an electricity running through the pavement like a current that keeps her breathing. She loves it."

Studying him, I knew I was taking a risk asking my next question, but I just had to know. "Do you?"

He kept his eyes glued to the road. "I like to visit. I know I'm going to have to make the leap and move there at some point if I want our relationship to work, but I'm not ready to say goodbye to LA just yet. I grew up in Jersey. I woke up to the New York cityscape every day. While New York is as good as LA for what I do, it's not the same. It's busy. People don't look each other in the eyes. They're all in such a rush to get where they're going, they let life pass them by. Granted, LA is a little like that, too, but it's different. Yes, our driving can be a bit aggressive, especially on the freeway, but there's more of a laid back mentality out here."

He pressed a button and the sunroof opened, bathing us in that California sunshine that had infected my soul over the past month. "Maybe all the sunshine has a good effect on people." He glanced at me.

"How did you two meet?" I pushed, wanting more of their backstory. Maybe it was wishful thinking, but something about the way he spoke of their relationship didn't add up. The way he defended her to Marcel painted a picture of a man hopelessly devoted to a woman men would bend over backwards to be around. But now, I was getting a different side of the story.

"On a shoot," he answered. "It was about five years ago. I was on location in New York at some high-class art gallery in SoHo."

"Was she an extra or something?"

"No." He shook his head. "Although she could be," he added quickly. "She's gorgeous." A wide grin spread across his face and I could almost see his eyes gleaming beneath his dark sunglasses. It was the first genuine reaction I saw from him when speaking of Mercedes, but it was fleeting. Too soon, his smile faded and he let out another small sigh. "Actually, she's the manager of the gallery. She's your stereotypical New York art snob, and I say that with the utmost respect to her." He glanced at me before returning his eyes to the road.

"She grew up wealthy, studied art, and is now one of the foremost art appraisers in the city. We started seeing each other while I was in town on the shoot. I even stayed in New York a little longer to spend more time with her. Right before I was slated to head back to LA, I was offered a job producing a series that was shooting in New York. It was kind of out of nowhere and, based on the connections she has, I couldn't help but think she had something to do with it. I turned it down."

"Why?"

"A series would be great. It's a steady job, instead of always wondering if you'll be able to line up another gig, and I was still kind of new in the industry at the time. But it wasn't a good enough reason to leave LA. My gut told me it wasn't the right time for a move, so I stayed here. I'm glad I did because not even a month later, I landed my first feature film."

"And she's okay with the long-distance thing?"

"I suppose." He shrugged as we pulled up to a stoplight. I got the impression this was probably a contentious issue between them, but Sebby didn't want to admit it. "It's only a six-hour flight, so it could be worse. And it gives us time apart to live our own lives." The light turned green and he peeled away, slamming the shifter from first to second.

"Well," I said, my voice bright. His body language made it obvious he didn't want to talk about his relationship anymore, but was too nice to say anything. "It sounds like you've got it all figured out."

He met my eyes briefly, a blank expression on his face as he studied me. I had only known this man for a little over a month, but I had become familiar with his little idiosyncrasies. Something about the way he regarded me at that moment, the torn and pained expression on his face, made me think he was starting to question whether he really *did* have it all figured out.

"I've definitely got a good thing going." He looked back at the road. Inhaling deeply, he glanced skyward and I followed his line of sight to see the brilliant sunshine above us. "Plus, why would you want to live anywhere else?" He gestured to the picturesque sky. The temperature was a comfortable sixty-five degrees. People in New York were probably shoveling snow and wearing heavy winter coats. "There's no place like California."

"You really love it here, don't you?" The unease that had engulfed him seconds ago was replaced with a child-like zeal.

"I do. Just knowing you're walking on the same streets where all these Hollywood legends once walked… There's something just so—"

"Magical," I breathed out, cutting him off.

"That's exactly how I would put it, too."

It was silent for a moment as he turned onto Wilshire, driving past the Veteran's Administration, then taking a few more turns.

"This is Century City," he pointed out. I had absolutely no idea where I was in relation to the famous Los Angeles landmarks I had seen on TV or in the movies. "This used to be the backlot of the old Twentieth Century Fox studios."

I stared out the window. Where I imagined there was once a sprawling complex now sat high-rise buildings and shopping centers.

"They sold the land to developers in the early sixties after losing a ton of money on *Cleopatra*," Sebby explained.

"Where are the studios now?"

"Just a few blocks over." He gestured with his head.

"Wow," I murmured in complete awe. "It's kind of surreal knowing people are creating movies just a few yards away."

"Isn't it? Starting to feel inspired?"

I leaned back in my seat, staring up at the palm trees lining the street. I remembered my father taking me to Disney World when I was a little girl. As we neared Florida, I always grew excited to see the palm trees. I always imagined living in a place where I would be surrounded by them. Now I was. I closed my eyes briefly, allowing the sun to warm my skin, and felt a sense of drive. Sebby was right. I had only been in the car for a matter of minutes, but I was already starting to feel inspired to find my story.

"I hate to admit it, but I am."

We drove in relative silence as Sebby navigated the streets of LA, pointing out landmarks every now and then. Our journey soon took us down Rodeo Drive and I gawked at the high-end stores lining the street.

"Want to go shopping?" he asked when he saw my impressed expression. I shuddered to think how expensive a dress from one of these boutiques would be. I could only estimate one stitch would cost more than my entire wardrobe. "We can stop and take a look if you want. I don't mind."

"I'm not really much of a shopper," I responded. "Don't get me wrong. I love clothes and shoes just as much as the next girl, but I don't shop for the sake of shopping…usually." I winked.

A smile on his face, he shook his head. "You and Mercedes couldn't be more different if you tried."

I shrugged, unsure of whether or not I should take that as a compliment, but when I saw him glance at me and our eyes met briefly, I knew it was a good thing. There was a longing in his eyes, as if he were struggling to come to terms with his friendship with me and his commitment to Mercedes. I had seen that look before…in Will's eyes.

"So, where are you taking me now?" I asked as he turned off Rodeo Drive and headed toward a more residential area.

"You'll see." He winked.

He navigated through a maze of streets and headed up into the hills, pointing out various estates hidden behind high walls covered with ivy… *The Beverly Hillbillies* mansion, the Spelling mansion, which had a guard shack bigger than most people's homes, the Playboy Mansion. As he drove through the narrow, winding roads, it was surreal knowing just on the other side of the high walls lived some of the legends in the entertainment industry.

After driving by a few more points of interest, we headed away from Beverly Hills and down the Sunset Strip toward Hollywood. The hours passed quicker than I anticipated as we drove by the various studios… Disney, Paramount, Warner Brothers. He treated me to a world-famous Pink's hot dog, and I was able to do some people-watching as we sat out back and observed all the other tourists. We stopped and had a martini at Musso & Frank's, another Hollywood landmark according to Sebby. The bartenders were all clad in tuxedo jackets, and I was pretty certain some of them had been there since the place opened in 1919.

"Back in the '30s, the Screen Writer's Guild used to be right across the street from here," Sebby explained as I sipped on what was the most delicious and smooth martini I had ever tasted. I didn't care that it was only three in the afternoon. "It was a lot different back then. Under the studio execs' watchful eyes, writers were recruited to pump out work after work. I'm sure you can imagine how that would hinder the creative process."

I nodded.

"Many of them came here so they could write uninhibited. Just think about it, Baylee," he said, his voice growing feverish. "You could be sitting where Julius and Philip Epstein sat when they wrote *Casablanca*! Can't you just feel the energy of this place?"

I tore my eyes from his and took in my surroundings. The bar area was small, maybe a dozen or so stools at the counter. The remainder of the restaurant was filled with tables and booths, white tablecloths covering them. There was even a lunch counter on the other side of the bar, which seemed out of place yet fitting at the same time. Everything was dark with deep wood accents, and I could tell they probably hadn't changed the décor in nearly a hundred years. It was dated, but in the best way. It wasn't run-down or in need of repair. It was preserving a piece of Hollywood history. After visiting so many places I had only dreamed of, I was starting to get it. I could understand why Sebby would never want to leave LA. I didn't want to, either.

"I can," I admitted.

When we left the bar, it was nearly dark. Consumed by our conversation, I had lost track of time. Having spent the day getting to know the real Sebby, I began to feel a kindred closeness to him. We were both creative, and he was more supportive than any of my friends

127

back home. He was determined to help me find my story, and I couldn't help but feel an overwhelming sense of gratitude toward him for taking the time out of what I imagined was an incredibly busy schedule to show me around town.

After driving through Hollywood once more, he turned the car onto a fairly deserted side street and began navigating a curvy incline. I had no idea where we were or where we were going, but as I glanced over my shoulder at the lights of Hollywood twinkling below us, I didn't care. The sun had gone down and the city was coming to life, energizing me.

He pulled his Camaro off to the side, grabbed his backpack from the trunk, and led me across the street toward a locked gate.

"Are you okay jumping the fence?" he asked.

I eyed him, then the fence, noticing the No Trespassing sign. "Umm… This sign says the park is closed from dusk until dawn." While I'd had my share of adventures in the past, I never really strayed from the rules all that much…or ever.

"Come on." He elbowed me. "Live a little. I promise. It'll be worth it."

Pulling my bottom lip between my teeth, I stared at the conviction on his face. As apprehensive as I was about getting caught, I couldn't say no. "Fine."

"I'll go first and help you down once you get to the other side," he offered, already scaling the seven-foot fence and dismounting with grace.

Shaking my head, I started to climb up the chain-link. "I have no idea why I let you talk me into this," I muttered. He had made climbing the fence look so easy, but it certainly wasn't. After a struggle, I finally flung my feet over the other side and slowly descended, already dreading having to do this again when it was time to leave. Unless, of course, we were caught and led out in handcuffs.

"Careful, Baylee," Sebby cautioned as I continued my shaky descent. When I put my foot in one of the openings, it slipped, making me grip the chain-link, adrenaline pumping through my system.

"Whoa! I got you!"

A pair of hands grasped my hips, steadying me as I clung on for dear life, although the drop was only a few feet. I inhaled quickly, the feel of Sebby's hands on me making the tiny hairs on my neck stand on end.

"Let go, Baylee," he instructed, his voice soft and calm. "I got you."

Nodding, I gradually released my hold on the chain-link and he carefully lowered me to the ground. His hands remained on my hips for a brief moment, both of us frozen at the contact. I was convinced we looked like a prom photo gone horribly wrong, both of us completely dumbfounded, my back to Sebby's front, his hands glued to my hips. A shiver ran down my spine when he rubbed his thumb in a circular pattern. There was something about this moment — the darkness, the light wind in the air, the romance of the LA city lights twinkling below me — that made me want to turn around and feel Sebby's lips on mine. I had to keep reminding myself that we were simply friends, that he was so incredibly off limits.

"This way," he said, snapping out of whatever daze he was in. In an instant, his hands were no longer on me and he was walking away through a small parking lot. He grabbed his cell phone and lit the way, illuminating a cement path leading up to a bunch of steps.

I followed him in silence, holding onto the railing and trying not to trip over my own two feet as we made our way up what had to be at least fifty steps. Reaching the top, he helped me climb over the railing, then led me to a small grassy area.

"Wow," I breathed in awe at the view before me. I could see everything. High on the hill across the freeway, the Hollywood sign was lit up, the town that was built on hopes and dreams bustling below. Skyscrapers in downtown LA were illuminated to the right. I could see planes preparing to land at LAX miles away. From this vantage point, I finally got a feel for how large LA really was. It was nothing like New York, where everything was congested in just a few compact miles. LA was sprawling, every section having a distinct character all its own.

As I was lost in awe, Sebby pulled a blanket out of his backpack and laid it on the grass. He gestured for me to sit next to him.

"It's something, isn't it?" he remarked as I lowered myself to the ground. I positioned my legs in front of me and leaned back on my hands, still soaking in my surroundings.

"It sure is."

"Worth scaling that fence?"

I glanced at him. Even in the darkness, I could see a playful expression on his face.

"Definitely."

He dug through his backpack once more and pulled out a bottle of red wine and a few plastic cups.

"You certainly came prepared, didn't you?"

Opening the bottle, he shrugged. "I suppose. This kind of reminds me of my high school days. A bunch of us would always go to this one place back home. We called it 'The Rock'. It was a rocky ledge high up on a hill. We'd bring some beer and just hang out, watching the lights of New York twinkle in the distance."

"Do you see your family often?" I asked, taking a sip of the wine.

"Once in a while. Not as much as I'd like, though. When I'm on a project, it takes up a lot of my time. When I have a free weekend, I usually spend it with Mercedes in Manhattan."

"Isn't that close to where you grew up? Couldn't you just hop on the train or take a cab to go see your family?"

"I could," he agreed, "but something always comes up. It's hard to get Mercedes out of the city, so I usually have to decide between her and my family, which is probably the reason my mom's not a big fan of her."

"Really?" I tried to mask the intrigue in my voice. The more he spoke of Mercedes, the more I was beginning to not like her, although I wasn't sure whether that was because she sounded like a selfish person or because a part of me wanted Sebby for my own.

"Well, my mom would never come right out and say so, but you just know when your parents aren't fond of something."

"How does that make you feel?" I knew all too well what he was talking about. My uncle, pretty much the only parent I had left, certainly did not approve of my marriage to Will. He warned me we were too young,

131

that I'd regret it later. As always, he turned out to be right.

"It's hard to say. Sometimes, I wish Mom could see the side of Mercedes I fell in love with. Other times, I wish *I* could see the side of Mercedes I fell in love with." He looked up as he toyed with his wine glass. My jaw dropped a bit at his candid response. I didn't know if it was the fresh, yet smog-filled night air, the buzz of the city below us, or the liquor we had consumed during the day that forced this unfiltered response, but I didn't care.

"Don't get me wrong," he corrected quickly. "There are times I see it, but I think being bi-coastal has been difficult for her. Maybe if I finally make more of an effort to move to New York, it will make things better. I mean, she's beautiful, smart, charming. She's any guy's dream girl…"

"But is she yours?"

When his eyes met mine, I could see the struggle within.

"Sebby?"

A small smile crossed his face, as if recalling a fond memory. "I guess that's the hardest part about the distance. Not being around the person, you forget why you put yourself through the pain of the separation. But all it takes is the memory of one amazing moment you shared for the reasons to come rushing back. Those moments, those small instances, make it worth it."

"Well, I hope I can meet this Mercedes one day," I said, not calling him out on the fact he didn't answer my question.

"She can seem a little aloof at first, but once you get to know her, she'll warm up to you. Everyone in New

York is that way."

I nodded, unable to shake the feeling that Sebby wasn't completely happy, regardless of what he just told me.

"How did your mom die?" he suddenly asked, probably to change the topic.

I took a deep breath. "She had a rare form of brain cancer. The doctors gave her a slight chance of survival if she went for treatment, but she was pregnant with me. She had to choose between her life and mine." I shrugged. "She chose me."

"I'm sorry," he offered in a sincere tone. "How do you—"

"Live with the fact that it's my fault my mom died?" I interrupted. I had gotten the same question whenever I shared my mother's story. Hell, there were moments I would look at my father and think he was wondering whether my being here was worth him losing his soul mate.

"I wasn't going to say that," Sebby assured me. "It's not your fault. You don't honestly believe it is, do you?"

"I don't know." I swirled my wine, focusing on the red liquid coating the side of the clear plastic. "When I was four, my dad remarried and Camille pretty much raised me. When they started having their own kids, I felt like I was intruding on their happy life. I became really close to my uncle Monty, my mom's older brother. He was always my role model. He left the small town I grew up in and is now one of the most successful lawyers in North Carolina."

"And your dad?"

"He died my junior year of high school. Heart attack. He owned a huge lumber company that transferred to me when I turned eighteen. That's why I don't work. I don't have to. I'm the majority shareholder of the company, even though it's run by the same people who have been managing it for as long as I can remember. They know what they're doing. I don't. At some point, I may sell my ownership in the company to someone who cares a little bit more about it, but it offers me security while I figure out what I want to do."

"Which is?"

"I'll let you know when I figure it out." I winked and our eyes met once more. We were in our own little world up here. Nothing else mattered. Only us, enjoying our time as we sat in a comfortable silence. Breaking his gaze with me, Sebby stared off into the distance. He toyed with the grass in front of him and let out a long breath, his shoulders sagging. It was clear he was struggling with something.

"I like having you as a friend, Sebby." I nudged him, bringing him back from wherever he went in his mind. I rearranged my body so there was more space between us.

"I like having you as a friend, Baylee," he replied, changing his tone of voice to sound more assured.

"And there's no way Dennis is gay," I added, smirking.

"We'll see about that," he said, a twinkle in his eye.

"You're pretty confident in your assessment of a guy you've never met. Why is that?"

"It's just a feeling I'm getting."

"Are you rooting for my relationship to fail?"

"No!" he responded almost too quickly. "Of course not! I want you to be happy, Baylee, but I don't want you to get your hopes up and then get hurt. That's all."

I crossed my arms in front of my chest. "That's very nice of you, but he's not gay."

"Care to wager on this?" He wiggled his eyebrows at me.

I pulled my lip between my teeth, considering his offer. He had already suggested betting on whether a man and woman could truly just remain friends, one bet I was starting to believe he was losing. But this… I didn't know why, but I was worried he was on to something.

"You don't, do you? Deep down, you know there's something off."

"Maybe," I conceded. "When we were talking before yoga class the other day, the only thing I could think of was there had to be something wrong with him. Why else would someone that absolutely beautiful find me attractive?"

"Because you are," Sebby shot back in an instant. "If I weren't—"

"Sebby," I interjected, needing to stop him before he said something we would both regret. "There's no need."

"You're beautiful, Baylee." He turned his head from me, almost scared to look into my eyes as he said those words. I would be lying if I didn't admit that a slight fluttering erupted in my stomach as his soft voice crooned his confession to me. "And what's better is you have an amazing and caring soul. Never trust anyone who doesn't love dogs… Well, that's what my mom always told me," he added, the mood between us becoming light once more.

"And how does Mercedes feel about dogs?" I asked.

He turned away, avoiding my eyes.

I had my answer.

~~~~~~~~~~

"It looks like you get to cross one more item off your list," Sebby said as we exited the elevator and headed down the hallway toward our respective condos. It was nearly three in the morning. After leaving his picnic spot, he took me to an Italian restaurant in Hollywood named Miceli's where all the waiters and waitresses sang. The talent was amazing. I was certain they were waiting to be discovered. Sebby's goal was to inspire me, and he succeeded. It was impossible *not* to be inspired surrounded by creative and talented people all day long…Sebby included.

The remainder of the night passed in a flash as we drove around LA…including West Hollywood. We passed several clubs, and Sebby slowed his speed so I didn't miss what he was trying to prove. I knew why he thought Dennis was gay. Attractive men were lined up on the street waiting to get into the different clubs, some of them clinging onto other men. A few of them even catcalled Sebby as he drove by. Many of the men were fit, attractive, masculine…just like Dennis. But after spending the day with Sebby, it didn't matter. Dennis' sexual orientation was the furthest thing from my mind.

"What's that?" I asked as we walked down the hall, my eyebrows scrunched in confusion.

"If I'm not mistaken, your mother wanted to break a few rules and not get caught. I think we successfully did that tonight."

I pulled the small journal out of my bag and

scanned the list. Midway down, there it was... *Break a few rules and don't get caught.*

My lips turned up at the corners and I pulled a pen from my bag. It felt good to have one more task completed. As my pen touched the paper, I paused. Looking at Sebby, I handed it to him. "Here. You should do the honors. If it weren't for your trickery, I never would have done it."

"Nah. You would have."

"But I want you to do this. My mom would have wanted it, too."

He groaned. "You're really going to give me the dead mother guilt trip? That's not fair."

"I know, but you were a part of this today."

Sighing, he took the pen and paper from me, striking a strong line over my mother's handwriting.

"Feels good, doesn't it?" I asked as he handed the paper and pen back to me.

He nodded. "It does."

An awkward silence fell over us. Something changed in our relationship today. We shared parts of ourselves with each other that we probably hadn't shared with anyone else in years...or ever. I was able to be myself and not worry what Sebby would think. And I think he was able to be himself around me and not worry whether or not Mercedes approved.

"Well, I should get some rest. I have a date tomorrow," I reminded him.

"Of course," he said, clearing his throat. "Have a good night, Baylee. If you ever need someone to help you cross more stuff off that list, I'm more than happy to lend a hand."

"I'd like that." I smiled a small smile at him, then pulled my keys out of my bag and unlocked my door, disappearing into my condo.

"Me, too," I heard him respond softly.

# CHAPTER ELEVEN

"WELL, LOOK WHO'S UP early on a Sunday morning!" my uncle Monty said in faux surprise when I answered his FaceTime call. I had just gotten out of the shower after taking Sport for his morning walk. Sebby was waiting for me on the same park bench, my coffee in hand, just as I had expected. We sat and talked for longer than usual, no longer playing our question game. Instead, we just said whatever came to mind...or nothing at all.

I couldn't remember ever being so connected and in tune with someone, even my family, which was confusing for me. One second, I was telling myself our friendship was doomed for failure, that it was impossible for a man and woman to simply remain friends. Then I thought about what it would be like if he didn't have a girlfriend and both of us acted on our obvious impulses. What if it didn't work out? I'd lose him as a friend, and I hated that thought. I kept reminding myself of that whenever I caught the glimmer in his eye that he should only reserve for his girlfriend.

I would have been fooling myself if I didn't admit I thought there was something between us from the very beginning, even when I gave him a bloody nose. Now that I knew who he was, it was time to stop thinking about him that way. Plus, I had a date with the very straight, very non-homosexual Dennis in just an hour's time.

"Yeah," I said, breaking from my thoughts. "Had a bit of a late night last night, though." I yawned. You know those people who function on just four or five hours of sleep a night? That wasn't me. I had been guzzling coffee all morning in the hopes I would be somewhat awake and bright by the time Dennis showed up.

"It's okay, Baylee Grace. You've been living your life. That's good to hear."

"I have been," I agreed, thinking about the previous day and how alive I felt touring LA with Sebby.

"Have you been making any progress on your mother's list?"

"Actually, yes," I answered. "I did yoga, then watched what my neighbor considers to be one of the greatest cinematic masterpieces of the twentieth century, although the jury's still out on whether it qualifies or not."

"And what was that?" he asked, a slight smile on his distinguished face.

"*Blazing Saddles*." I rolled my eyes in playful irritation.

"Really?"

I shrugged. "Well, he's a producer out here, so maybe he sees something we don't."

"Making friends with people in high places, aren't you?"

"I guess." I struggled to hide my smile when I thought of Sebby. "Yesterday, I broke a few rules and didn't get caught."

He narrowed his eyes, a mock stern expression

140

crossing his face. He was a lawyer, after all. "What did you do?"

"We scaled a fence after dusk and broke into this little park overlooking LA. Oh, Uncle Monty," I exhaled, briefly closing my eyes. "It was unlike anything I've ever seen before. The lights of LA, the Hollywood sign... It was inspiring. If it weren't for Sebby, I never would have experienced it."

"Your neighbor?" he asked, raising his eyebrows. Pulling my bottom lip between my teeth, I nodded. "Sounds like you're spending a lot of time with him."

"I guess," I replied dismissively, trying to play it off. I knew the more I spoke of him, the more questions he'd ask. I didn't need him to berate me about spending so much time with a man who was, for all intents and purposes, unavailable.

"Is there something else you should be telling me about this Sebby?"

I looked at him. "Like what? We're neighbors. That's all. You know, a woman and a man *can* spend time together without there being any sort of romantic involvement."

"Mmm-hmm."

"What? It's true! Plus, I have a date with a guy I met at yoga class the other day. A hot, built, muscular guy...unlike many of the male specimens I grew up with back home."

"You have a date with someone you met in yoga class?" I could hear the caution in his voice. "You don't think he's..." He narrowed his gaze at me and I knew exactly what he was thinking.

"No!" I exclaimed. Taking a breath, I lowered my voice. "Well, it may have crossed my mind a time or two…" *Or three or four.*

"Well, regardless, enjoy yourself and don't take it too seriously. You deserve some fun after everything."

"Thanks, Uncle Monty."

"On that note, there *is* a reason I wanted to talk to you this morning." He hardened his expression to one I had seen whenever he was in a meeting or court.

"What's that?" I asked, nervous. "Is something wrong?"

"No, not at all. I was just thinking… This is going to be the first Thanksgiving since I can remember where you aren't around. What do you think about me flying out for the week? I know you have your new life and all, but—"

"Are you crazy?!" I screeched. "I'd love to see you!" My face lit up.

"Good. I'm going to have my assistant send my travel details to you once they're all ironed out. I'll try not to interfere with whatever you have going on, but I'd like to see you as much as possible when I'm there."

"You better believe it!" My eyes settled on the time, not realizing how late it had gotten. "Shit. I'm sorry. I have to go. My date's going to be here any minute and I haven't put my face on yet. Can we talk later?"

"Sure. Call anytime."

"I will. Love you."

"Love you, too, Baylee."

I closed out of our video chat, brimming with excitement over the news that my uncle was coming to visit in just a few weeks. I ran upstairs to the master bedroom and hastily began to get ready for my date with the very handsome, very straight Dennis. That was what I kept telling myself, anyway. By repeating the mantra, I hoped it would make it so. Choosing a flowing white sundress, I paired it with coral wedge sandals and a yellow cardigan. After carefully applying makeup, I headed back down the stairs just as a gentle knock sounded.

Pulling open the door, there was a slight fluttering in my stomach when my eyes fell on the slice of heaven standing in front of me. *Good,* I thought. *Flutter away.*

"Good morning, Dennis," I murmured. The dark jeans he wore fell from his hips as if they were tailor-made for his body. The sleeves of his checkered button-down shirt were rolled up, revealing his strong forearms.

"Wow. I love those shoes, Baylee. They're fantastic!"

"Thanks," I answered guardedly, silencing the voice in my head telling me that no straight man would be commenting on my shoes. Giving him a smile, I tried to convince myself there was no way in hell this man was gay, not with the way he looked and carried himself. He licked his lips as he surveyed my appearance. *He wouldn't do that if he were gay, would he?*

"Ready?" He held his elbow out to me.

"Yes. Let's go."

I took his arm and allowed him to lead me down the hallway toward the elevator, unable to stop humming the chorus of "It's Raining Men" in my head.

"Morning, Miss Morgan," Jeffrey greeted when he saw me emerge from the lobby. "Enjoy your day." He tipped his hat and smiled politely as Dennis led me to an idling Ford SUV. The perfect gentleman, he opened the door and helped me in. Running around to the other side, he got behind the wheel, giving me a small smile as he pulled onto the street and headed east.

During our short drive, I catalogued everything about him, from the placement of his hands on the steering wheel to the way he looked at people on the sidewalk. One minute, as I watched him groove along to "The Bitch is Back", I was convinced he was gay. It wasn't just because of his choice in music, though. I knew plenty of straight men who got down and funky to Sir Elton John. There was something about his mannerisms that was decidedly feminine. Then he would clear his throat, the noise guttural and masculine, and I was convinced I was playing into some sort of ill-conceived stereotype.

Had I never told Sebby about him, causing him to plant the notion in my head that Dennis was gay, I wouldn't have been dissecting every sound and movement he made. Part of me wanted to come right out and ask him, but I was worried he would be offended. Worse, I was worried Sebby was right and he *was* gay.

"Did you do anything fun on your Saturday night?" I asked, breaking the tension building between us.

"The usual," he admitted. "Hung out with the guys."

I turned toward him, studying him once more. Sure, Will said that when he was heading to watch a big game with some of his friends, but Will didn't give off the impression of sexual disorientation like Dennis did.

"Had some drinks," he continued. "Nothing exciting. The club scene is getting kind of old. It's always the same people, so we just decided to stay in."

"Who's 'we'?" I asked, waiting for him to say him

and his boyfriend.

"My roommate and a few of the guys who live down the hall from us."

My mind was going a mile a minute. I could just hear Sebby's voice in my head saying something ridiculous, like "Roommate? So that's what they're calling it these days?" A wide smile crossed my face and I had to stifle a laugh.

"What's so funny?" Dennis asked.

I bit back my smile. "Nothing. Just remembering something."

"Anything you care to share?" He narrowed his eyes.

"Nah. It's nothing important. So where is this farmer's market?"

"Just a few blocks up the road." Dennis gestured with his head before pulling down a side street and parking the car. "Today's such a beautiful day, I thought we'd walk."

If it were anyone else, I'd grow excited about the prospect of a leisurely stroll up the street, hand-in-hand with a man who could only be described as God's gift to the female population. Instead, I continued to question everything about him. This was my first date since high school and I couldn't even enjoy it.

Plastering on a fake smile, I said, "Sounds wonderful."

"Perfect." He ran around to help me out of the car. "You look great today, Carolina," he commented, making small talk as we journeyed up the street. I fidgeted with the hem of my skirt, unsure of what to do with my hands. He kept a respectable distance from me, only brushing against my arm when we passed other people on the narrow sidewalk. "Yellow really suits you. It washes some redheads out, but not you. You've got great style."

"Thanks."

As we approached the entrance to the farmer's market, Freddie Mercury's voice belted out "Killer Queen". I looked at Dennis as he grabbed his cell phone from his pocket.

"Sorry," he said after glancing down at the screen. "Do you mind if I take this? It's my boss."

*Queen?* I thought. This wasn't looking good for me.

"Of course." I waved him off with a cheery smile. Needing to get the opinion of an expert, I took the opportunity to pull my own phone out of my bag. Thankfully, I knew of such an expert who could shine some light on the situation. Searching my contacts, I typed a quick text.

*Marcel, I need your professional opinion on something.*

A reply appeared instantly.

*Yes. Orange was so last season.*

I rolled my eyes as I entered my response.

*No. That's not it. I met a guy in yoga class the other day and he asked me out. After I told Sebby what I knew of him, he insists there's no way he's straight. Now everything he does is making me second-guess his sexual orientation. I don't want to come right out and ask, but I'd kind of like an expert opinion.*

*Where are you?*

Glancing around to make sure Dennis wasn't peering over my shoulder, I gave him an innocent smile when I saw he was still on the phone. Returning my attention to my cell, I typed.

*At the farmer's market on San Vicente.*

*Oh, Miss Dixie, I can tell you right now that boy is not straight, even if he says he is. I'll come down and give him a thorough exam, though. One can never be too sure about these things.*

*I bet you will.*

"Everything okay?" Dennis asked.

I spun around, dropping my phone back into my bag.

"Of course. Just answering my friend's text."

We made our way through the crowded market and I continued to study him, tempted to see how much further I should take this. "He lives in my building. There's a group of us who get together every Thursday for game night, and we've kind of grown close. He's probably the first openly gay man I've ever met." I laughed, waiting to see his response. If he were gay, surely he'd mention it at this point, wouldn't he? This was the perfect opportunity.

Instead, he simply smiled back. "Sounds like you're making lots of new friends in town."

"I am," I agreed, slinging my bag over my opposite shoulder, leaving my hand open for him to hold if he wanted to. Instead, he maintained that same respectful distance as we strolled through the market. It was set up on a blocked off street, vendors standing behind long tables piled high with some of the freshest produce I had ever seen…strawberries, corn, zucchini, oranges. The aroma of herbs invaded my senses and I felt inspired once more. Inspired to stock up on fresh produce and cook something with my finds, crossing another item off my mother's list.

I continued through the open-air market, wanting to scope it all out before making any decisions. As we neared a grassy area, a bounce house for the kids set up, a smell that brought back childhood memories hit me. "Is that funnel cake?"

"Smells like it."

"Reminds me of all the county fairs back home," I said under my breath, closing my eyes and inhaling, instantly transported back twenty years.

Nearly every summer, my father would take me to the annual county fair. It was one of the few things I looked forward to because it was a day reserved just for us. He didn't bring along my step-mother, step-brother, or step-sisters. It was like old times. He would let me go on as many rides as I liked and would cater to my every whim. Before heading back home, we would always make one last stop… The funnel cake stand. I would try to savor the delicious doughy concoction as much as I could, knowing my time alone with my father was coming to an end. To this day, whenever I tasted the combination of deep-fried dough and confectioner's sugar, I could hear my father's booming laughter in my head.

"Me, too," Dennis agreed, bringing me back from my memory. "That's what I miss the most about Texas. The county fairs. You just look at some of the food they

148

have and immediately gain twenty pounds."

"Doesn't look like it was a problem for you."

"Really?" Raising his eyebrows, he faced me.

"Absolutely. I'm sure you had all the girls chasing after you back home." I willed him to take the bait and say something, *anything*, in response. Maybe Sebby was wrong. I had given him several opportunities to admit he was gay, yet he didn't. "Well, now that we've scoped it out, time to get our hands on some of this stuff, don't you think?" I gestured with my head back toward the way we had come.

"Sounds good to me."

"So…," I began after several awkward silent moments passed. "What do you do for a living? After our conversation the other day, I kind of thought you were an actor."

"I audition for roles in my spare time, but I *do* have a real job, something that pays the bills when I'm between acting gigs."

"And that is…?"

"I work for a large accounting firm downtown."

"How does one make the jump from accounting to acting? It reminds me of *The Producers*."

"God, I loved Matthew Broderick in that," he said with an excitement in his voice that was completely new. "Didn't you?"

"I prefer the original, to be honest." I wondered if the only reason he preferred the remake was because it was a musical. "Don't get me wrong, I loved the musical version of it. I howled with laughter during 'Keep It Gay'." I eyed him.

"Imagine seeing it live," Dennis countered, a smile

on his face. "The stage production did a run out here at the Pantages Theater in Hollywood a few years ago. I went with one of the guys who lives in my building…"

I tried to ignore the giant red flag waving in front of me at the mention of him going to see a musical with a man from his apartment building in West Hollywood. Or maybe his friend was a struggling actor, as well.

"That entire scene had us roaring with laughter. Nothing like watching a bunch of gay men dancing on stage."

And, just like that, the giant red flag waving in front of me turned rainbow-colored.

Heading toward the closest stand to subdue what could only be described as an immature case of the giggles, I said, "These strawberries smell delicious." I surveyed them, the red, juicy fruit bigger than anything I could get back east. "I'm going to have to buy some. They'll be perfect for my grandma's famous strawberry shortcake."

"Sounds delicious."

"A pound of strawberries, please," a familiar voice cut through…but not Dennis'. I snapped my head to my left, my mouth agape when I saw Sebby standing next to Marcel, grins on both their faces. I had expected Marcel to show up to provide his expert opinion, but I didn't anticipate seeing Sebby standing next to him.

"Oh, hi, Baylee." He feigned surprise at seeing me there. "What a coincidence."

"Sure is, *Sebastian*." I smiled through my clenched jaw, placing my hands on my hips in irritation. "*Marcel*," I continued in the same tone, making it apparent I wasn't pleased with him for bringing Sebby along.

"Who are your friends?" Dennis asked, surveying both Marcel and Sebby from head to toe. There was a heat in his eyes that he never had when he was looking at me. He licked his lips, his eyes still raking over Marcel's tall, lean body. I could sense that his interest in Marcel went beyond just politely wanting to know who my friends were.

"Hi. I'm Sebby." Grinning, he held his hand out for Dennis to shake. "I'm her neighbor."

"And I'm Marcel," my typically non-theatrical friend said rather flamboyantly, making it obvious that he was gayer than Liberace.

"Nice to meet you," Dennis responded, keeping his eyes glued to Marcel's as they shook hands amicably...although it certainly lasted longer than necessary.

"Likewise."

"Do you live in Baylee's building, too?"

"I do, but not in one of the penthouses like these two." Marcel gestured between Sebby and me. "I'm slumming it on one of the lower levels."

"I've been in that building," Dennis interjected. "I wouldn't exactly call it slumming. I don't even want to think about what one of those places costs."

"What can I say?" Marcel replied. "The interior design industry is jumping these days."

"You're a designer?" He closed the distance between him and Marcel. I started to feel like a third wheel. "I'm actually in the market for someone to come and add some life to my place."

"I bet he is," Sebby whispered to me, his voice barely audible.

"Stop it," I hissed back. "He could be interested in Marcel because he's a designer. I latched onto him when I found that out, too, ya know."

I returned my attention to Dennis and Marcel's conversation, but I was no longer listening to the words coming out of their mouths. All I knew was that Dennis seemed to be very interested in whatever Marcel was saying, laughing every so often as he brushed his hand on Marcel's toned arm.

"Dennis? Fancy running into you today," a booming male voice called out.

Dennis tore his attention away from Marcel for the first time since he laid eyes on him, his demeanor changing when he saw the source of the voice. Turning back to us, he looked at me, then to Marcel. "Will you all excuse me for a minute? I'll be right back." He rushed off, which struck me as odd. Maybe things were different out here, but when I was with someone and ran into a friend, I would always introduce them, not run off.

Turning to Marcel, I timidly asked, "So, what's your professional opinion?"

"Oh, Miss Dixie," he began, placing his hand on my shoulder in a consoling manner. "If that man isn't gay, someone should give him a SAG card for that amazing performance."

"SAG card?" I turned to Sebby.

"Screen Actor's Guild."

"Right." I nodded, then faced Marcel. "But I gave him more than enough opportunities to come clean and tell me. When I mentioned girls falling all over him, he didn't correct me. Don't you think—"

"Not necessarily," Sebby said. "There may be some

152

reason he wants everyone around him to believe he's straight. Maybe his job. Maybe his family. At the very least, you owe it to yourself to just come out with it and ask him. You both need to be on the same page."

My eyes widened at the thought. "But what if he isn't? Then he'll think *I* think he's gay and it will ruin whatever this could be."

"I doubt he's straight," Sebby insisted. "And I'll prove it to you." He nodded toward Dennis, who had broken into a light jog to rejoin us.

"Sorry," he said, approaching. "That was just a friend."

"An old *boy*friend," Sebby mumbled in my ear. I elbowed him in the gut, causing him to let out a barely audible groan. "Dennis," he continued, not even missing a beat. He turned his attention to the stand in front of us, large fruits and vegetables displayed on the line of tables. Sebby picked up a gargantuan-sized zucchini. "You appear to take care of yourself. Maybe you can settle a disagreement between Baylee and me. Which do you prefer as a snack? Melons or zucchini?"

My eyes grew wide, my face burning. I should have been absolutely livid with Sebby, but I found myself stifling a laugh.

"Melons have more natural sugars," Dennis responded, ignoring the double entendre. "I love zucchini, though. Look how big they are right now, even this late in the season! It's certainly more than a mouthful, isn't it?"

"It sure is," Sebby agreed, a satisfied smirk on his face.

I glared at him and Marcel, who was also trying to hide his laughter, albeit unsuccessfully.

"Well…," Marcel said when I gave him the death stare. "We don't want to intrude on your *date*."

"You're not," Dennis insisted.

"No, we are," Sebby added. "We'll leave you to your afternoon. Hope to see you around, Dennis." They shook hands before Sebby turned to me, mouthing, *Just ask him*.

"Likewise." Dennis shook Marcel's hand, the exchange again seeming to last longer than necessary.

I spent the rest of the afternoon forking out a small fortune on fresh produce, cheese, meats, and anything else that caught my eye, all while trying to work up the courage to ask Dennis if he was gay. I didn't know why it was so difficult for me. Maybe I just hated to admit I was so naïve that I didn't have the wherewithal to see the signs.

After loading up his car with all my purchases, Dennis drove me back to my building and pulled my bags out of his trunk, handing them to me. If this was a date, now would be the perfect time for him to kiss me. We stared at each other for several long moments, but the awkwardness I imagined building between us right before our first kiss was absent.

Sighing, I briefly closed my eyes. "Dennis…" I paused. "Are you gay?"

He stiffened his spine, taken aback. "What? Where is this coming from?"

I shuffled my feet, wondering if maybe Sebby and Marcel were wrong. If Dennis *was* gay, why wouldn't he just come out and admit it when asked? I couldn't imagine wanting to keep that a secret, especially out here, where it appeared most everyone was open to different races, cultures, and sexual orientation.

"It's just something I've been thinking about. That's all."

He stared at me, not responding.

"Dennis…" I took a step closer. "It's okay if you are. I don't think it's anything to be ashamed of, and you shouldn't, either."

"So…what?!" he exclaimed, slightly exasperated. "Just because I live in WeHo, like musical theater, and do yoga, that makes me gay?"

"No," I insisted, although those were certainly on my list of things pointing to him being gay. "That's not it at all. It's just… Well, to be honest, it looked like you were more interested in Marcel than me…which is perfectly okay," I added quickly, noticing his annoyance rising.

"Well, thanks for your concern, Baylee," he hissed, spinning on his heels dramatically. If he were wearing a scarf, I could just picture him whipping it over his shoulder for added flair. "But I'm not gay. I'm as straight as they come." He jumped into his car and peeled out of the porte-cochere. As he pulled away, I could have sworn I heard the opening lines of "Lullaby of Broadway" from *42ⁿᵈ Street* blaring from his car.

I was going to have to find a new yoga studio.

# CHAPTER TWELVE

GUILT SEEPED ITS WAY into my conscience as I unloaded all my produce and put it away. Marcel and Sebby seemed so sure Dennis was gay. I kind of was, too. I didn't mean to stereotype him based on his likes and interests, not to mention the way he occasionally carried himself, but I thought all the signs were there. Even Marcel with his "finely-tuned gaydar", as he called it, insisted he was. Where did we all go wrong?

After changing out of my sundress, which didn't even get me a kiss because I had to open my big mouth, I collapsed on the couch and turned on the TV, flipping aimlessly through the channels. Not finding anything, I put on a movie I had seen at least a dozen times and simply stared at the screen, lying snuggled up with Sport. I wavered between being angry with Sebby and Marcel, and being upset with myself for thinking it was a good idea to ask Dennis whether or not he was gay. I hated thinking there could have been something between us. Now I would never find out.

At the height of my pity fest, party of one, there was a knock on my door. Sport perked up, a low growl building in his throat. Knowing it could only be one of a handful of people, I padded toward the front door and pulled it open.

"How did it go?" Sebby asked, running his hand through his hair. He peered into my condo, probably to see if I had a guest. Thanks to him and his prodding, I didn't.

"Well..." I spun on my heels, heading into my kitchen. He followed, taking a seat on one of the barstools at the island. "For your information, he's *not* gay." I bent down and rummaged through my pantry, pulling out the flour, sugar, and baking powder. I intended to cross one more item off my mother's list — cook something with all the goodies I got at the farmer's market.

"You're shitting me." He leaned back and crossed his arms over his chest, his voice oozing with disbelief. "Or are you just saying that to make me think you were right."

I looked up at him and rolled my eyes. "Yeah. I don't think so." I turned from him and opened my refrigerator, pulling out the carton of strawberries he had bought me earlier in the day. "Especially considering he stormed off after I pushed it a little. All the signs are definitely there. I guess we just read them wrong." I rinsed the strawberries and handed them to Sebby. "Make yourself useful and slice those for me."

He jumped off his stool and headed to the sink to wash his hands. Then he returned to the kitchen island and got to work on chopping the strawberries. "What are you making?"

"Strawberry shortcake," I answered, my eyes glued to a recipe that had been handed down in my family for generations.

"The list?"

"Yup." I grabbed a measuring cup and sifted the precise amount of flour the recipe called for.

The next half-hour passed in comfortable silence as

Sebby and I worked on the strawberry shortcake. The tension and guilt I had been feeling for the past hour slowly eased its way out of my body as I mixed, chopped, and tasted. The aromas coming from my kitchen reminded me of Sunday dinners at my grandmother's house. She would always make strawberry shortcake and regale me with stories of my mother, a nostalgic twinkle in her eye as she reminisced.

*"She always sat exactly where you're sitting, Baylee Grace,"* she had said. *"Whenever I was baking, she made sure to lick the bowl and spoons clean, covering her face with chocolate or whatever the dessert of the day was. She loved strawberry shortcake, too. It was her absolute favorite, mainly for the whipped cream."*

*"Why?"* I had asked.

*"She loved having it squirt in her mouth. I couldn't even make fresh whipped cream with her around. Whenever I asked if she'd like whipped cream on any of her desserts, she'd smile and respond 'In my mouth, please' and open her mouth wide."*

I laughed to myself as I recalled my grandmother's stories. My memories filled me with warmth, and I could have sworn I felt my mother in that kitchen. Every little girl has memories of learning to cook and bake with her mother. I didn't. However, as I popped the shortcake into the oven, I knew she was there with me. With each item I crossed off that list, I had a deeper understanding and connection to the woman who gave her life for mine.

"This smells delicious," Sebby commented a short while later, dishing out a portion of the lemon chicken and ratatouille we made for dinner. I didn't remember the precise moment I went from simply baking a strawberry shortcake to preparing dinner for the two of us. I didn't want to stop cooking, needing to feel that bond with my mother.

"If you weren't here, I'd go straight for that strawberry shortcake and bypass dinner. It's been one of those days."

Sebby met my eyes as we sat down at the kitchen island. The dining room table Marcel had urged me to sign off on would take a few more weeks until it was ready. "I can get on board with that."

We indulged in our dinners as if we hadn't eaten in days, all conversation ceasing. It wasn't an awkward silence, like it was when we first met. It was comfortable, like we had known each other most of our lives and didn't need to say anything to fill the void. I *had* known Will most of my life. I even had photos of us in diapers together. Still, during the course of our relationship, I never felt this at ease with him. As I sat eating my dinner, I struggled to come up with one thing Will and I had in common, even if it was the same favorite cheesy movie.

The old adage that opposites attract was never the case with Will and me. We were polar opposites. He didn't envision a life outside the small town we grew up in. I wanted to spread my wings and see the world. He liked the fried comfort food so typical of southern country living. I preferred fresh organic food full of flavor and low on fat. Hell, we even had trouble agreeing on what song we would use for our first dance at our wedding. I wanted something a bit more traditional, like "The Way You Look Tonight". As ironic as it was, Will insisted on Journey's "Faithfully", claiming that was what the radio was playing when he picked me up on our first official date. I never corrected him, although that should have been a giant red flag. The radio in his car was broken that night. It stood out in my mind because he had acted like a child, complaining that his parents wouldn't give him the money to get it fixed. Apparently, getting a job never crossed his mind.

"Earth to Baylee," Sebby's voice called out, snapping me back to the present. "Where'd ya go?"

I glanced down at his plate and saw that it was practically licked clean. Mine still had a few bites of ratatouille and half my chicken left. "Sorry." I shrugged, slicing into the chicken. "I was just thinking."

"About?"

"Polar opposites."

"What about it?"

"You know the saying that opposites attract?"

He nodded.

"Don't you think it's complete bullshit? I mean, how can two polar opposites find happiness together when they have absolutely nothing in common, especially when one or both of them are pretty stubborn and set in their ways?"

"I don't think it's bullshit," Sebby responded. I could sense I might have struck a nerve in regards to his relationship with Mercedes. From the little information he had shared, they seemed to be on opposite sides of the spectrum, too.

"Well, I've been there," I said.

"Will?"

I nodded, taking a sip of my wine. "We were complete opposites. It's exciting at first, but when my dreams and aspirations conflicted with his, there was no compromise. He always won. I was the one having to sacrifice what I really wanted to make him happy. So

160

no. I don't think two people who are complete opposites have a real shot. Not in the long run."

"If there's compromise, like you mentioned, two people who appear to be opposites could certainly make it work. Plus, being with someone like that keeps things interesting. You're both constantly learning from each other, keeping each other on your toes. How boring would life be if you had the same interests, same dreams, same taste in wine? It would get monotonous and, after time, you'd be desperate for something different, wouldn't you?"

"I suppose, but what if one person isn't willing to compromise?" I asked guardedly, recalling his stories about Mercedes and how she refused to entertain the idea of ever leaving Manhattan.

"If you truly love someone, you'll do whatever it takes to make it work, even if it means sacrificing your dreams to support your partner's aspirations."

I wanted to say it sounded like there was a thin line between making a sacrifice and being a pushover. Instead, I kept my thoughts to myself. "Then I guess it wasn't true love between Will and me," I said, lightening the heavy air as I stood up from the table. Grabbing our plates, I headed into the kitchen. "Hell, when you're eighteen, your concept of love is pretty much limited to the first guy who buys you flowers and some cheap necklace at a shitty department store jewelry counter. Not to mention he was the first guy I had slept with, and I wouldn't have done that if I didn't love him, right?" I laughed. "If you can even refer to our first time as having sex. I still have my doubts."

Sebby followed me into the kitchen, taking the plates from me and helping to clean up. "From a guy's point of view, there's a lot of pressure to...perform that first time." He raised his eyebrows.

"Perform is a nice way of putting what Will referred to as having sex. It felt like he was on a pit crew for Nascar, rushing through everything to get back to the race. Just as soon as the car pulled into the pits, he was sending it back on its way, confused about what the hell just happened."

Sebby turned the water off, keeping his back toward me. He was still for a moment before an all-consuming laugh bellowed against the walls, his shoulders shaking. He turned around and leaned against the counter, crossing his muscular arms in front of that defined chest I had the pleasure of seeing bare a few days ago.

"Baylee," he began, wiping his eyes, "you may be the first person I've ever known to equate having sex to being in the pit at a Nascar race."

"Not just any sex," I corrected. *"Bad* sex."

He shook his head, wiping down the counters. "For your sake, I hope you find someone to help erase that experience from memory."

"Think I should put an ad on Craigslist?" I joked. "Short white female looking for sex that isn't like screwing an impact wrench."

"Impact wrench?"

"Yeah. That's one of those things they use to take off and put the tires back on. Will made me learn all the terminology," I explained, plating strawberry shortcake for us, finishing it with whipped cream on top of each. I resisted the temptation to squirt the whipped cream into my mouth, although it was nearly impossible. "He loved watching racing, football… You name the sport, he followed it. I tried to be the supportive wife and watch with him as he drank cheap beer from a can." I shivered dramatically, walking from the kitchen with my strawberry shortcake and sitting on the couch, Sebby following my lead. "We had plenty of money, but Will refused to drink anything of higher quality than Milwaukee's Best."

"How about you?" Sebby asked, eyeing me.

"What do you mean?"

"What did Baylee like to do?"

I shrugged as I shoveled a bite of the strawberry shortcake into my mouth, moaning when the sweet buttery combination hit my senses. "It was never my decision. Whenever Will came home from work, even if I was watching something on the TV in the family room, he took the remote and put on whatever he wanted. He definitely had that good ol' boy mentality. When the man's home from work, the wife should cater to his needs." I rolled my eyes. Will often forgot I was the main earner in the family, despite my light work schedule.

"Well, Will's not here now." Sebby grabbed the remotes off the coffee table and handed them to me. "What do you want to watch?"

A childish grin on my face, I placed my strawberry shortcake on the table and greedily took the remotes, scanning through all my movies to find the one I was looking for. "This," I said, smiling. "A *real* cinematic masterpiece of the twentieth century."

"That's a matter of opinion," Sebby scoffed as the opening measures of "The End" by The Doors filled the room, the image of palm trees and helicopters appearing on my large screen television.

"Are you really going to sit there and tell me that *Apocalypse Now* isn't a great fucking movie?"

"I would never demean Coppola in such a way."

"Good." I settled back into the couch and watched Martin Sheen stare at the ceiling fan in his hotel room in Saigon. The conversation with Sebby ceased as we were consumed with a movie both of us had probably seen more times than we cared to admit. During some of the scenes, we mouthed certain well-known lines with the characters as they spoke them.

The sun had set, leaving my entire condo dark, apart from the glow from the television. Exhaustion caught up to me and I lay down on the couch. Sport snuggled up next to me, and I propped my feet on Sebby's lap. As if on autopilot, he took one in his hand and massaged it, lulling me into a deeper sense of comfort. The last thing I remembered before dozing off was The Chef screaming about never getting off the boat.

~~~~~~~~~~

"BAYLEE." I FELT A slight shaking on my foot and struggled to open my heavy eyelids.

"What?" I whined.

"The movie's over. You dozed off."

"I know I did," I retorted. "And I'd still be sleeping if some inconsiderate prick didn't wake me up."

"I couldn't just leave you sleeping on the couch. Only a true inconsiderate prick would do that."

Groaning, I stretched and opened my eyes to see Sebby's form looming over me. He held his hand out to me and I took it, allowing him to help me up.

"Whatever you say, Nosebleeder."

I shuffled away from the living area, Sebby following me as I walked to the front door. "Sorry I fell asleep on you," I offered, then grew flustered when I thought of the double meaning behind my words. "I mean, I didn't fall asleep *on* you, but fell asleep with you."

He raised his eyebrows at me, his butterfly-inducing smile growing wide and more devious. I loved his smile. I could stare at it for hours. There's nothing creepy about that, right?

"Ya know what?" I shook my head, knowing there was no way for me to say what I was trying to without the double meaning. "Let's just drop it."

"You're the one who fell asleep on me." He winked. A stiff silence settled between us as we stood there. I should have been angry that he essentially ruined my date earlier, but tonight was the perfect ending to my day. I couldn't picture it any other way now.

"Well, thanks for dinner." Sebby broke through the awkwardness, shifting from foot to foot.

"Thanks for the company."

He studied me for a brief moment. Maybe I was simply imagining something that wasn't there, but I could have sworn I saw desire within those eyes. It was the look you gave someone when you were about to kiss them. I swallowed. I had wanted Sebby to kiss me from our first meeting, but things were different now. It wasn't just the girlfriend. It was the friendship we had been nurturing over the past few days. I valued that more than my unruly libido.

"Have a good night." I took a step back from him.

Nodding, he looked at me for a split second longer, then turned and opened the door, heading toward his condo. I leaned against the doorjamb, watching him walk away from me.

"Sebby, wait!"

He spun around and faced me.

"All that stuff I said earlier about opposites…" I fidgeted with my hands. "I didn't mean anything by it. If you're happy…"

He looked down.

I took purposeful steps down the hall, approaching him. "Sebby, *are* you happy?"

He tilted his head back, our gaze meeting. I could see the indecision in those stormy eyes. I waited for what seemed like hours for him to finally answer my simple question. Then he let out a long breath, shaking his head.

"Yes. I am."

*Liar*, I thought.

# CHAPTER THIRTEEN

MY PHONE BUZZED WEDNESDAY night as I was lounging on my couch eating a bowl of ice cream, snuggled next to Sport. Apart from my usual morning walks and coffee with Sebby, I hadn't left my condo much. Inspiration had finally seeped its way into my brain and I didn't want to lose my momentum. I had been searching for my story for years when I didn't have to look too far. The old adage that you write what you know turned out to be true. I was writing my story, more or less, with some changes and embellishments. I didn't know how it would end yet, but I knew that would all come in time.

Sebby kept asking to see what I had written, but I didn't want to let anyone read it until I had a better grasp on the story. I was just writing whatever came to mind, not knowing where it would all fit, and that was okay for now.

Convinced that the only person who would be looking for me tonight was most likely Sebby, I ignored my phone, devoting my full attention to the two men in my life who had never let me down...Ben and Jerry.

My phone stopped buzzing, then instantly began again. Groaning, I looked at the screen and saw Marcel's dapper and brilliant face beaming back at me. If I didn't answer, a search party would be sent to my condo.

"You're interrupting my threesome," I answered.

"Oh boy, Miss Dixie!" he bellowed over the background noise of wherever he was. I could hear voices shouting over some crappy techno remix, so I could only assume he was at a club. "I expect full details!"

"Don't get too excited," I replied. "It's the usual suspects. Ben and Jerry are the only men in my life who know exactly what I need when I need it."

"Speaking of men in your life, I'm sleuthing."

"Sleuthing? What do you mean?"

"Well, when you told me about the fallout between you and Dennis, I refused to believe I was wrong. I mean, there are times when it could go either way, but Dennis certainly doesn't."

"What did you do?" I asked cautiously. By the tone in his voice, I knew he was up to something.

"Don't get mad, but I may have tracked down where he lives."

"You what?!" I couldn't believe my ears. Why would he do such a thing? What if he got caught? Would Dennis think I put him up to it?

"It wasn't that hard," he insisted. "Hell, he ended up contacting the design company I work for to get a consult. Initially, he asked for me, but I didn't think I could take him on as a client. Anyway, I went through our system and got his address. When I got there, he was leaving with another guy."

"That doesn't mean anything. He has a roommate."

"But this guy picked him up. They went to a romantic little Italian restaurant in Hollywood, and now they're at a swanky martini bar, which just so happens to be where I am at the moment, too."

"That still doesn't prove anything."

"Dixie, stop fighting me on this. If you want to see for your own eyes that Dennis lied to you, get off your butt, put on a hot dress, and come to the address I'm about to text you. Drinks are on me." He hung up before I could even respond.

I remained on my couch, unmoving, staring at the laptop in front of me. Minutes passed as I tried to refocus my energy into writing. I read my words over and over, not really comprehending them. My thoughts kept shifting to Marcel and what proof he had that Dennis was gay.

"Well, since I'm now officially blocked, I may as well go," I huffed, throwing my legs off the side of the couch. If nothing else, this invitation would get me out of my condo for a while. I was beginning to feel like a hermit, spending the past few days in front of my laptop, typing away. After fixing my appearance and throwing on a slinky green dress and leopard print heels, I was on my way to the address Marcel had texted me.

I pulled up to a brick building off Sunset a short while later, the sound of drunken frivolity greeting me once I entered the darkened club. Behind the bar was an extravagant water feature, rain-like streams cascading over a stone backdrop. Bartenders demonstrated their skills as they prepared brightly-colored drinks in martini glasses, a perfectly orchestrated symphony of alcohol and more alcohol with a floater of alcohol for good measure.

As I made my way through the crowd, I spied

Dennis at the opposite end of the bar and I looked down, trying to hide myself. Running into him hadn't crossed my mind, even though I knew he'd be here. I would have been lying if I said I wasn't hopeful Marcel was right. It would at least make me feel better about how things ended between us. I wasn't immature to the point that I wanted to rub his lies in his face, but I was hoping for some sort of vindication if he, in fact, did lie and made me look like a complete fool.

"Whoa, hot stuff!" Marcel draped his arm around me and pulled me toward the bar, taking me by surprise. "You clean up good!" He continued moving his hips, not even missing a beat. He had this energy and liveliness that could only be described as being akin to a kid rushing down the stairs Christmas morning to see that Santa had come the night before. He didn't have an off switch, and you couldn't help but feel an added boost of energy whenever you were in his presence. Who needs caffeine when you have a friend like Marcel around?

"You've seen me in a dress before," I shouted over the music.

"I know, but this is a quick turnaround from you wearing an oversized t-shirt and yoga pants less than an hour ago."

I scowled, placing my hands on my hips.

"I know these things." He winked. "Now, what do you want to drink?"

"Manhattan, please. Up."

"Hitting it hard. My kind of girl."

Marcel signaled the bartender, a tall, lean man with dark hair and soft, creamy skin. He was probably in his late twenties or early thirties, although he didn't look a day over twenty-one.

"What can I get you?" he asked, his attention devoted to Marcel, who rattled off our drink order, leaning closer than necessary to our bartender. Once he left to make our drinks, I elbowed Marcel in the side.

"What was that for?"

"Is this a gay bar?" I hissed under my breath.

He placed his hands on his hips. "Just because I'm here and flirting with the bartender, you think it's a gay bar?"

"Apparently, based on recent experience, I can never be too sure about these things."

When the bartender returned with our drinks, Marcel paid him, throwing a generous tip down on the counter. "Relax, sweetie. It's not a gay bar."

"Then why were you hitting on the bartender?" I asked, taking a much-needed sip of my Manhattan.

"Like I said, Dixie." He wrapped his arm around me, ushering me away from the bar and toward an empty booth in a dark corner where we could observe the dance floor and not be spotted. "When it comes to knowing who's gay and who's not, I just know."

Rolling my eyes, I slid into the booth. "Like with Dennis? You messed that one up pretty good."

"Did I?" He nodded toward the dance floor. My eyes followed his line of sight, landing on tall, dark, and muscular Dennis dancing to an upbeat song with a shorter blond man.

I had seen men dancing together before, but usually only when they were drunk as they slurred the words to "Sweet Home, Alabama" or something, their arms draped over each other's shoulders. I wasn't even sure you could consider swaying and stumbling over your own feet dancing, but that was what I had witnessed during my wedding at the glamorous VFW Hall and any other social event I had been to with Will. But as my eyes lingered on Dennis and his dance partner, I knew this wasn't simply a friendly dance between two men. This was something different, something bigger, something much more…intimate.

Their eyes were glued to each other. The connection was so strong, I had a feeling even an earthquake couldn't break it. Dennis' hips moved in a sensual way, his body nearly touching his partner's. The way their two bodies moved together was almost erotic, like they were each other's perfect match.

The music grew to a climax and, as if scripted, Dennis grabbed his partner's neck and pulled, ensnaring him in his arms. Giving me further confirmation, he crushed his lips passionately to his partner's, their kiss eliminating any doubt left in my mind.

I bolted up from the booth, my eyes glued to Dennis and the kiss that seemed to last forever. I didn't know what I thought I would do. Confront him? Why? He lied to me. So what? Maybe he had a good reason. What would it solve if I did confront him with his lie? Most likely nothing. Would I ruin his chance at happiness? I couldn't live with that on my conscience.

Unclenching my fists, I took a deep breath and lowered myself back to the booth. "Well, looks like you were right," I said to Marcel.

"I told you, Dixie," he replied. "I just know these things."

"I still don't understand why he wouldn't just admit

it."

Marcel shrugged. "I can understand, I guess. I remember being afraid of people finding out who I truly was, but then I finally stopped caring. When I told my parents, you want to know what they said?"

"What?" I asked, sipping my drink.

"My Dad goes to me, 'Tell me something I didn't know.' My entire family knew I was gay."

"And they didn't say anything?"

"No. They figured I'd tell them when I was ready. Even after I told them, it took me a while to be open with my friends and co-workers. It doesn't matter how far we've come as a nation in support of gay people. There are still a lot of close-minded people out there."

"Tell me about it," I agreed, rolling my eyes. "I used to live in a town full of them."

"So maybe there's something going on in Dennis' life that is still scaring him so much, he wanted to be able to go into work on a Monday morning or pick up the phone at night and tell people how he met a beautiful girl and have the proof to back it up. Hell, he may have even taken you somewhere knowing he'd run into someone and could prove he wasn't who they all assumed he was." He narrowed his eyes at me.

"The farmer's market," I mumbled as I recalled Dennis excusing himself and talking to someone he knew. The exchange seemed cordial and almost professional in nature.

"I've been there and have done the exact same things. Eventually, he'll get sick of constantly pretending to be someone he's not and he'll finally be brave enough to show everyone who he truly is. Until then, I wish him all the luck in living the double life he's made for himself."

He raised his glass and I followed, downing the remainder of my drink.

"Like Dennis really matters anyway," Marcel continued, lightening the mood. "From where I'm sitting, it looks like you've got your sights set on someone else." He raised his eyebrows at me, a lascivious smile crossing his face.

"What are you talking about?" I feigned ignorance. I knew all too well about whom he was speaking.

"You can play that innocent card with everyone else, but not me. I know you and Sebby have been spending quite a bit of time together lately."

I rolled my eyes. "You're looking for something that isn't there, Marcel," I replied. "We're neighbors. We get along. We have a lot in common. It's only natural for us to spend some time together."

"Mmm-hmm." He pinched his lips together. "Then why did he cancel the trip he was supposed to take to New York on Saturday?"

"What?"

"You heard me, Dixie. Your darling neighbor, Sebastion, was supposed to be heading to New York City for the next month to see his girlfriend and family, as well as promote his new film. Then, out of the blue, he canceled the trip and, from what Sophia told me, had the studio rearrange his schedule so he could promote it from the West Coast instead."

My jaw dropped as I tried to think of what that could all mean. He wouldn't have changed his plans just to spend time with me. There had to be another reason.

"It's not because of me," I insisted.

"Mmm-hmm," Marcel repeated. "Whatever you say."

"We're just friends. He has a girlfriend—"

"Whom he never sees."

"That doesn't matter. I've been cheated on. I don't care whether you know the relationship is doomed to fail or not—"

"So you think Sebby's relationship is doomed to fail?" he interrupted.

"I didn't say that!" My voice grew irritated. "What I meant to say is that, regardless of the status of the relationship, I refuse to come between them."

"Even if he's not happy?" Marcel pushed.

"His happiness isn't at issue here."

"It's not?" He tapped his glass. I felt like I was in a sparse interrogation room, the police officer tripping me up with each question.

"Of course, I want him to be happy. Like I said, I've been cheated on, Marcel. It didn't matter that I wasn't in love with Will anymore, if I ever truly was. It still hurt that he cheated on me. I could never hurt anyone else like that, regardless of whether I know them or not."

"Just take Mercedes out of the picture for a minute. What if he decided to end it with her? Then what would you think?"

"I…" I stopped short. I hadn't given much thought to that scenario because it wasn't reality. Still, there was something refreshing and familiar about being with Sebby, knowing there was no hidden agenda. We were just two friends hanging out. I had the horrible fear that if he were to break up with Mercedes to pursue something with me and it didn't work out, it would end our friendship. I shuddered at the thought.

"Even then, nothing will change between us," I said, my voice firm. "Sebby and me… We're friends. Really good friends. I can't destroy that."

"And you think a more intimate relationship would?"

I shrugged. "I don't know, but I could never risk finding out."

"He means that much to you?"

"His friendship does. I know it's crazy, but since the day I gave him a bloody nose all those weeks ago, I felt a connection to him. At first, before I knew who he was, yes, I was attracted to him. Then I realized that friendships are just as important as having an intimate relationship with someone. I've only slept with one person in my entire life. Hell, I've only *kissed* one person. This is my chance to finally experience what life has to offer me, including friendships I never thought I'd have with people like you and Sophia…"

"And Sebby," Marcel finished my thought.

"Exactly." I leaned back in the booth, a satisfied expression on my face. I wondered if he believed me. I wasn't even sure *I* believed what I was saying.

"Well, Miss Dixie, I can certainly see where you're coming from. Friendships are important…" He stood up. "But regret can be a bitch, too." He kissed my temple and headed toward the bar and the cute bartender.

I remained in the booth and allowed the atmosphere to consume me. Since I had started writing, people-watching had become one of my favorite sources of inspiration and material. New ideas never seemed to be in short supply, and tonight was no different. Young professionals crowded the bar, ordering whatever trendy drink they could. Some people were on the dance floor, moving to the rhythm of the mix the DJ was playing. It was the kind of place people went just to say they were there. I felt somewhat intimidated, surrounded by tall blond women who all looked like cookie-cutter versions of each other. I wondered when they had eaten last, each of them waif-like with made-up eyes and paper straight hair. I wasn't overweight by any stretch of the imagination, but I liked knowing that a gentle breeze wasn't going to blow me away.

"Is this seat taken?" A strong voice broke through my observations. I raised my head to see a man whom I estimated to be in his late thirties looking down at me. He had a two-day stubble on his jaw, haunting silver eyes, and a full head of dark hair. His nose was slightly crooked, making me wonder whether he was a hockey player. He had that kind of vibe about him, despite the sport jacket he wore over a collared shirt with the first few buttons undone, exposing a hint of dark chest hair.

Glancing over my shoulder to make sure he was, in fact, speaking to me, I returned my eyes to his, noticing a hint of eagerness as he awaited my answer. I gestured to the opposite side of the booth. "Help yourself, I suppose."

He beamed his too bright for words smile at me and I felt like a giddy schoolgirl, flustered that the hottest guy in class was actually talking to me. And, for once, it wasn't a joke. I imagined this guy was an intellectual type who knew enough to take care of his body. The dark glasses he wore perfectly accented his distinguished features, bringing forward fantasies of a hot student-teacher roleplay. And yes, "Hot For Teacher" was totally blaring during said fantasy.

Drawing my lip between my teeth, I knew it was readily apparent that I was ogling this fine specimen of a man. Worse, I was pretty sure *he* knew I was practically drooling over him. I was in lust, and not just normal lust. I was in *take me in this booth right now and clear out the cobwebs of the past decade* lust, possible arrest for indecent exposure be damned.

"I'm Declan," he said in an even tone, holding his hand out.

"Baylee," I barely squeaked out. My brain was yelling at me to imitate his gesture and allow him to take my hand, but I was still frozen in place, mesmerized by his voice. I had to suppress the urge to answer "Yes, Professor" to any further inquiries.

Finally snapping back to reality so this complete stranger didn't think I wasn't all there mentally, I reached my hand across the table, allowing him to take it in his. He didn't break eye contact as he shook it, his motions slow and deliberate. His hand was large in comparison to mine, his skin rough and manly. All I could think was that he must work with his hands.

I wanted him to work *me* with his hands.

"What's a beautiful woman like you doing here all alone?" he asked smoothly, Rico Suave-like.

"Technically, I'm not alone. I came with a friend, but I got ditched for a guy." I shrugged, sipping my drink.

"I'm sorry," Declan offered.

"Don't be." I waved it off. "If you can't enjoy your own company, whose can you?"

A small smile grew on his lips, the right side slightly higher than his left. I'd call it a smirk, but that didn't adequately convey the cool attitude this guy exuded. "That's something I don't hear often."

"Why is that?"

"Most girls I meet seem to be of the mob mentality."

I scrunched my eyebrows. "I don't follow."

"They're so insecure, they refuse to even go to the bathroom without an escort."

A look of disgust crossed my face. "I like my privacy. There's something to be said of solitude."

"I couldn't agree more." His bold eyes met mine again. He gave off an air of mystery that I found myself being drawn to. He was in complete control of his actions. He wasn't nervous or flustered. He was confident and assertive with a hint of cockiness. The longer he sat across from me, studying my every move, the more intrigued I was about him...and the more I was no longer thinking about Sebby and our "friendship", which was exactly what I needed, wasn't it?

"So, Declan." I lowered my gaze, completely unnerved by the intensity of his mere presence. "What do you do?"

He ran his finger around the top of his pilsner glass as he considered my question. I was kind of expecting him to tell me he was a porn star. Marcel had informed me that the San Fernando Valley...more specifically, Chatsworth...was the porn capital of the world. Then again, I had walked in on Will watching porn on more than one occasion. From what I had seen, the men in those movies weren't exactly attractive.

"I'm a doctor," he responded. I would have been lying if I said a flurry of excitement didn't rush through me at that moment. I flashed back to all those corny soap operas I watched with my friends when I was a teenager. We always swooned over the tall, dark, handsome, mysterious doctor. He would always be treating a wealthy woman with whom he had secretly been having an affair, unbeknownst to her husband. The tension in the hospital room could be cut with a knife as the woman had to decide between a moderately wealthy sex on a stick doctor and an older man with more zeros in his bank account than one could imagine. And the crazy bitch always chose the extremely wealthy old guy who worked countless hours and never paid her any attention. I would have chosen the doctor every time.

"You must have your pick of women then," I joked. "What made you come over here to talk to me?"

"In my line of work, you learn to read people fairly well, and there was something about you that interested me. Not to mention," he continued, leaning in closer, "most of the women in this bar have had more plastic surgery than anyone should undergo. I prefer natural beauty to the fake, Botox-injected attempts to be beautiful." He paused and raised his glass to his lips. "Plus, I'm a sucker for a natural redhead."

I tried to hide my smile, but it was useless. It didn't matter how many times you heard it. There was nothing like a man calling you beautiful. I had never been one of those women who was timid or shy around men. I never put myself down just to fish for a compliment. I wasn't self-absorbed, and I never put on an act just to get a handsome man's attention. Still, I never got tired of hearing a man call me beautiful…particularly a man as handsome, intriguing, and professional as Declan appeared to be.

"Well, who is *this*?"

I tore my gaze from Declan's and smiled at Marcel standing just to the side of the booth, interrupting our moment.

"Marcel," I began, seeing how interested and probably even surprised he was that an incredibly attractive man had stolen his seat, "this is Declan. Declan, this is my friend, Marcel."

"Pleasure to meet you." Marcel held his hand to Declan and shook it lightly.

"My friend who ditched me for another guy," I explained to Declan, causing a look of understanding, perhaps even relief, to cross his face.

"A man's got to do what a man's got to do," Marcel joked in a slow drawl.

"Well, I'll let you two continue with your evening." Declan got up from the booth. "It was lovely talking to you, Baylee." He grabbed my hand and brushed his lips against it, sending a delicious chill down my spine. I didn't know if it was the combination of his smooth voice, the mysterious way he carried himself, or those piercing eyes, but I was completely mute, my voice nowhere to be found. All I could do in response was giggle. I fucking giggled. At a seriously drool-inducing man.

"It was nice meeting you, Declan," Marcel said, saving me from embarrassment.

"You, too." He winked at me one last time before retreating from our table. I couldn't take my eyes off his attractive backside the entire time he made his way across the bar and toward a high-top table, rejoining who I assumed to be his friends.

"Holy Doctor McDreamy," I exhaled, leaning back in my seat. I wiped my lower lip of the remnants of my Manhattan. I wanted to believe it wasn't drool.

"You've been watching too much *Grey's Anatomy*."

"No," I insisted. "For real. He's a doctor."

"Or so he says. You can't always trust what comes out of the mouth of a guy you meet in a bar. He could have just been saying that to get into your pants."

"Maybe," I shrugged. "Hell, he could be gay, too, for all I know. I don't exactly have a great track record with these things."

Marcel glanced across the bar to where Declan was drinking with his group of well-dressed, well-groomed friends. "I wouldn't rule it out, but I'm not getting a strong vibe that he is. Plus, he came over here to talk to you."

"Dennis went out of his way to talk to me, too. That didn't mean shit."

"True, but I noticed something when Doctor McDreamy, as you call him, was looking at you that makes me almost certain he's straight."

"What's that?" I asked, my stomach clenching.

"When he—"

"Marcel," a deep voice cut through and we both snapped our heads up to see our bartender standing off to the side of the booth. "I'm off now. I just wanted to come over and say goodbye."

"Baylee, this is Nicholas. Nicholas, Baylee."

"Nice to meet you." I smiled.

"Likewise." He returned his attention to Marcel. "Stop by again. I work most nights."

Marcel lowered his head, surprising me. For the first time since I had met him, he didn't act like the self-assured man I knew him to be. He was timid and uncertain.

"I'll do that," he said, blushing. It was obvious he liked this guy.

I fidgeted with my martini glass. I had no problem with people who were gay, but I felt awkward as the two men said goodbye, like I was intruding on a private moment. Still, I couldn't turn my head. I was mesmerized with how into each other they appeared to be. I wished love was this easy for everyone.

"Please do." Nicholas placed his hand over Marcel's and squeezed, then left us alone, glancing over his shoulder one last time before disappearing into the crowd of people.

"Marcel," I urged, "go after him. Get his number. Ask him out. Do *something*."

"What are you talking about?" he replied nervously.

"You like him. Why wouldn't you want to see where this could go?"

"He probably only came over here because I'm a big tipper."

I rolled my eyes. "Come on. He likes you. He wants to see you again. Put your big girl panties on and ask him out. Remember... Regret can be a bitch." I smirked as I threw his own words back at him.

"Oh, you hussy!"

I gestured toward the front door of the bar where Nicholas was saying his goodbyes to the doorman. "Go!"

Resolved, Marcel straightened his spine and stood,

taking a few small steps toward the door before turning back to me. "But what about you?"

"What about me?" I shot back. "I'm going to sit here, enjoy my drink, and people-watch. Then I'll go home. Go. And I want to hear all about it tomorrow night!" I ushered him away.

He remained still as he looked between me and Nicholas.

"Do I need to drag you over there?"

"All right. All right. I'm going." He started across the room, adjusting his jeans and jacket as he did. I tried not to stare as he approached Nicholas, but I couldn't help it. Both men were smiling nervously as they spoke to one another. I had no idea what they were talking about, but when I saw Nicholas grab Marcel's hand and lead him out of the bar, I got a good feeling about them.

Half the trouble of finding the right person is opening your eyes to see what's right in front of you. Sometimes you're blind to everything around you so you need someone else to act as your glasses.

After finishing my drink with little interruption, I decided to call it a night. As I approached the door to leave, a strong hand grasped my arm. I whirled around, only to be greeted by those piercing silver eyes once more.

"Declan," I said, breathless, trying to maintain my composure that was slowly leaving me. Gay or not, doctor or not, porn star or not, there was a part of me that wanted him to haul me out of that bar at that instant.

"Baylee…" He hovered over me. I hadn't noticed his height earlier, but he had to be nearly a foot taller than I was. I felt so small compared to him. "I know this sounds crazy, but I couldn't stop thinking about you all night."

"It does sound a bit crazy," I said, trying to break the intensity between us. "You don't even know me."

"No, but I'd like to *get* to know you. Can I take you out next Wednesday? It's the only night I'm not on call."

I studied him, wishing Marcel had finished his thought about how he knew he was definitely straight. After everything with Dennis, I was second-guessing myself.

"I'm not exactly in the habit of going out with men I meet in bars."

"I rarely ever go to bars, and I certainly never ask for a woman's number when I do, but there's just something about you... You're different. A breath of fresh air from all these LA women."

"How can I be sure you're not a serial killer? Or that you're really a doctor? Or that you're not gay? I've made that mistake before."

"What?" he asked, a smile crossing his face. "You've dated a serial killer?"

I smirked. "No. But I did go out with a man thinking he was interested in me only to find out he was gay."

He studied me for several long moments. I grew uneasy with the silence between us, unsure of how he would respond. I half expected him to confess that he *was* gay. Instead, before I could comprehend what was happening, he wrapped his arm around my waist and pulled my body against his, crushing his lips to mine. My libido was doing backflips, singing "Let's Get It

185

On", as his tongue brushed with mine. His body against mine was strong, powerful, commanding. So was his kiss. It erased any memory of every kiss I'd ever had.

Out of nowhere, I began to imagine what Sebby's kisses would feel like. They wouldn't be as forceful as Declan's. They would be more passionate, more meaningful. Every brush of his tongue against mine would be thought-out and measured. His hand would roam my body, telling me with the way his fingers traveled across my skin that he revered me, that we were equals, instead of the way Declan held me against him, as if he needed to be in complete control.

He pulled away, leaving me panting as I still thought of Sebby's kisses, unable to stop myself.

"Tell me, Baylee. Would a gay man kiss you like that?"

Staring at him, I simply shook my head, speechless.

"Good. Dinner Wednesday?"

Still in a daze, I nodded, a puppet to my starving libido.

"Great," Declan responded, the fire in his gaze softening a bit. I didn't know what possessed me to agree to dinner with him, especially considering I thought of another man during his kiss. Maybe dating someone like Declan would help me finally get my mind off thinking about Sebby that way.

"Can I have your phone number?" He handed me his phone and I input my name and number into it.

"I'll call you later," he said when I handed it back to him. "Have a wonderful evening, Baylee." He leaned down and placed one last soft, sensual, powerful kiss on my lips.

"You, too, Declan." I pulled away and left the bar, still thinking about Sebby's kisses.

# CHAPTER FOURTEEN

"THERE SHE IS!" MARCEL exclaimed when I walked into Sophia's apartment Thursday for our weekly game night. I glanced around the table at all the familiar faces, Sebby included. "I've been trying to get in touch with you all day to find out what happened after I left last night!"

I shrugged, avoiding everyone's eyes as I poured myself a glass of wine from the bottle I brought. "Not much to tell."

"Where did you go?" Sebby asked.

"Out with me," Marcel answered. "Turns out I was dead on with Dennis. He's gay. What's the verdict on Doctor McDreamy?"

"Doctor McDreamy?" Sophia turned away from arranging a tray of hors d'oeuvres.

I shrugged again. "Some tall, dark, and handsome doctor who hit on me at the bar last night while Marcel was flirting with our hottie bartender...whom he just so happened to leave with, but it appears he left out that little piece of information."

"You what?!" Lacey exclaimed, shoving Marcel.

"Yup. Let me just say that our little Marcel talks a big game, but around a hot guy, he closes up like an inexperienced virgin."

"Nothing wrong with a little modesty," Sebby

argued in a harsh tone. I shot my eyes to him, my smile fading when I saw his tightened jaw.

"Of course not," I agreed, brushing off his odd reaction. "It just caught me off guard. That's all."

"So who's this new beau?" Sophia sat at the table and everyone lunged for the trays of food she set down, breaking the growing tension between Sebby and me. "Does he have a name?"

I took slow steps, sitting in the only vacant chair...next to Sebby. I turned toward Marcel, trying to ignore the heat of Sebby's eyes on me.

"Nicholas," Marcel said dreamily. "And, for your information, nothing happened last night," he added, waving a finger at me. "We just went out for coffee and talked."

"Are you going to see him again?" I asked.

A wide grin crossed his face and he nodded. "Yes."

"Me, too." I raised the glass of wine to my lips.

"What?!" All eyes at the table turned to me, except for Sebby, who remained facing forward, his grip on his beer bottle tightening.

"Doctor McDreamy," I explained, addressing the rest of the table. "His real name is Declan. He asked me out to dinner next Wednesday night and I agreed."

"This one's not gay, right?" Darren laughed.

"One can never be too sure of these things," I quipped, "but after the amazing kiss he left me with, all I can say is he's a damn good actor if he is. There's no way a gay man would kiss like that."

"How was it?" Cora asked, a whimsical look on her face.

I leaned back into my chair and thought back to the

night before. "It was hot. Honestly, it took me by surprise. He cut me off in mid-sentence and before I could even react, his lips were on mine."

"Sounds like a real stand-up guy, forcing himself on you," Sebby commented, pushing out of his chair and stalking toward Sophia's wet bar. He poured a large tumbler of a dark liquid before retaking his seat.

I narrowed my eyes at him, furrowing my brow at his impetuous and childish reaction. "It wasn't like that," I insisted, although it kind of was. "Women sometimes like men who take control in certain situations."

"Hell yes, we do," Lacey added.

"See," I said smugly.

"So you mean to tell me you all prefer to date complete assholes who only think of themselves?"

"He's not an asshole," I countered, noticing the tension in the room building the longer the conversation went on.

"How do you know?" Sebby shot back. "You just met him. And at a bar, no less. You don't know anything about him, other than he's allegedly a doctor, which he could have just made up to impress you."

"Well, I guess I'll find out on my *date*, won't I?" I swiped my wine glass off the table and gulped down the liquid. Sebby's glare unnerved me. I didn't know why I wanted his approval so badly, but I did.

"I suppose you will." He pushed out of his chair. "I'll be right back. Nature calls," he announced, but instead of heading to the bathroom, he stormed out of the condo, slamming the door behind him.

We were all silent for a moment as Sebby's outburst

hung in the air.

"I'll go talk to him." Sophia raised herself from her chair and followed him out of her condo.

"See, Dixie," Marcel mumbled into my ear. "What did I tell you last night?"

"Whatever." I rolled my eyes. No matter what Marcel wanted to believe, whether it was true or not, I refused to be the other woman.

"You can ignore it all you want——"

"And I will *continue* to ignore it," I interrupted, shooting out of my chair. "He has a girlfriend!"

"Who he's been miserable with for the past several years," Lacey said. "Although he puts on a damn good show. He's loyal to a fault."

"Not to mention they're all wrong for each other," Darren added. I couldn't believe what I was hearing. These people were supposed to be his friends. They were supposed to support his choice in girlfriend, not encourage him to be unfaithful. "Do you think it's just a coincidence he's here tonight? He's never made time to come to game night and yet all of a sudden he does?"

"He can't have his cake and eat it, too." I grabbed my bag and headed toward the door.

"Where are you going?" Marcel asked, following me.

"Home. I'm not exactly in the game night mood anymore," I fumed, leaving Sophia's condo. As I was about to turn the corner toward the bank of elevators, I halted when the familiar timbre of Sophia's and Sebby's voices echoed.

"What do you mean?" Sebby whispered.

"Exactly what I said, Sebby," Sophia shot back. "I

know you. You have a thing for Baylee, but you can't act that way around her, then hop on the next flight out to see your girlfriend. It's not fair to either one of them."

"I haven't cheated on Mercedes. I'd never——"

"Yet," Sophia interrupted. "You can't say that you and Baylee are simply friends, then go into a jealous rage when she meets someone. You don't have that right. Unless you want to ruin what appears to be a great friendship, I'd suggest apologizing to her, and proving with your actions how sorry you truly are."

When I heard Sophia's heels clicking on the marble flooring, I scrambled to hide my presence, not having thought that far ahead. I contemplated running in the opposite direction, but I'd be spotted. Having only seconds to decide what to do, I dashed to an alcove in the opposite side of the hallway and crouched behind a large pot containing some sort of decorative tree. Trying to control my labored breathing, I concentrated on not moving an inch as Sophia walked past me and toward her condo. Closing my eyes, I held my breath and waited for Sebby to walk by, too. Several painfully long moments passed as I kept my eyes firmly closed. If I couldn't see him, he couldn't see me, right? Thinking he must be gone by now, I let out my breath and opened my eyes.

"*Aaaggghhh!*" I screamed as I looked into Sebby's eyes just on the other side of the tree. I lost my balance and grabbed the closest thing I could to try to steady myself...the tree. Unfortunately, it was no match against my weight and it came tumbling down on top of me as I fell to the ground, bringing Sebby along for the ride.

I didn't know how long I lay on the surface of the
192

cool marble tile covered with dirt, a faux plastic terracotta pot broken between Sebby and me. I had lived through many embarrassing moments over the past few months, but I was fairly certain this one took the cake. Not only did he catch me eavesdropping on a private conversation, but I then proceeded to fall ass over tea kettle, covering him with potting soil in the process.

Remaining still, the only sound in the hallway was that of our breathing...until a low rumble sounded from his chest, growing louder and louder until he was laughing wholeheartedly. I glanced over to see him holding his stomach, trying to control his infectious laughter. Soon, I laughed at the situation, as well. It was typical Baylee...turning what was supposed to be a serious conversation into something we'd laugh at for months.

Once our laughter finally died down, our eyes met. "I'm sorry about my behavior earlier," Sebby offered.

I took a deep breath, my smile faltering. "Sebby, you can't react that way every time I meet someone."

"I know," he admitted, shaking his head. "It's just... There are a lot of assholes out there...."

"I know. I moved across the hall from one," I joked, nudging him with my elbow.

"I deserve that, I suppose."

"Sebby..." I sighed, my expression turning serious. "I appreciate that you're looking out for me, but I'm an adult and I can take care of myself. Not to mention I'm not looking for anything serious right now. I just want to have some fun. Do I see this thing with Doctor McDreamy going anywhere? Not really." I shrugged. "But that doesn't mean I'm not going to go out for dinner and a few drinks. My mother's bucket list has taught me to step out of my comfort zone, to experience things I typically would have shied away from. That's all I'm doing." I hesitated for a brief moment, debating whether to bring up the fact that he had a girlfriend and his reaction would lead anyone to believe he was interested in me. As much as I wanted to address it, I just couldn't. I didn't want our friendship to become weird over this.

"I get it," he said finally. "But I swear, if he hurts you, he'll have me to answer to."

"I know." I leaned over and planted a friendly kiss on his cheek. "And that's why I'm happy to be able to call you a friend."

He turned his head toward me, our lips just a breath away. There was something serene about this moment and I didn't want it to end. "Baylee, I—"

"Sebby," I interrupted. I didn't know what I expected him to say, but by the tone of his voice, I had a feeling he would regret it later on. "Don't. It's not worth it. I'll admit I was kind of upset when I found out you had a girlfriend, but now I see it as a blessing in disguise. You were right. Men and women *can* just be friends, and I wouldn't want to ruin this friendship for anything, regardless of whether or not you have a girlfriend."

Deflated, he looked up at the ceiling. "Me, either."

I thought I heard disappointment in his voice.

# CHAPTER FIFTEEN

I SCANNED THE COLD exam room I sat in, illustrations of the female reproductive system surrounding me. I never understood why gynecologists felt the need to decorate with images such as these. I'd much rather look at a calming seascape, not be reminded I was here to have a cold metal instrument shoved up my hoo-ha.

I shifted on the exam table, the crinkling of the thin paper gown against the protective tissue echoing in the room. I wished there were some sort of music being piped in. Maybe it would help me relax. I just kept reminding myself that this would all be over soon, then I could go home to get ready for my hot date with Doctor McDreamy. I absently wondered what kind of medicine he practiced. I could envision him in some fast-paced emergency room, barking foreign medical lingo at the nurses.

Just as I was wondering whether the doctor would ever be coming to do my checkup, there was a soft knock on the door, followed by the sound of it opening. I'd tried to recreate that exact moment in my mind time and time again since then, but it was just a blur. All I could remember were my eyes nearly popping out of my head as my entire body grew stiff when the doctor emerged from behind the privacy curtain. With frantic hands, I tried to cover myself more than the flimsy gown would allow.

"Baylee?" He cleared his throat glancing down at the tablet he held in his large, muscular hands.

"Declan?" I muttered, my voice rising in pitch. I crossed my legs, trying to warm my body. *Why did they keep these exam rooms so chilly?* "You're a gynecologist? You said you were a doctor," I spat.

"A gynecologist *is* a doctor."

I threw my head back, barking with laughter. The ridiculousness of the situation shouldn't have surprised me. It was just my luck that my dreamy doctor just so happened to be a gynecologist. But not just any gynecologist. Oh no. Life liked to take Baylee Morgan's dating fails to the next level. Doctor McDreamy had to be *my* gynecologist.

"I know that, but you made it seem like you were some ER doctor, being on call and all that," I hissed, flustered.

"It wasn't my intention to mislead you," he responded in that same deep, soothing voice. "I am on call several nights a week in case any of our patients go into labor."

"But…," I floundered, trying to figure out what to say next. I couldn't wrap my head around my luck. What were the chances that the guy I was supposed to be going to dinner with tonight would end up being my new "lady parts" doctor? I admit I didn't exactly do research on any of the doctors at this practice. All I cared about was getting this appointment over as quickly and painlessly as possible so I'd no longer have it hanging over my head.

"I can have one of the other doctors do your checkup."

"I should hope so."

Agitated, he stared at me for an embarrassing moment, then quickly retreated from the exam room.

Instead of waiting for another doctor, I hastily dressed, wanting to get out of that office without running into Declan again. As I was darting through the parking lot toward my car, a voice called my name. Stopping, my hand on the door handle, I cursed under my breath. *So close*, I thought, turning to meet Declan's eyes.

He shifted from foot to foot, running his hands through his hair. I glared at him, waiting for him to finally say whatever was on the tip of his tongue. "So…," he began, his voice barely audible. "Are we still on for tonight?"

"What?" I shrieked, taken aback. "Are you out of your mind?"

"Nothing's changed," he insisted. "Now you know what type of medicine I practice. I'm not your doctor. You're not my patient. I've never seen your medical charts, and have instructed my support staff to shred all your records."

I shook my head. None of that mattered. I couldn't date a man who looked at hoo-has all day long. Even if he assured me he could leave the job at the office, I knew from experience that was never the case. After working as an editor of the local newspaper, whenever I read other articles, I always rewrote them in my head to make them more poignant and interesting. How could he not do the same thing?

*"Nice vagina, Baylee, but I've seen better."*

"I don't think so, Declan." I opened the door and climbed into my car. "Have a nice day."

I cranked the engine and sped out of there before he

could persuade me to change my mind. I just knew Sebby would get a kick out of this one. Baylee - 0. Men of LA - 2. It seemed the odds of ever dating again were certainly not in my favor.

~~~~~~~~~~

"HOW WAS YOUR DATE?" I asked Marcel upon entering Sophia's condo the following night. I hoped to be able to get the attention off me and my dating disaster from the previous day. I knew I couldn't avoid sharing what had happened forever, but I wanted at least a few glasses of wine in me before telling everyone that Doctor McDreamy was a gynecologist. I wondered how long it would be until they'd all stop bringing that one up. I was fairly certain this disaster surpassed the Dennis mix-up on the embarrassment scale.

Marcel looked up from the table everyone was gathered around and beamed a brilliant smile at me.

I smirked. "Well, that answers my question."

"He's been raving about him all night." Sophia drapped her arm around his shoulders, batting her eyelashes flirtatiously. "Or at least constantly in the ten minutes he's been here." She winked as I took my usual seat on the opposite side of Marcel.

"I need to hear all about this guy!"

"He's amazing," he gushed like a teenager with his first crush. "Everything about him is amazing. He took me to a top-of-the-line waterfront restaurant in Marina del Rey."

"How do you know who's taking whom out?" I blurted, intrigued.

"I could tell just by looking at him that he's a

topper."

"A topper?" I furrowed my brow. This lingo was completely foreign to me.

"That's what I said." He acted as if this were all common knowledge.

"What's that?"

There was a brief moment of silence around the table before everyone broke out in laughter. I made a mental note to do some research on gay terminology so I wouldn't be completely lost during conversations with Marcel.

"What's everyone laughing about?" Sebby's voice broke through and we all turned our heads toward the foyer to see him strolling in, carrying a bottle of wine.

"Baylee asked what a topper is," Marcel responded, still giggling.

Sebby lowered himself into the last empty seat next to me and grinned his sly smile at me. "Think about it."

I pinched my lips and studied Sebby's face for a few moments before looking back at Marcel. "You mean...?" I began, putting the pieces together.

"Exactly, Miss Dixie," he said. "There are some gay men who give, if you know what I mean. Some of us are happy to go either way, but others aren't. They're what we refer to as a topper."

"How can you tell?"

"Sometimes it's hard," he admitted. "But Nicholas made it pretty clear from the very beginning. *He* asked me out. *He* picked me up. *He* initiated the goodnight kiss, which led to a goodnight... Well, use your imagination." He winked. The table erupted in cheers and whistles as Marcel fanned himself. "Plus, he came right out and told me."

"You could have just said that from the beginning," I chastised.

"I know." He wrapped his arm around me, pulling me close. "But I love watching you squirm, Miss Dixie."

I pushed away from him, laughing.

"So when are you seeing each other again?" Lacey asked.

"When *haven't* we seen each other?" He popped a slice of cheese into his mouth.

"Apparently, he's been coming by Marcel's condo every night after his shift at the bar," Sophia announced.

"What can I say?" He shrugged, a devilish grin on his face. "My man is insatiable."

"And what about *your* date, Baylee?" Sophia asked. All eyes were on me in an instant, including Sebby's.

"It's not going anywhere, so why even talk about it?" Raising my wine glass to my lips, I took a sip of the full-bodied Cabernet.

"Who cares where it's going?!" Cora exclaimed, leaning toward me. "We still need details on Doctor McDreamy. Where did he take you?"

Swallowing hard, I mumbled, "Nowhere."

"Staying in on your first date?" Marcel elbowed me. "You hussy, you!"

"That's not it." I drew in a long breath, meeting the eager eyes of everyone around the table. "He didn't take me anywhere because the date never happened," I focused my eyes on the wine glass in front of me.

"What do you mean?" Sebby interjected. "I asked you this morning how last night was and you said it was good."

"Yes," I answered. "You asked me about my *night*…not about my *date*. The devil is in the details."

"So what happened?" he pushed. "How did you go from looking forward to your date to not going in just a few hours?"

"Nothing." I fidgeted with the stem of my glass. "It's not important, so let's just drop it and start playing." I grabbed the box of cards off the table and opened it.

"I don't think so!" Marcel exclaimed. "There's a story here, and from the rate at which your cheeks are turning red, I'd say it's probably a pretty good one, so let's hear it."

I continued sifting through the cards, ignoring Marcel.

"You know damn well I'm not going to stop hounding you until you tell us what happened, so just save yourself the hassle and fess up, girlfriend."

Sighing, I reached for the bottle of wine on the table and refilled my glass. "Yesterday, I had a doctor's appointment," I said once I had taken a large gulp of wine. "It was *that* appointment." I raised my eyebrows as the table let out a collective breath of acknowledgment. "As I was sitting there in a thin paper gown, looking at all the illustrations of vaginas and whatnot, the door opened and in walked my doctor, except it was *my* doctor." I raised my eyebrows again, hoping they'd understand so I didn't have to explain. I was met with a mixture of confused and amused expressions.

"What do you mean?" Lacey asked with a smirk. She clearly knew what I meant, but wanted confirmation.

"Doctor McDreamy is a gynecologist, but not just any gynecologist." I buried my head in my hands, my ears burning as I relived that embarrassing moment. "He was supposed to be *my* gynecologist," I said in a muffled voice, the entire table erupting in laughter. "Go ahead. Laugh at my expense."

Sebby flung his arm around my shoulders, the vibrations of his laughter warming me. "We're not laughing at you, Baylee," he insisted. "More like the situation. It's kind of funny, don't you think? You can't make this shit up."

"I'm not sure anyone else in LA has as bad luck dating as I do."

"So you didn't go out with him just because he's a gynecologist?" Marcel pushed.

"It was game over once I found that out."

"He didn't do the exam though, right?" Cora asked, a horrified look on her innocent face.

"Of course not! I hightailed it out of there. But as I was running to my car, he had the balls to chase after me and see if we were still on for our date."

"He still wanted to go out with you?" Sebby asked.

I nodded. "I told him no."

"Why?"

"Because!" I exclaimed. "He's a gynecologist!"

"So? You were all hot to go out with him when he told you he was a doctor. He's *still* a doctor."

"Yeah, but…"

"But what?"

"How will I be able to tell the difference between foreplay and an exam?!" I shouted, bolting up from my chair.

The room was silent as everyone stared at me. As if on cue, they all erupted in laughter, tears streaming down some of their faces. Sebby pulled me back into my chair, wrapping his arm around me once more. "Point taken, Baylee. Point taken."

"Foreplay or an exam," Marcel said through his laughs, barely able to even get the words out. "You're something else, Miss Dixie."

Once the laughter died down and the conversation had turned to other people's love interests, Cora shot up. "Wait! I have an idea!" Her eyes turned to me. She had a devious grin that I knew meant she was planning something I wouldn't like.

"What?" I asked cautiously.

"There's this guy at one of the charities I volunteer at. A freelance photographer. He's the epitome of tall, dark, and handsome."

"Why am I worried about where this is going?"

"I'm going to set you guys up!"

"Why don't *you* go out with him?" I glared at her.

"I don't like to mix business with pleasure. You'd be perfect for each other."

"What makes you think that?"

She shrugged. "It's just a feeling I get. He's an artsy type like you. He loves classic movies. I just think you'd have a lot in common. And if you don't, at least you get a free meal and some good wine out of it."

"I don't think so." I waved her off. "After my last two failed attempts at dating here in LA, I'm going to take some me time. Maybe work some more on my mother's list."

"Oh, come on, Baylee," Cora pouted. "Just one

date. Don't you want to be able to rub it in your ex-husband's face that you've moved on and have some hot new beau with six pack abs and a panty-dropping smile?" She grinned. "Because he has all of those qualities."

Pinching my lips, I considered her offer. Granted, I wasn't ready to have another failed date, but maybe it would be different this time since it was someone Cora knew. If there ended up being something wrong with him, at least I would have her to blame. And I would certainly pay to see the look on Will's face when he found out I was dating a man with a physique he could only dream about having. Superficial? Perhaps, but he deserved it.

Letting out a long breath as I stared around the table, everyone eager to hear my response, I met Sebby's eyes.

"Fine," I agreed, my gaze still locked on Sebby's. "Set it up. Just let me know when and where."

# CHAPTER SIXTEEN

"YOU'RE MAKING AN ABSOLUTE mess!" Sebby bellowed, throwing a larger helping of flour at me than I had just flung at him.

Laughing, I glanced around my condo on Sunday afternoon a week later, the kitchen covered with flour. These were the moments I had begun to look forward to and crave. It was almost like déjà vu, as if we had done this exact thing together at some point in a former life. Sport and Gidget had lost interest in begging for table scraps and had assumed their regular positions on my couch. Every so often, a seagull would land on the railing of my balcony, sending both dogs into a barking frenzy. Regardless of their noise, the seagull stayed in its spot, most likely for the sole purpose of trying to irritate both dogs even more.

Sebby and I had been spending more and more time together as the weeks wore on. Not only had we met for coffee every morning, as had become tradition, but I could count on him barging into my condo nearly every day, wanting to do something, whether it be taking me to his favorite Thai, Mexican, or sushi place in town, or helping me check yet another item off my mother's list. Today was no different. He had appeared at my door with a bag full of flour, yeast, homemade pasta sauce, mozzarella cheese, and a bunch of other ingredients he deemed necessary for the task at hand.

"Just keep rolling. Add more flour if it gets too sticky," Sebby instructed as I struggled to make a circle out of the dough we had made from scratch. Apparently, he had worked at a New York-style pizza shop during his high school days and had become quite the master at tossing dough, making him the perfect person to help me cross *Learn how to toss pizza dough* off my mother's list. I was eager to see him in action, wondering if he had become rusty over the years and would splatter dough all over my condo.

"I think I'm a complete lost cause at this." I glanced between my pizza dough and his, which looked to be expertly rolled out into a slightly larger ball than he had begun with.

"It takes practice, Baylee," he encouraged.

"I've always sucked at this kind of thing. I can make cakes and stuff like that, but rolling dough? Never been my forte." I wiped my brow with my arm, probably smudging flour on it in the process.

"There's nothing to it," he insisted. "The hardest part is making the dough. Once that's done, all you have to do is get it into the right shape and you're good to go." He winked.

Sighing, I returned my attention to the disaster in front of me, ready to throw in the towel. A loud knocking broke through the silence, followed by the sound of someone barging into my condo. We both shot our heads up simultaneously to see Cora running through the foyer, coming to an abrupt stop when she realized I wasn't alone.

"What's going on here?" she asked, smirking and crossing her arms in front of her chest.

"Sebby's torturing me by trying to teach me how to

toss pizza dough. Little did I know I'd have to learn *how* to make pizza dough first."

"Oh, jeez." She took a seat at the large kitchen island opposite us, eyeing our projects with interest. "I thought you said you weren't a great cook."

"I'm not," I responded, rolling my eyes.

"I'm not taking any excuses," Sebby explained. "She's crossing another thing off that bucket list today if it kills me."

"It just might if you eat this pizza later," I joked.

"I supervised. I should be okay. If not, well… It's been nice knowing ya."

"Ditto."

We shared a smile, then I returned my attention to Cora. She raised her eyebrows at me, questioning. No matter how many times I had assured her and the rest of our circle of friends that there was nothing going on between Sebby and me, they always gave me that same look, as if they knew something I didn't. Sometimes I wondered if they did.

"So… To what do I owe this visit?" I asked, ignoring the expression on Cora's face.

"Right," she started, an eagerness about her. "I just got home from a promotional shoot for one of my charities. That freelance photographer I told you about was there and I talked to him."

"Great." My tone displayed my lack of enthusiasm. I didn't know what came over me when I agreed to her little plan. Part of me was hoping this photographer of hers wasn't interested.

"He was *very* intrigued by what I told him."

"And what was that?"

"That doesn't matter…"

"It does if you told him stuff that isn't true."

"I didn't," she insisted. "He's free on Tuesday if you are."

I glanced at Sebby, whose attention seemed to be entirely devoted to his pizza dough, but I saw his jaw tense, his back growing rigid. I raised my eyebrows and he gave me a strained smile, kneading the dough in front of him with so much force, his formerly perfect ball became torn from being overworked.

"I am." I smiled, ignoring Sebby's jealous antics.

"Good. Initially, he tried to plan something for Saturday, but I know you said that's your birthday, so—"

Sebby's head shot up. "Your birthday's coming up?"

I shrugged. "Yeah. So?"

"Were you going to tell me so we could celebrate it?"

"I don't celebrate my birthday."

"Why not?"

"No reason." I grabbed my rolling pin and started butchering my pile of pizza dough once more, most of it sticking to the pin and the counter. "There's too many expectations on birthdays…expectations that are never met. So I figured if I stopped celebrating it, I could never be disappointed."

"That's Baylee's way of saying Will never remembered her birthday," Cora offered. "Trust me. I've been there."

"Really?" Sebby questioned.

"It's not a big deal." I tried to sound as nonchalant

208

as possible about it. In truth, it bothered me that Will never put in the effort to do anything for my birthday. No card. No flowers. Nothing. Not even a phone call or text wishing me happy birthday. It was never mentioned. "Saturday would have been fine," I assured Cora, "but Tuesday will work better so I can prepare for my uncle's arrival on Sunday."

"Perfect." Cora jumped up. "I'm out of here. Tuesday night, Baylee. Seven o'clock at The Lobster."

I nodded and turned my attention back to Sebby, watching with intrigue as he began prepping his dough to toss. In an instant, it went flying in the air and back down again, growing in diameter with each toss, taking on the shape of a large pizza.

"Wait!" I shouted just as Cora was about to walk out the door. She spun around. "What's his name?"

A sly grin crossed her face. "I guess that kind of information is necessary."

"Yeah. Not so sure I want to approach every whack job at the restaurant asking if he's my blind date. Never know what kind of unsavory character I could meet that way."

"Never know what kind of unsavory character you'll meet on a blind date anyway," Sebby mumbled under his breath so only I could hear him. I glowered at him and he shrugged apologetically.

"True. His name is Owen. Owen Macallan."

I studied her, my lips turning into a small smile. "Like the scotch?" I tried to stifle my laugh.

"Yes, Baylee. Like the scotch, except he's not Scottish. He's Irish, and he has the accent to prove it." She spun on her heels and left.

Silence hung in the condo for a brief moment before Sebby turned to me. "You're going on a date with a man named after a scotch?"

"Why not? Macallan is a good scotch. It could be worse. I could be dating someone named after a crab in a Disney movie."

"Touché, Dixie. Touché."

# CHAPTER SEVENTEEN

WHEN TUESDAY ROLLED AROUND, my nerves about my impending blind date were at an all-time high. I couldn't remember being as nervous about my gay date or gyno date. There was something daunting about being forced into a social situation with someone to whom I had never spoken a single word. What would we talk about? What if we had nothing *to* talk about? What if he were an egotistical asshole? What if he didn't like dogs? *Gasp!* I would give anything to be able to pick up my phone and call someone for advice. These were the moments in life I hated. The moments when I could use a little motherly encouragement.

Flopping onto the couch, my eyes fell on my mother's journal sitting on the coffee table. *She must have some sort of wisdom about this kind of a thing*, I thought, picking it up. I flipped through the pages, scanning each one for something relevant. She wrote about her bucket list and all the things she accomplished during her last year of life. She saw the Great Wall of China. She snorkeled the Great Barrier Reef. She even swam with the sharks. My mother was absolutely fearless. When death stares you in the face, I suppose you learn to conquer your fears.

I stopped flipping the pages when something caught my eye.

*Dear Diary of a Dying Cancer Patient,*

*Today is the anniversary of my first date with Perry. I'm not going to say how many years. That would date me. I feel old and sluggish enough these days. Apart from the fact that I'm building a human inside of me, my body is fighting it. Part of me wonders whether I'm making the right decision, but when I see the little baby bump starting to form, I know I am.*

*It's a little bittersweet knowing that this is the last first date anniversary I'll celebrate with Perry. He's tried to remain strong, but I can tell today has been difficult for him. We never really celebrated this anniversary before, but we did this year. He bought out the drive-in theater for the night. It's still standing, even after all these years. We even drove his old pick-up truck there. You can imagine my shock when the movie* Gidget *began playing on the old beat-up screen. I felt as giddy as I did during that first date all those years ago.*

*As we lay in the bed of his truck, watching the movie that had brought us together, I tried to stay strong for Perry. But as I was watching Gidget's mom tell her all about how she would know when she was in love, how it would feel as if she had been hit over her head with a sledgehammer, I broke down in tears. I never wanted to leave that moment. For that brief moment in time, I felt it… I felt magic.*

*I don't want the magic to end.*

"Magic," I breathed, caressing the faded papers that were scrawled on by the woman I never knew but wished I did. Comforted by my mother's words, I felt a renewed outlook on my evening; however, that didn't mean I was still ready to go in completely blind, no pun intended. This was the twenty-first century, after all. There was no such thing as a blind date anymore, not with how pervasive social media was…unless my date was one of those strange people who abhorred technology. Something inside me didn't think that was the case. So I did what any normal twenty-something would do living in this modern day and age. I grabbed my laptop, booted it up, and set out to Facebook stalk him.

I found it disconcerting how many profiles returned with the name Owen Macallan. I could understand if his name were John Smith or something like that, but I didn't think I would have a hard time narrowing down my date with a somewhat obscure name like Owen Macallan. Apparently, I was wrong.

As I scrolled through all the Owen Macallans on Facebook (296 of them, to be precise), I finally stopped on one that looked about right. His profile indicated that he lived in Los Angeles and was a freelance photographer. I could have been wrong, but I found it hard to believe there was more than one freelance photographer named Owen Macallan running around the streets of this city. Confident I found him, I clicked on his profile.

"Hmm," I muttered. "It's not set to private." Rubbing my hands together, I grinned mischievously. "Let the Facebook stalking begin!" Sport yipped and I scowled in his direction. "Don't yell at me. If he didn't want anyone looking, he wouldn't have made it public." I returned my attention to the laptop, feeling like a kid walking into a candy shop with a hundred dollar bill.

I clicked on his photo album and was immediately inundated with a multitude of pictures. I had to hand it to Cora. She had good taste. He had a full head of dark hair and was very well-groomed, although he did sport a bit of scruff in some photos, but not in a way that made him look unkempt. It was hot and sexy. "Rugged man." I smiled, taking a sip from my coffee mug. I continued my sleuthing, scrolling through photo after photo...some at bars with his friends, some of him working on one shoot or another.

"Well," I said to Sport. "At least Cora set me up with someone who isn't completely hideous."

Returning to his Facebook profile, the wheels started turning in my head when I saw he had recently checked-in at a hotel down the street. "What's he doing there?" I wondered out loud. "Oh, here it is, Sport. It says he's 'Pool-side, catching up with a few college buddies'."

Tapping my fingernails on the laptop in front of me, I couldn't resist the devil on my shoulder who was prodding me that I had a perfect opportunity to settle my nerves about tonight. There was only so much I could find out about him by snooping through his profile. What I needed to do was see this guy in person.

I ran up the stairs and into my bedroom, rummaging through my dresser to find my bathing suit. Sport jumped up on my bed and stared at me as I went about grabbing my things. "Don't give me that look. If he didn't want anyone to know where he was, he would not have broadcast that information for all to see." Sport tilted his head toward me, as if he were waiting for further explanation...or a treat. I couldn't be sure which. "I'm not going to talk to him. I'm just going to observe from afar."

After throwing my e-reader, sunscreen, and sunglasses into a tote bag, I put on my bikini, checking my reflection in the mirror. "Not bad, I guess," I said, turning around as I raised myself on my tiptoes to check my backside. I was lucky that I had inherited my

214

mother's petite frame, although I would have done anything to be a bit taller.

"What do you think, Sport?" I asked over my shoulder before returning my attention to my reflection and the navy blue and white polka-dot two-piece I wore. "Well, I guess it really doesn't matter anyway, does it?" I grabbed a white sundress cover-up, then headed out the door. Within a few minutes, I was driving down Ocean Avenue toward the hotel on the other side of Santa Monica Pier.

I lowered my windows, allowing the wind to blow through my hair. It was an unseasonably warm day for mid-November. The past few weeks had been chilly for Southern California, the temperatures barely making it above sixty degrees. Today, however, summer had momentarily returned. The sun was shining, there were only a few small clouds in the sky, and the temperature was beginning to reach eighty. It was the perfect day to sit by the pool and soak in the sun. Who knew when we'd get another day like this before winter hit, although winter here seemed to have nothing on winter back in the mountains of North Carolina.

After getting stuck at practically every stoplight during the two-mile drive between my condo building and the hotel, I finally reached my destination and handed the keys to a waiting valet. I entered the lush hotel through the revolving door, resisting my innate temptation to keep going around in circles, deciding to act my age instead.

"Well, I came all the way here. May as well follow through with this," I said to myself, pulling out my large, floppy sunhat and placing my sunglasses on my face so my potential date didn't see me spying on him, just in case he had also done some Facebook snooping.

I walked through the lobby and out a set of doors overlooking the Pacific Ocean. I was surprised to see how empty the pool area was. There were a few guests catching some sun, as well as some people grabbing a late lunch on the patio, but it wasn't crowded like it would normally be during the busy summer tourist season. Finding a vacant lounge chair by the pool that had a great view of the entire area, including the pool bar, I made myself comfortable, pulled out my e-reader, and settled in for my afternoon of stalking…I mean, observing my blind date.

After reading a page or two of my book, I stretched, craning my neck to scan the area as inconspicuously as possible. James Bond, I was not, but for my first attempt at spying on someone, I was feeling good about how well I was doing. I could have wandered around with his picture pulled up on my phone, comparing it to each person, but I remained firmly seated.

A child squealed as he ran from his parents and jumped into the pool, catching my attention. And that's when I saw Mr. Blind Date. He and three other men were sitting at a table underneath an awning overlooking the ocean. He was facing me and was gloriously shirtless. I could tell this was a man who took pride in his appearance. His skin was dark, probably from working outside on various photo shoots. He seemed to be completely carefree and at ease as he laughed and spoke with the other men at his table, all of them shirtless and wearing swim trunks. But the sight of Owen put the rest of them to shame, their beer bellies protruding over the drawstrings of their shorts. But Owen… There was no beer belly. There was no belly at all. His muscles were well-defined, all the way to the little bit of abdominals I could faintly make out from yards away. I just wished the table wasn't obstructing my view of how he looked below the waist.

He was the picture of perfection. Perfect hair. Perfect smile. Perfect body. He was the type of guy any girl would drool over…but it did nothing for me. I thought he was *too* good-looking. He looked untouchable, unreachable. Or maybe I just wanted to think that because, no matter how many times I kept telling myself we were better as friends, I was still drawn to Sebby. I compared every potential date to him. It needed to stop.

"No, Baylee. Owen's hot. You're going out with him tonight. Enough with the Sebby thing. Girlfriend, Baylee. He has a girlfriend. Friends. That's all you can be."

I returned my attention to the e-reader in front of me, glancing up every so often to catch a glimpse of Owen across the pool. *He has a great laugh*, I said to myself whenever someone he was with said something amusing. *I like a guy with a sense of humor… Like Sebby.*

"How's the view?" a voice cut through my thoughts.

I snapped my head to my left, my eyes practically bulging out of their sockets. "What are you doing here?" I shrieked. "Are you stalking me?"

A smile crossed Sebby's face as he leaned back in the lounge chair and signaled a waiter. "What do you want to drink?"

I continued staring at him, my mouth gaping open. I didn't know if it was the surprise of seeing Sebby at that precise moment or the fact that he was dressed in something other than his usual cargo shorts and t-shirt. My gaze roamed over the tan suit jacket he wore over a crisp light blue shirt, matching pants that hung perfectly from his waist, and brown designer shoes that probably cost more than most people made in a month. He was clean-shaven, his skin appearing smooth to the touch.

And I *really* wanted to touch.

"Or do you want me to order for you?" He narrowed his eyes, waiting for me to respond, but I was without words. My heartbeat seemed to fill the pool area with its increasing *thump, thump, thump,* and a tingling sensation settled in my fingertips, my hands yearning to feel Sebby's skin. "Baylee?"

"S-something with bubbles," I stuttered.

"You got it." He turned to the waiter and ordered champagne and a beer, ignoring my bewildered expression. Several protracted moments passed while Sebby simply sat on the lounge chair next to me, a gratified smirk on his face. Unable to resist the temptation, I stole a glance at him every few seconds. He was the epitome of eye candy.

"Are you going to answer my question?" I barked, snapping out of my Sebby-in-a-suit-induced daze.

"Don't flatter yourself." He flipped his sunglasses down and relaxed into the chair, allowing the mid-November rays to warm his face. "I'm not stalking you."

"Then what are you doing here?" I glared at him. He remained blissfully carefree and serene. I could see his eyes closed behind his sunglasses. He seemed so unhurried, I expected him to start snoring at any moment.

Able to sense my presence all but hovering over him as I waited for him to explain why he was here, he finally opened his eyes. "I was supposed to have a lunch meeting with my assistant here, but he got stuck at the studio. *That's* why I'm here." He raised his sunglasses so I could peer into his eyes. "Not because I followed you from our building. That would just be creepy," he added, giving me a maniacal look.

"Knock it off." I smacked him playfully before settling back into my own lounge chair. "Sounds like you need a new assistant."

"He's pretty useless anyway. I'm very hands on, ya know," he explained slyly, invading my personal space. Actually, it wasn't as much of an invasion as it was a welcome encroachment. I would grant Sebby an easement onto my property any day of the week.

The combination of his body wash and toothpaste found their way to my senses, and I lost myself in the intoxicating aroma. I tried to slow my racing heart, but it was useless. I couldn't control the way my body reacted to him. He had a magnetic pull on me, making me want to forget everything for a minute…that things were complicated, that we were neighbors, that we had a strong bond I could possibly destroy if we pursued any sort of romantic relationship…

That he had a girlfriend.

Our server returned, breaking the tension between us. I readjusted my position, straightening my spine and pulling away from Sebby. Placing our drinks on the table between us, the server handed him the bill to sign. Once he left, Sebby raised his beer and I followed suit with my champagne. "To a fortunate change in circumstances."

Meeting his piercing gray-blue eyes, my gaze lingering just slightly too long on his full lips, I said, "I'll drink to that." Taking a sip of the delicious champagne, I leaned back into my lounge chair and kept my vision trained on Owen, trying to ignore Sebby's proximity.

"So, who's the guy?" he asked after several quiet moments.

"What guy?" I feigned ignorance.

"The one you keep looking at over there." He nodded toward where Owen was sitting. "Think he's hot?"

"No," I responded. "Well, actually, yes. I find him to be absolutely delicious. God-like, if you really want to know." I avoided his eyes, pretending to read. I could feel his penetrating gaze on me, studying my every movement. It didn't matter that we had only known each other for a few months. Sebby could read me better than anyone I had ever known.

"*Baylee!*" he exclaimed. "That's *him*, isn't it? The blind date Cora set you up on!"

"Keep your voice down." I lightly slapped him. "He might hear you, you ass!"

"You just accused me of stalking you, but look at you!" He chuckled heartily. "You're giving him the *Rear Window* treatment!"

"I can always count on you to make a movie reference."

"How did you know he would be here?"

I shrugged, trying to be dismissive. "I *may* have found his profile on Facebook. And said profile *may* have been set to public. And I *may* have seen that he checked-in here and I *may* have wanted to scope him out for myself. I prefer to call it research, not stalking."

I gauged his reaction, the silence awkward as he contemplated my words. Finally, he laughed, the sound loud and full of life. "Whatever you need to tell yourself to make you feel less creepy. Let's just hope you don't do anything to draw attention to yourself before your blind date. I wouldn't want you to have a repeat of how *we* first met."

"What can I say? I have a way of making a fool out of myself on a daily basis." I winked. "And you love that about me."

"Baylee," he said in a seductive tone, leaning toward me. "Our first meeting is one I'll never forget. And you're right..."

I turned my head, swallowing hard at the fire in his gaze, the intensity in his face, the tingle of his breath as it met mine.

"I *do* love you."

My heart dropped to the pit of my stomach when he uttered those words. His voice was so warm, so sweet, so perfect, as if he truly meant it. Closing my eyes, I lost all control over my body as I shortened the distance between us, our lips almost touching. I felt lightheaded, everything about Sebby and that moment drawing me to him. We were two magnets. No matter how hard I tried to resist the attraction, there was no denying the rule of science. It was...magic.

"Baylee..."

When I opened my eyes, he licked his lips, his gaze focusing on my mouth. A subtle ache settling between my legs from his proximity, I braced myself, my hormones taking over all logic and rationale.

"I love so much about you..." He cupped my cheek and ran his fingers through my hair.

The angel on my shoulder was shouting at me to put the brakes on immediately, telling me I would ruin a great friendship if we proceeded on this course of action. But the devil was louder, reminding me how much I was craving his kiss, how much I had fantasized about this precise moment since meeting him.

"As a friend." He pulled back abruptly.

Pausing for a beat, I straightened and adjusted my composure, taking a hearty sip of my champagne. I plastered a smile on my face. "Of course. What else would we be?" I said in a shaky voice. I guzzled down the remainder of the champagne, the effervescent liquid burning my throat. "We're neighbors. And you have a girlfriend." I hastily gathered all of my things, throwing them in my canvas bag. "And we're neighbors."

"You already said that." His voice was even, a direct contradiction to my hurried and nervous tone.

"I mean, we get along, but I would never want to date you, Sebby. Not anymore. What did you think I meant? You think I want to date you? I don't. I have a date tonight. Plus, I've said time and time again we're better off as friends. I would hate to ruin what we have by taking things—"

A strong hand on my arm startled me, cutting me off. I stilled, wanting to curse life for being this unfair. It didn't matter how many times I had told myself and everyone else we were better as friends. I felt a stronger connection to this man than anyone who came before him. That didn't negate the fact that his heart belonged to someone else. I wanted to scream and curl into a ball, wondering when I would find my someday.

"Baylee…," Sebby soothed.

"What?" I hissed.

"Stop."

"Stop what?"

"This. I…" He glanced at the ocean, pulling his lips between his teeth.

"What? Spit it out, Sebby."

Returning his gaze to mine, he drew in a long breath. Out of the corner of my eye, I noticed Owen stand up from his table. Sebby must have seen it, too, because we simultaneously turned in his direction, both of our mouths gaping.

"Oh. My…," I began.

"*God*!" Sebby finished. "Baylee…" He lowered his voice. "Is it me, or is he wearing a banana hammock?"

I snorted, covering my mouth so no one could overhear my juvenile laughter. "I think the correct term is speedo."

"I thought only retirees from Florida wore those things!"

"Stop laughing, Sebby," I ordered, unable to control my own laughter. "It's not funny."

"No, it is. It *really* is."

"He's European," I argued, wiping the tears that were forming in my eyes. "Maybe it's a thing over there."

"But he's in America now." He tilted his head, eyeing Owen up and down, finally throwing his hands up. "Well, I feel intimidated. I can't compete with that."

"Oh, my god… On *that* note, I'm leaving. I got what I came here for."

"Which was?"

"To see if this guy is worth my time. I think he might be."

A tense moment passed between us. I wished things

223

were different. I wished he would declare his love for me and tell me he was leaving Mercedes to follow his heart.

"Baylee, I…"

"Yes?" I asked, hopeful.

He took a deep breath. "I…"

My chest rose and fell, my lips parting.

His shoulders slumping forward, he held his hand out to me. "I wish you luck on your date tonight."

Deflated, I simply nodded. "Thanks." I swung my bag over my shoulder and retreated from Sebby, unable to shake the feeling that he wanted to tell me something else.

"Just remember to stay away from Big Kahuna's surf shack, though, will ya?" he called after me, his tone light.

"Is that what they're calling it these days?" I winked over my shoulder.

# CHAPTER EIGHTEEN

As I took a long bath that afternoon, sipping on a glass of wine, I was finally able to relax for the first time since my run-in with Sebby. The sun was setting over the ocean, and there was something calming about the combination of the bubble bath and my peaceful surroundings. I needed this. I had finally shaken off my almost kiss with Sebby, the feel of his breath so close to my skin, how much I wanted to toss out my own stupid rules and take a risk, friendship be damned. I had been on edge since seeing him. Now, thanks to the tranquil bubbles and super-sized glass of wine, I was focused solely on my impending date with Owen...his beautiful smile, perfectly sculpted chest, fantastic laugh, silky-looking hair, banana hammock...

*Dammit!* I screamed in my head, a snort escaping my nose as I relived exactly how I felt when Owen had stood up, exposing his choice in swimwear. I prayed I would be able to get through the date without being reminded of that image, regardless of how appealing it was. I didn't have to wonder whether he wore boxers or briefs. That question was already answered for me in living color.

Starting to prune, I decided it was probably time to get out of the bath and prepare for my date with Mr. Banana Hammock. I perused my overflowing wardrobe, selecting a bright red sundress. Most redheads couldn't pull off wearing red, but something about the vibrant color, the deep auburn hue of my hair, and my fair skin made red stand out on me. Checking my reflection in the mirror, I was satisfied with the way the halter top of the dress looked. It was fitted to my waist, then flowed out to my knees. Sliding on a pair of zebra print heels, I instantly gained three inches.

As I was applying my makeup, my phone buzzed. I shuffled across my bedroom and grabbed my cell to see a text from Sebby.

*Getting ready for your date?*

I typed a quick reply.

*Yes. Why are you checking up on me? Don't you have better things to do on a Tuesday night?*

*Nothing's more important than making sure you're okay. Have fun with Mr. Banana Hammock. I expect a full report tomorrow morning.*

My fingers hovered over the screen of my phone as I tried to come up with some witty, sarcastic response. I wondered whether it was simply a coincidence that we had given Owen the same nickname, but snapped out of my thoughts when I spied the time. Tossing my phone onto the bed, I applied the rest of my makeup and took one last look at my reflection, happy with the final result. I sent one more text to Sebby.

*I'm leaving. Wish me luck.*

Grabbing a cashmere wrap, I placed my phone in

my clutch just as it buzzed again. I almost fell down the stairs when I looked at the screen and saw a photo of a banana between two large walnuts. I should have hated him for that, but I couldn't help but laugh at his twisted sense of humor. It was silly and a bit immature, but it was what I had always been attracted to in a man. Hell, that was what had drawn me to Will all those years ago…his easy-going, good-natured attitude. He was the class clown, always lightening the mood, but over the years, his sense of humor became more crass and awkward, never maturing past the age of sixteen.

After saying a quick goodbye to Sport, I left my condo. Music blaring from Sebby's place filled the corridor. I shook my head and grinned as I made my way toward the elevator, *Cruel Summer* serenading me while I waited. The irony of Sebby playing Bananarama was not lost on me.

The butterflies in my stomach grew stronger as I drove south down Ocean and toward the pier, pulling into the parking lot beneath the restaurant. I handed the keys to the valet and headed toward the entrance. As I walked on the sidewalk, a man with disheveled sandy hair strode past me carrying a bright yellow surfboard, reminding me of a banana. I halted momentarily to regain my composure before I began laughing like a mad woman.

"Fucking Sebby," I mumbled, climbing the stairs to the foyer of the restaurant. "It was a speedo."

"Welcome to The Lobster," an effeminate twenty-something man said as I entered.

"I'm supposed to be meeting someone at the bar."

"Baylee?" a deep voice with a slight Irish brogue sounded. The way my name rolled off his tongue sent shivers down my spine, but the second I looked at him, I feared I wouldn't be able to keep a straight face. I was already picturing him in a big banana costume. I needed to get that image out of my head.

The host raised his eyebrows at me, gesturing to where the voice obviously stood, and I took a long, measured breath, slowly turning around.

"Owen?" I tried to hide that I already knew it was him.

He beamed, walking toward me. Placing his hand on the small of my lower back, he leaned toward me and kissed my cheek. "Pleasure to meet you, love."

I subtly inhaled his scent, not wanting him to think I was some crazy girl who went around sniffing everyone she encountered. It was a musky aroma, just like I imagined. He smelled like an aftershave commercial, he was as sleek and smooth as a designer car commercial, and the way his smoldering eyes were trained on me reminded me of an underwear commercial.

For briefs, naturally.

"How did you know it was me?" I asked breathlessly, pulling away. My voice was throaty and seductive, completely unlike me. Maybe that was what relationships were about. Allowing that one person to bring out a side of you that you never knew existed.

"Cora told me to look for a beautiful redhead with an adorable southern accent. She was spot-on in her description." He winked and a small smile crossed his chiseled face, highlighting a set of boyish dimples. By appearance, I estimated he was in his late thirties, but when he smiled and showed me those dimples, he shaved at least ten years off his age. He looked mature, yet fun at the same time, and I found myself intrigued, despite his questionable choice in swimwear. The devil was back on my shoulder, telling me to just get on with it and drag my tongue along his face, rip his clothes off, and jump on him so I could feel his beautifully defined and sculpted body against mine. The image in my head was quite nice...until my fantasy version of Owen wasn't completely naked. Instead, he was pressing me against the wall, thrusting between my legs...wearing a freaking banana hammock...

*Speedo!* It was a goddamn speedo!

"Baylee... Where did you go, darling?"

A smile grew on my lips as I tried to keep my eyes trained on his. I was scared that if I looked below his waist, he would no longer be wearing the dark jeans he had on, but would be sporting a bright yellow speedo instead.

"I'm sorry. I..." What could I possibly say? That I was picturing him in a speedo because I had spied on him earlier and saw him in one? That would go over well. *Hi. Nice to meet you, Owen. I'm Baylee. I know it's your first time meeting me, but I decided to stalk you on Facebook, then spent the afternoon by the pool with my friend, ogling you in your banana hammock...*

*Speedo!*

"I could use a drink."

"After you, love." He placed his hand on my lower back, leading me up a short flight of stairs into an open-air bar, space heaters warming the area now that the sun had set over the ocean.

"Is that an Irish thing?" I asked.

"What?"

"The word love."

"It's a term of endearment. Here." He gestured to a table overlooking the pier and ocean below us. "I had them reserve a table for us. Hope this is okay."

"Of course." I smiled at him, giving him a bonus point for holding the chair out for me. Will had never done that. "Thank you."

"My pleasure." He slid into the chair opposite me, and I sat enjoying the music of the lapping ocean waves combined with the typical sounds of busy Santa Monica. "It's gorgeous, isn't it?" he commented, staring at the horizon.

"It is. I always dreamed of coming out here."

"Me, too," Owen said.

"How long have you been here?"

"In California, about fifteen years. In the States, nearly all my life."

"Yet you still have the accent."

"It comes and goes. I just got back from visiting some extended family who still live overseas." A waiter approached our table and Owen turned his attention from me. "We'll each have a glass of the Moet & Chandon."

"Yes, sir," the waiter responded, nodding as he retreated from our table.

I was completely taken aback by Owen's bold personality. "Umm… I'm perfectly capable of ordering for myself."

"I apologize." He raised his arm, summoning the waiter back. "I may have misspoken," he said to him. "The lady would prefer to order for herself."

My face flushed in embarrassment, but I hated the idea of any man thinking he could get away with

230

making decisions for me. I had enough of that during the past ten years of my life. "The Moet is fine. Thank you."

The waiter simply nodded once more, running from our table before he was summoned back again.

"So I was right," Owen said, breaking the awkward silence.

"About what?"

"About what you like to drink. It's a talent of mine."

"And what made you think I wanted champagne?"

"Your dress." His eyes sprang to life, fire building inside them.

"What about my dress?" I asked flirtatiously, momentarily forgiving him for assuming he knew what I wanted to drink.

"It's sophisticated, yet fun. That seems to be the type of girl you are. You're boisterous, your personality loud at times, but you're still full of grace and poise. So forgive me for being presumptuous, but all that points to you wanting a glass of champagne."

"You've known me less than five minutes," I commented, skeptical. *Not counting the few hours I spent spying on you.* "How did you figure all that out?"

A dazzling smile crossed his face, those sinful dimples popping, just as the waiter returned with our drinks. "I'm a photographer. It's my job to be observant, to see things most people don't. You can't get those one-in-a-million photographs if you don't take in your surroundings."

"I'll drink to that." I raised my glass and took a sip of my drink. Owen's eyes never strayed from me, penetrating me, unnerving me. Placing my glass back on the table, I fidgeted with the hem of my dress, crossing and uncrossing my legs in the stiff silence.

"Cora mentioned you just moved into her building a few months ago," Owen commented finally. I nodded. "The penthouse, right?" I smiled sheepishly. He whistled, drawing my attention to his full lips. "I'm impressed you can afford that place, if you don't mind me saying."

"I inherited my dad's lumber company when he died," I explained. "Someone else runs it because, let's be honest, I don't know the first thing about that company...or lumber, for that matter. I'm the majority shareholder so I reap a lot of the benefits. If I so choose, I don't have to work a day for the rest of my life."

"Aren't you bored?"

"I haven't had time to be bored," I answered, thinking how quickly two months had passed. Truthfully, when I first moved out here, giving up my life and career back home, I definitely thought I'd be bored living off my inheritance and not working. "I've been keeping myself pretty busy."

"Doing what?"

"The usual stuff." I shrugged, not sure I wanted to share any details. It was personal to me.

"Like what? I can tell there's a story there."

I studied him, trying to find a way to change the subject so I didn't have to talk about it. But wasn't I here to see if we clicked? Weren't first dates all about sharing bits and pieces of yourself with someone else?

"When my mom was pregnant with me, she kept a journal chronicling her adventures during those eight months."

"What happened?" he asked. I furrowed my brow. "I could be wrong, but something about the wistful look on your face makes me think something happened to her."

I nodded and proceeded to tell him how my mother was diagnosed with brain cancer just weeks after finding out she was pregnant with me, how she kept a journal, and how, one day, I found her bucket list tucked inside the pages of that journal.

"A bucket list?"

"Yeah. She had scrawled a list of things she wanted to do before she died."

"Did she get to all of them?"

I shook my head. "No. Considering she was pregnant and sick, there were things on there she definitely couldn't do, but that didn't stop her from dreaming of doing them. So that's what I've been doing. Finishing her bucket list for her. And I've been writing about it as I go."

"So you're keeping a journal, too?"

"Not exactly…"

"Then what?" he pushed, intrigued.

"I'm using the list more like an inspiration."

"Inspiration for what?"

"To write a book. I've always wanted to, but never knew what my story was. I'm still not sure what it is, but this experience, doing all these things I never would have had the courage to do… It's kind of opened up my mind."

"Well, cheers to a new adventure." He raised his glass and I followed suit, taking a polite sip of my champagne. I really wanted to guzzle it back to settle my nerves, but even I knew there was a thin line between social drinker and raging alcoholic.

"So," I started, trying to clear the serious air at the table, "is there really a pub on every corner in Dublin like I've read?"

He laughed, and I was happy our conversation had turned to something lighter. Death was never good first date dinner conversation. "More than on every corner. Dublin has more pubs per capita than any other city in the world. I'm also pretty sure it has a higher rate of alcoholics, but I can't be certain." He winked. "Are you hungry? We can order some food, if you'd like. They have this amazing halibut that's cooked in a banana leaf—"

I choked on my champagne, spraying it everywhere.

"My god, Baylee. Are you okay?" He was out of his chair in less than a second, trying to help me through my choking and coughing fit that quickly turned into laughter. He slinked back to his side of the table and stared at me with an inquisitive gaze. "What's so funny?"

Wiping the tears that had formed in my eyes, I couldn't help but giggle. "Sorry. I'm just remembering something my neighbor told me earlier." I took a deep breath, trying to settle down, Bananarama playing in my mind.

*Freaking Sebby.*

~~~~~~~~~~

"CAN I SEE YOU again?" Owen asked as he walked me toward the valet stand after a surprisingly enjoyable dinner that lasted longer than I was anticipating. He told me about all the exotic places he had visited on various shoots. I mostly listened, living vicariously through him, dreaming about the day I'd hop on a plane to some South American jungle or remote tropical island.

"Really? My laughing fit didn't scare you off?" I pulled my shawl tighter around me. The summer-like temperatures that had been present earlier in the day had given way to a slight chill. That was one of the things I had learned about living in California. The temperature could swing from eighty degrees in the afternoon to barely fifty once the sun went down, especially this time of year.

His fingers grazed my arm. Before I knew what was happening, he had me ensnared in his embrace, one hand on my lower back, the other cupping my cheek. "No, Baylee. It did not." He licked his lips while he studied my face, as if he were imprinting each dip and curve to memory. "In fact..." He pulled me closer, trapping me in place. And I wanted to be trapped by this strong, powerful, dominating man, if for no other reason than it had been so long since I had been intimate with someone. "I think that's what I'm drawn to."

"What? My laugh?" I giggled nervously.

"No." He leaned down, his six-foot-plus frame towering over me. A rush spread through me when his lips grazed my neck. The hair on my nape stood on end, my skin hypersensitive to every touch of his fingers, every caress of his breath. "Your essence," he murmured. "Your heart. Your vitality. I want to get to experience that again."

My eyes fluttered and I was completely weak in the knees. You know those movies where the heroine swoons in a dramatic fashion and the hero has to catch her? Well, if Owen wasn't already supporting me, I was pretty sure that would have been me. However, based on my propensity for injuring people, I probably would have fallen to the ground, and not in an endearing manner. It would have been ass over tea kettle.

Hmmm… My tea kettle is yellow.

"Bananas are yellow," I mumbled as I craned my neck, giving him permission to explore my skin further.

"What?" Where his lips were a second before was now cold and vacant.

"Nothing." I opened my eyes. "Sorry. I was somewhere else for a minute."

"A good somewhere else, or somewhere else because you didn't enjoy yourself tonight?"

Softening my expression, I allowed a small, coy smile to cross my lips. "A good somewhere else," I breathed against his mouth.

"Good. You had me worried there."

Our eyes remained locked, horns honking as cars sped down Ocean Avenue.

"You didn't answer my question," he said, his lips just out of reach of mine.

"Which was?"

"Can I see you again? I'd really like—"

"Yes," I exhaled before he could finish his sentence. "I'd like that."

"I was hoping you'd say that, love." He leaned down, his lips brushing mine momentarily. "I had a wonderful time getting to know you, Baylee. Can't wait to find out even more." He pulled back, leaving me somewhat frustrated. It was an amazing kiss for what it was, but after all the buildup, I was expecting more. I didn't want to make-out with him on the city street, but a little respectful tongue would have been nice. Hell, the way his sinful tone caressed my name, his strong arms pulled me to him, and his forceful and dominant demeanor, I anticipated an intense, passionate exchange.

"Baylee?" he said as I remained deep in thought, dissecting our first lackluster kiss. "Is this your car?"

I looked to see my little red BMW idling in front of us. I nodded.

Owen held the door open and tipped the valet attendant for me. "I'll call you this week. Good night."

"Night," I mumbled as he closed my door. All this dating was putting my libido into overdrive. I considered Googling the address for the closest sex shop on my way home.

# CHAPTER NINETEEN

ON SATURDAY, A LIGHT knock sounded on my door mid-morning as I was sitting on my couch, staring at the whitecaps of the ocean. So far, I was having the best birthday I could remember in a long time. I had met Sebby that morning and, in addition to my coffee, he brought me a blueberry muffin with a candle in it. To most, it wouldn't seem like much, but to a girl who was used to practically everyone forgetting about her birthday, it meant everything.

I spent the rest of my morning writing, but nothing seemed to stick. I had written and deleted more pages than I could remember. I felt like I was losing the inspiration I had when I first started this project. It had been a few days since I had crossed an item off my mother's bucket list and I wondered if that was why I was feeling blocked.

Getting up from my couch, I made my way to the front door and pulled it open, only to be greeted by Sebby's cocky smirk.

"Sebby." I leaned against the doorjamb, imitating his confident demeanor. "To what do I owe this visit? I thought you had to work today."

"I lied." He shrugged. "Go put on something comfortable. We have plans."

"Plans?" I raised my eyebrows.

"That's what I said. It's your birthday, and it's my

goal to make it one you'll never forget."

I hesitated. "I already have plans with Owen later."

His expression fell momentarily before he recovered. "I'll have you home in time for your date. Don't worry."

My curiosity getting the better of me, I stepped back, allowing him to enter my condo. Sport dashed to him, showering him with all the love he typically reserved for me. I was used to it at this point. Over the weeks, Sebby had become like a second father to my little man.

I clambered up the stairs, almost tripping as I neared the top, and headed into my bedroom. As I rummaged through my closet, not knowing what to wear, other than something comfortable, I considered what Sebby had planned. I was happy to spend my birthday on my couch, toiling over my half-written manuscript. I never anticipated Sebby would knock on my door and drag me out to do God knows what. All I knew was it would be a day I wouldn't soon forget.

The truth was, even if we did nothing, a day with Sebby was always one I wouldn't soon forget.

"Get a move on, Baylee!" Sebby shouted up the stairs. "We don't have all day!"

"Right." I snapped out of my unhealthy preoccupation with my neighbor and refocused on my closet. I grabbed some jeans and a light sweater, finishing the look with a pair of Converse. I hoped this was appropriate for whatever Sebby had planned.

"Ready for this?" he asked when I bounced back down the stairs and into the living room.

"I'm not sure. If you tell me what we're doing, I'll let you know."

"It's a surprise." Winking, he grabbed my hand and pulled me out of my condo. As we walked toward the elevator, he didn't drop my hand and I didn't make any motions to pull it out of his grasp.

We didn't speak a word as we rode down to the lobby, our hands still glued together, Sebby running his thumb across my knuckles. It was so light, barely noticeable, like it was second-nature. His scent filled the small space and I sidestepped closer to him, wanting to eliminate all distance between us. I didn't know what it was about elevators, but it was taking all my resolve not to throw caution to the wind and find out how his lips tasted.

Finally, the doors opened and Sebby dropped my hand, my sanity returning due to the absence of his touch. Steeling myself, I followed him through the lobby. When he held the door open for me, I expected to see his Camaro waiting for us with a valet attendant standing by. Instead, the porte-cochere was void of any car.

"Let's go, Baylee," Sebby called out. I turned to see him hopping onto a vintage BMW motorcycle, holding a helmet and a leather jacket toward me.

I took a few cautious steps, eyeing the motorcycle with hesitation. I had never been on one before and I was certainly on edge about ending up splattered on the pavement. I trusted Sebby. I just didn't trust the rest of the drivers in LA.

"Come on," he urged. "Don't worry. We're only going to be on the freeway for a second, then on PCH."

"Where are we going?"

"You're not going to find out until we get there. Wouldn't want to ruin the surprise."

Masking my excitement with an annoyed sigh and an eye roll, I approached the motorcycle and grabbed the helmet and jacket from Sebby. "More like you don't want me to head back to my condo," I muttered, zipping up the jacket, then securing the helmet on my head.

"Pretty much." The engine roared to life as I climbed on. "Now, hold on tight."

I wrapped my arms around his mid-section, certain I was cutting off his circulation, and before I could change my mind, he pulled onto Ocean Avenue. At first, it wasn't so bad. There was a stoplight practically every block, so the bike never broke thirty miles an hour. Then he veered off the main drag, merging onto the freeway momentarily before it ended, dumping onto PCH.

There was a fair bit of traffic on the four-lane road abutting the coast of California, which I was more than happy about. As Sebby weaved between the lanes at a cautious speed, I absorbed my surroundings. To my right, majestic mountains rose into the sky. To my left, sun-glistened ocean waves stretched for miles. Too soon, traffic began to dissipate and stoplights grew more infrequent. Shoreline skyscraper hotels and condos gave way to smaller houses, which probably still cost several million dollars.

Increasing his speed, Sebby zoomed up the road, making me tighten my hold around his waist.

"How ya doing back there?" he shouted in response to my death grip.

"Fine," I answered quickly, shutting my eyes. I figured if I couldn't see how fast the cars on the opposite side of the road were racing by, it wouldn't be as bad.

"Relax, Baylee." The motorcycle slowed to a stop at a light. "I'm not going to let anything happen to you. Riding on a motorcycle is all about feeling free, having the world at your fingertips. Stop worrying and just enjoy yourself."

Taking a deep breath, I loosened my grip and lifted my head away from Sebby's back, where I had buried it. When the light turned green, I fought my instinct to close my eyes and wait until we arrived at our destination to reopen them. Instead, I took in the sights, the smells, the feel of the California shoreline. The coastal area of Malibu soon gave way to a more mountainous terrain, and I marveled at my surroundings.

"Beautiful, isn't it?" Sebby asked, noticing I had relaxed my grip.

"Yes," I answered just as he turned off PCH and navigated his motorcycle up one of the mountain passes.

The road slowly climbed and curved through the dips and valleys of the terrain. Gorgeous, sprawling estates appeared every so often, and I gazed in awe at the view of the Pacific Ocean from this altitude. The water rippled and rolled as it always did, but up this high, it went on and on, disappearing into the horizon. I tried to come up with a way to adequately explain how I felt on the back of Sebby's bike, the wind in my face, the sun on my skin, the world wrapped around me, but words escaped me. I felt free, adventurous.

I know it sounded crazy and maybe a little melodramatic, but on the back of that bike, up in those mountains, I felt my mother's spirit surrounding me. I grew up in a semi-religious household. Church was an every Sunday thing. I never bought into any of it, though. I never understood why you had to go to a building to be saved. That moment reinforced my beliefs. I felt something out on that road, something stronger and more awe-inspiring than I ever did within the four walls of the church.

Drawing in a long, relaxing breath, I leaned my head back and stared at the sky above me. A few white clouds added a pleasing texture to the otherwise endless blue canvas. Regardless of what Sebby had planned for the afternoon, this was already the perfect day.

The road continued to climb, and just when I thought we couldn't go any higher without requiring oxygen, the path dipped and we began our descent. After about ten minutes of navigating down the mountain, we were back among civilization once more, gas stations and fast food restaurants popping up. The euphoric feeling I had experienced back on the mountain was gone. I now understood why people disappeared to the middle of nowhere to get away from it all. Maybe that was what I needed to do to finish my book.

Soon, Sebby veered the motorcycle onto a somewhat hidden street and, after about a mile, we pulled past an open chain-link gate and drove toward what looked like a small airplane hangar.

"Where are we?" I asked as Sebby parked the motorcycle by the entrance to the building.

"We're here," he answered, killing the engine and hopping off his bike, helping me find my footing. My legs and arms vibrated from sitting on the back of his bike for so long. Surprisingly, I loved it.

"I understand that," I began, taking my helmet off, "but where exactly is here?"

"You'll see. This way." He gestured to a door toward the rear of the hangar, a sign that said *Main Office* hanging over it. It was a gray metal building that looked like it would collapse if you sneezed too hard. The large bay doors at the front of the hangar were wide open, revealing a small plane. A sinking feeling formed in my stomach and I wanted to turn around and hop back on the motorcycle.

Then again, I had overcome that fear rather quickly. No matter what awaited us inside that beat up airplane hangar, I knew I would be okay.

Approaching Sebby as he held the door open for me, I stepped over the threshold into a small waiting room with a desk and several chairs, practically jumping out of my skin when five of my closest friends screamed "surprise".

My hand flew to my chest and I let out a small gasp. "What are you all doing here?" I was met by the excited faces of Sophia, Marcel, Lacey, Darren, and Cora. "What am *I* doing here?"

"We're here to celebrate your birthday!" Marcel announced.

I glanced at Sebby, giving him an incredulous look, waiting for an explanation. He smiled at me, revealing those boyish dimples I had been attracted to since our first meeting.

"And *you're* here to do something to make this a birthday you'll never forget," he said. "I know you've been avoiding crossing this one off your mother's list, so we all decided to do it with you."

"Do what?" I scanned the small office, wishing I

could ignore all the clues. I was surrounded by posters of people plunging to their deaths from an airplane, happy little clouds in the background.

There was no avoiding it anymore…

Today, I would skydive.

~~~~~~~~~~

AFTER SITTING THROUGH SEVERAL hours of videos and instruction detailing exactly what fate awaited us, we all suited up in our jumpsuits and were paired with a certified skydiver, whom we would each be strapped to for the jump. I had contemplated backing out at least a dozen times over the course of the afternoon, but I knew I couldn't. All of my friends were going through this with me. If they were scared, they did a good job of hiding it…laughing, joking around with each other. Hell, Lacey was talking about getting a new tattoo to memorialize her first skydiving experience.

"Want to come with me and get one of your own?" she asked.

I snorted at her. "Y'all are lucky I didn't leave when I first got here. There's no way in hell I'm jumping out of a plane, then getting my skin jabbed with a needle. My limit is one crazy adventure per day."

"So tomorrow then?" She wiggled her eyebrows at me.

I shook my head and laughed, securing the helmet straps under my chin. Once we were all set to go and the instructor said we'd been cleared to take off, I blindly followed the group to a small plane, all of us hopping in, taking a seat in one of the bench seats lining the sides of the aircraft. As the plane lurched forward and we taxied toward the runway, a hand squeezed mine. I looked to my left.

"You okay?" Sebby shouted over the roar of the engines.

"Never better!" I grinned a toothy smile at him, trying to hide my obvious nerves.

The next twenty minutes were a blur as the plane climbed into the sky. I would have given anything to have more time to pep myself up. Instead, the minute hand of my watch seemed to race, time passing with lightning speed. The higher the plane climbed, the more my body was overtaken by nerves. I tried to fight off the chills running through me. I plastered a smile on my face as I listened to my friends talk about their evening plans, as if they weren't about to plummet back to earth. A ding sounded, cutting through the conversation, and we all turned our heads to see the ready light illuminated. We unbuckled from our seats and found our jump partners.

"Ready, Baylee?" my instructor, Bruce, asked. He was in his fifties and just an inch or two taller than me.

"Ready as I'll ever be," I responded.

He smiled. "Let's do this."

Nodding, I turned around, allowing him to clip himself onto the harness I was wearing on the back of my jumpsuit. After he checked all the straps and connections to make sure we were secured to each other, he squeezed my arm.

"We're set, Baylee."

We lined up and I watched my friends jump out, one by one, until I was the only one left. It was so tempting to tell Bruce I wanted to back out, but I had already come this far. Approaching the open door, the sound of the engines and wind grew louder, and I didn't even hear the jump signal. One minute, I was in the airplane, my feet firmly planted on the solid floor. The next, I was free-falling through the sky, screaming.

Keeping my eyes closed, I clutched onto the straps of my harness, as if it would slow me down. I wanted to curse my mother for her adventurous spirit. Humans weren't meant to jump out of airplanes and fall back to earth. Based on my luck, our parachute wouldn't open, like always happened in those *Bugs Bunny* cartoons I watched growing up. It didn't matter that I knew there was a backup 'chute, too.

Then something unexpected happened. As the wind hit my face, I felt that same euphoria from on the mountain. An air of serenity filtered through me, erasing the tension that was there moments ago. I finally opened my eyes and let the world around me come into view. I knew we were falling fast toward the ground, but it didn't feel like that. I felt like I was flying.

Within minutes of beginning our free-fall, Bruce opened the parachute, slowing our descent, giving me a bird's eye view of my new home. To the south, I could see Hollywood, Beverly Hills, and downtown LA. To the north, nothing but mountains. In front of me, the waves of the Pacific Ocean crested in the distance. This was heaven on earth. I swallowed through the lump in my throat at the thought that my mother never got to experience something as incredible and momentous as this.

All too soon, houses that seemed to be specs of dust grew larger and larger, and our landing site came into view. When we had first jumped, I wanted nothing more than to be on solid ground. Now that it was almost over, I didn't want it to end.

I was still on cloud nine when we hit the ground and ran across the grass, slowing to a stop. I felt such a rush from how liberating the experience was. After Bruce unclipped my harness, I walked to my friends waiting in the distance, clear of the landing zone. As I approached, I was swarmed by all of them throwing their arms around me and congratulating me.

I was always met with a strong sense of accomplishment each time I crossed something off my mother's list. This time, however, it was different. Yes, I felt accomplished, but having this strange group of misfits who had become my second family by my side made it worth all the nerves. When I first moved out here, I wondered if this place would ever feel like home.

It finally did.

# CHAPTER TWENTY

SEBBY SPED DOWN PCH toward Santa Monica, driving more carelessly than I imagined he wanted, but it was getting late. After finishing our jump, we all went to a bar in Malibu to have a few birthday drinks. I had lost track of time, now on the verge of missing my date with Owen. He was supposed to be picking me up at seven, which was in fifteen minutes. I had debated canceling and spending the night with my friends, but Owen would be leaving town tomorrow, making tonight our last chance to go out for a week. I wanted him to think I was willing to sacrifice a few things to see if whatever was going on between us had the potential to grow into something more.

I kept telling myself that the more time I spent with Owen, the less I would think of the man I had my arms wrapped around as he navigated down the road. After this afternoon, however, I knew it was a lie. Today was a turning point in our "friendship". I couldn't quite explain it, but there was something bigger between us now. Maybe it was because he remembered my birthday. Maybe it was because he helped me cross another item off my mother's list. Maybe it was because he pushed me to face my fears, promising to stand by my side the entire time. Maybe it was because, over the weeks, Sebby had brought out a side of me I never knew existed. Regardless of what triggered the transformation, it was there. It was…magic.

Pulling up to our building, Sebby parked his bike off to the side of the porte-cochere and ran through the lobby, dragging me along with him. Despite my impending date, I didn't want to go back to my condo. I was worried that whatever spark or change that had occurred between us today would be erased the moment we returned home.

I glanced at him as we rode up to the top floor of our building. "Thanks for today." I shuffled my feet, closing the distance between us.

Peering down at me, he brushed a strand of hair, which had come loose from my ponytail, behind my ear. It didn't matter that, during the course of our friendship, his fingers had grazed my skin on countless occasions. That gesture was more charged and thrilling than any of our previous ones.

His fingers lingered on my face, cupping my cheek. Breathless, I melted into him, closing my eyes. When I opened them, he was gazing at me with a yearning that was unmatched in all my now twenty-nine years. I wanted to freeze time. That was the moment I knew.

Sebby lost the bet.

Men and women couldn't just be friends.

The unwelcome ding of the elevator reaching our floor echoed, the sound deafening as it broke our moment. Reality slapped me in the face the second I stepped into the hallway. All day, we had lived in our fantasy world, the rush of doing something crazy making me forget about the real world for a minute. Now that my body had returned to earth, so did my conscience. Regardless of what happened between us today, nothing changed the fact that Sebby had a girlfriend. No matter how much my heart truly believed he would be a man worth taking a risk for, I couldn't come between him and Mercedes.

Turning from him and dashing toward my condo, I halted when I saw a tall, intimidating man standing at my door.

"He looks different with clothes on," Sebby remarked, approaching me from behind.

I let out a small laugh. Owen looked in our direction, his brows furrowing when he saw I wasn't even remotely close to being ready for our date. A pang of guilt knotted in my stomach before disappearing. I wouldn't trade today for anything.

"Owen," I started, "I'm so sorry. I got dragged out earlier today under the false guarantee that I would be home in plenty of time to get ready for dinner." I rushed to the door and unlocked it. "I just need to shower, but I can be ready in thirty minutes." I stepped back, allowing him to enter.

"Blame me," Sebby added, following Owen into the living room of my condo, much to my surprise. "We took her skydiving for her birthday." He headed toward my kitchen, grabbing a bottle of wine off my counter and pouring three glasses. Owen appeared dumbfounded as to why this man just made himself at home in my condo. I knew Sebby all too well at this point. This was his way of marking his territory. Territory he had no claim over.

"And you are?" Owen hesitantly took the wine glass Sebby held toward him.

"Oh. Sorry." Sebby brushed his hands on the legs of his cargo pants. "I'm Baylee's neighbor, Sebby. I live across the hall."

Both men stared at each other for several awkward

moments, as if they were having a silent conversation. I pictured them in fur skin loin-cloths, hunched over, grunting like cavemen, gesturing that they were my keeper and protector.

"Well," I said, breaking up the pissing contest, "I'll let you two get to know each other while I go shower. I'll make it quick." I stood on my tiptoes and placed a soft kiss on Owen's neck before dashing up the stairs. I knew it irritated Sebby, and I'd be lying if I said I wasn't hoping to get some sort of reaction out of him. As misplaced as his jealousy was, considering his own relationship status, I craved it.

Jumping into the shower, I washed in record time, worried I would walk in on a wrestling match when I made my way back downstairs. I briefly considered the possibility that Sebby could have said something to scare Owen off, but when I heard two voices echoing against the high ceilings, making their way to me in my bedroom, I grew relieved that he was still here.

After towel drying my hair and running some gel through it to settle the waves, I put on a cream-colored form-fitting dress, coupled with a chunky black jeweled necklace and bracelet. Sliding on a pair of dark stilettos, I made my way down the stairs to see Sebby and Owen joking about something as they sat on the couch. It was a complete one-eighty from the state I had left them in moments ago, but I was glad to see them getting along. Sebby was an important part of my life. If this thing with Owen was going anywhere, I needed them to be civil toward one another. I wasn't expecting them to form an unhealthy bromance, but I didn't want there to be any animosity between them, either.

I tried to hide my presence to see what they were laughing about, but my heels gave me away. Both men spun their heads in my direction, silence falling over the room. I stood in place awkwardly while Sebby and Owen stared at me, an identical heat in their eyes.

"Wow," Owen exhaled, making Sebby snap out of his trance and struggle to regain his composure. Jumping off the couch, Owen strode toward me, pulling my body against his. Instead of closing my eyes and enjoying the feel of his arms around me, his body flush with mine, I kept them trained on Sebby. I couldn't look away. His brows were furrowed and he swallowed hard. It didn't take a genius to know what was going through his mind… He was wishing he were in Owen's shoes.

*I* wished he were in Owen's shoes, too.

"Ready for your birthday dinner?" Owen asked, and I forced my attention back to him.

"Of course." I released myself from his hold and grabbed a green-belted coat out of the hallway closet. Being a true gentleman, he helped me into it.

"Well, you kids have fun," Sebby said. His voice was fraught with sorrow and disappointment that he tried to mask with a chipper and upbeat tone. He headed toward the foyer and opened the door.

"Thanks." Owen reached his hand out and shook Sebby's once more.

"You bet." He turned away from us, heading toward his condo. "And happy birthday, Baylee," he added, his voice soft.

I glanced over my shoulder at him and my smile fell, a silent apology spoken between us. Owen remained oblivious to our exchange as he pulled me down the corridor toward the bank of elevators.

"Sebby seems like a good neighbor," Owen said as

we waited for the elevator to arrive. "He's very protective of you."

"What do you mean by that?" The elevator doors opened and I stepped inside.

"Nothing." He pressed the button for the lobby. "You can tell how much he cares about you, especially when he said he would make sure I could never get another freelance gig for the rest of my life if I did anything to hurt you."

"And what did you say to that?" I should have been horrified that Sebby had threatened him, but a warmth ran through me instead.

"I promised he had nothing to worry about."

Nodding, I faced forward as the doors closed, remaining silent.

During our extravagant dinner, I tried to make Owen think I was thrilled to be with him. I smiled at his compliments. I laughed at his jokes. I blushed when his hand caressed my skin, but it felt wrong. My mind was elsewhere. It was locked in that moment of time when Sebby saw me walk down the steps of my condo and into the living room, longing and devotion etched on his face…

Because I felt the same way toward him, girlfriend be damned.

All the months of reading my mother's journal culminated in that instant. If I had learned anything from her it was to take a risk because tomorrow isn't guaranteed.

Tomorrow, I would finally tell Sebby the truth, that I *didn't* think we were better off as friends, and let the chips fall where they may.

# CHAPTER TWENTY-ONE

SUNDAY MORNING, I WOKE up after a restless night's sleep. I couldn't get Sebby out of my mind. After as romantic a date as I had ever been on the previous evening, you'd think Owen would be on my mind, even in my bed, but he wasn't. Instead, I had spent the majority of my date formulating exactly what I was going to say to Sebby. If Owen noticed my distant demeanor, he didn't say anything. He remained the perfect gentleman...opening doors for me, holding my chair out, walking me back to my condo after dinner. I felt awkward as we stood outside my door. He gazed at me with such heat, such unrequited want.

He moved toward me and we shared a kiss that was more passionate than I was anticipating. My body grew rigid and I knew I should push him away, tell him I couldn't see him anymore, but his lips on mine felt so good. I had missed this connection during the years of my marriage so much, all sense of what was right disappeared and I lost myself in his arms. I think I may have even moaned a little. Still, all I could think about during that amazing exchange was Sebby. I wondered if he was on the other side of his door, witnessing our kiss. I hated the thought. So instead of inviting Owen in, I thanked him for a wonderful evening and left him in the hallway. I could feel his confusion from beyond my closed door.

This morning, I put more effort than I typically did

into making myself look presentable. Instead of simply throwing on a pair of yoga pants and a jacket, I dressed in jeans and a sweater. I even went so far as to add a hint of blush and eyeshadow. When declaring your love to a man who was otherwise attached, one should at least look presentable, right?

"Well, this is it, buddy," I said to Sport as I checked my reflection one final time in the full-length mirror. "There's no turning back after I cross this bridge. It's sink or swim, pal."

Familiar with our routine, Sport ran around in circles, knowing we were about to go for his morning walk. I hooked him up to his leash and left my condo, heading to the same bench that had been the scene of so many wonderful memories. Strolling through the park, the sky a dim gray, I tried to imagine what Sebby's response would be. I pictured him smiling wide, sweeping me into his arms, and making some joke about it taking me long enough to finally see what had been in front of me for months.

But what if I was reading it wrong? What if I was just imagining his jealous reaction whenever I had a date with another guy? What if he really had no interest in me, other than as friends? Now that I had talked myself into finally admitting my true feelings, I didn't know if I could handle the rejection.

Slowing my steps, I wondered whether I should follow through. There was a risk he would turn me down. I was starting to think I had imagined it all in my head. I stared at the ocean, hoping to draw strength from the powerful waves. Then there was an unexpected tug on Sport's leash, much like that day all those months ago. I lost control of his leash and darted after him toward our bench, only to come to an abrupt stop when it sat empty. Sport didn't know what to make of it, either. In all the weeks I had been meeting Sebby at this spot, he had always been waiting for me, apart from the few times he was out of town. Maybe he was just running late.

Lowering myself to the bench, I tugged my jacket closer, a strong offshore breeze blowing. The sun was hiding behind the clouds, and there was a cold dampness in the air that chilled me to my core.

Five minutes passed.

Then ten.

Then fifteen.

After twenty, Sebby still hadn't shown up. I grabbed my cell phone and sent him a quick text.

*Everything okay? I'm at the park. Sport is missing Gidget.*

I kept my phone in my hands, bouncing my legs as I waited for a reply. For the first time since we met, one didn't come right away. I waited longer, only to be left waiting. When the wind grew stronger, I couldn't take the cold anymore. I got up from the bench and headed back to my condo. I kept an eye out for Sebby and Gidget. Every time I heard a dog bark, I snapped my head in that direction, only to be disappointed.

With slumped shoulders, I walked into my building, brushing off Jeffrey's attempts at making small talk. Sebby's mysterious absence and lack of communication made me uneasy. I tried to think of something else, like my uncle's arrival later in the day, but that didn't help. My mind was elsewhere.

As I stepped out of the elevator and rounded the corner to my condo, I was caught by surprise when I heard Sebby's door open. Pausing momentarily, I found myself speechless when he emerged with a stunning blonde. I had put in the effort to make my appearance presentable this morning, thinking I did an adequate job, but I couldn't hold a candle to the woman staring back at me. Her hair was straight, not one strand out of place. She was thin and tall, her legs seeming to go on for miles. She wore black knee-high boots pulled over skinny jeans, and an oversized tunic sweater. Her smile was charismatic and my heart sink. I knew all too well who this woman was. There was no way I could compete with the picture of perfection leaving Sebby's condo.

I was amazed he even noticed I was standing in the hallway opposite him, but he did, stopping abruptly. "Baylee." A nervous expression grew on his face. Sport lunged for them, his tail wagging excitedly, and I had to reel in his leash to stop him from jumping on Sebby, especially when I saw the look of disgust on his blonde companion's face.

"Good morning," I responded curtly, turning to unlock my door. I tried to hide how unsettled I was. Seeing his girlfriend in person made her real. Just an hour ago, I was ready to beg him to leave her for me, but I couldn't do that, not anymore.

"This is Mercedes," he said.

Turning, I plastered a fake smile on my face. "Mercedes..." I held my hand out to her and we shook cordially. "I've heard so much about you. What brings you to town?"

"Well, I heard this one was planning on staying here for Thanksgiving and I couldn't stand him being alone during the holidays." She squeezed his arm, a beautiful smile crossing her face. She wasn't what I had expected at all. The picture Sebby had painted of her was completely different than the woman standing in front of me, her eyes alight whenever she met Sebby's gaze.

"Well, that's not the only reason." Sebby shifted his feet. "She's opening a new gallery in Beverly Hills and needed to come out here to approve the space."

"Then I'm sure you'll both be seeing much more of each other," I said cheerily, trying to mask my true feelings.

"Perhaps. Or he can just finally move back to the East Coast like I've been trying to get him to do for years. New York is great for his line of work. Plus, he'd be so close to his family. It's a win-win, don't you think?"

"Sure sounds like it," I replied solemnly. "Well, I don't want to keep you two from wherever you were headed. It was lovely to meet you, Mercedes."

"You as well, Becky."

"It's Baylee," I mumbled as they headed down the hallway.

Frantically unlocking my door, I tore through my condo, grabbing an open bottle of red wine and pouring a glass. I didn't care that it wasn't even ten in the morning yet. I needed something to shake off meeting Mercedes. The timing couldn't have been worse.

Just as I was about to take another long slug of my wine, my phone vibrated in my pocket. Pulling it out, I saw a text from Sebby.

*I'm sorry.*

My hands hovered over the screen, about to respond, but what would I say? I couldn't possibly say everything I wanted to, that he should have let me know Mercedes was coming to town. But why did that matter? Guilt seeped into my conscience. Sebby and I had never done anything inappropriate, but there was a spark between us that had been stoked with each second we spent together. Nothing had been able to dull it, not even meeting Mercedes, but it put the reality of our friendship into a cold, hard truth.

Throwing my phone on the counter, I ignored his text, plus all the subsequent beeps indicating more incoming messages. I just wanted to forget for a minute… Forget that he had a girlfriend, and forget that I was about to throw myself at him, encouraging him to make me the other woman. Heading to the couch, I grabbed my mother's journal, staring at the leather cover, running my fingers over her embossed initials.

"You don't have any pearls of wisdom in here for when you fall in love with a man you can't have, do ya?"

# CHAPTER TWENTY-TWO

IT WAS EVENING WHEN I pulled up to the valet of a swanky hotel in downtown Los Angeles, looking forward to seeing my uncle. After the morning I had, I needed a familiar face who had absolutely no connection to Sebby. I needed someone to distract me from having my heart crushed in the hallway outside my condo. I prayed my uncle would do just that, as he often did back home when I was having a bad day.

I pulled my coat close to my body. The gray clouds present earlier had given way to a heavy downpour, which was much-needed out here in drought-ridden California. The wind was fierce, chilling me to the bone. I felt bad for all the people who had come here on vacation in the hopes of enjoying some sun and sand. Still, I knew the rain pummeling the coast at this moment would give way to sun tomorrow. That's how it was out here.

After tipping the valet, I walked through the revolving doors and into the lobby of the hotel. It was bustling with people coming and going, voices echoing in the cavernous entry. Back home, the nicest hotel was a budget-friendly place whose most marketable amenity was an outdoor swimming pool. The only people staying there were those unlucky enough to be in town to conduct business with one of the many mills or my father's lumber company. This hotel was a palace compared to the one back home, and it should be. It cost my uncle at least $700 a night. The marble flooring was so clean and lustrous, I could almost see my reflection in it.

I strolled past a sitting area with a coffee bar and up to a desk set in front of an elegant stone wall boasting the name of the hotel in gold lettering.

"Excuse me," I asked a man at the desk. "Which way is the bar?"

"Just past the wall here," he instructed, gesturing beyond where he stood and toward a circular bar with a towering stone wall in the middle.

"Thank you." I smiled and proceeded toward the bar. It was packed with people all decked out. In LA, it seemed most people pretended to be someone they weren't. This was the case in here, too. Nobody needed to wear sunglasses inside on a dark, rainy night.

I scanned the area, searching for a set of familiar eyes I hadn't seen in two months. It felt like such a short time. So much had happened since the fateful day that I took my dog for a walk and gave a stranger a bloody nose. I had been looking for a fresh start, an escape from the only life I had ever known. I never anticipated losing my heart all over again.

"Baylee Grace!" a voice cried out as I approached a table toward the back of the bar. In that instant, all my troubles and heartache of the past twenty-four hours vanished, if only for a second. "Aren't you a sight for sore eyes." He raised himself from his chair and I found my way into his arms.

"It's so good to see you, Uncle Monty." I inhaled his scent, immediately reminded of home. But it wasn't really home anymore, if it ever was. And, after today, I wasn't sure LA was home, either.

"It's great to see you, too." He pulled back, releasing me from his embrace, and helped me into a chair.

He smiled, then signaled to a server. Although he was in his mid-sixties, my uncle didn't look a day over forty. He always joked that his lack of wife and kids attributed to his youthful appearance. He had a full head of gray hair that showed no signs of receding anytime soon. In Charlotte legal circles, he was referred to as North Carolina's Richard Gere. I had to admit that there was a resemblance between the actor and Montgomery Chester Crawford, III. Having that name, if he wasn't destined to work in the legal profession, I don't know what to tell you.

"What can I get you?" a bubbly brunette asked, approaching us almost instantly. My uncle always had a commanding but gentile presence wherever he went. The charming smile, the sparkling eyes, the perfectly tailored and pressed designer suits made heads turn daily. He was impossible to ignore.

I opened my mouth, about to order my typical drink...a Manhattan. But that just reminded me of Sebby and Mercedes. "Old Fashioned," I said to the waitress, channeling my southern roots.

She nodded, focusing her attention on my uncle. "Can I get you another scotch?" She gave him a provocative smile, her eyes leering at him. I simply shook my head. No matter where he went, women flirted with him, many of them young enough to be his granddaughter.

"Sure thing, sugar," he responded, winking. He had a smooth and inviting Carolina accent, as opposed to the full-blown twangy one that surrounded me growing up. Don't get me wrong. I loved my childhood in a small town, which most people never heard of, with a population of less than 4,000. Everyone knew everyone else. Front porch sitting and sweet tea sipping were common occurrences during summer days. I just wasn't meant to live there the rest of my life. Like my uncle always told me, I am my mother's daughter. I was meant to spread my wings.

The waitress retreated from us, swaying her hips in such a way that made it obvious she was trying to draw attention to her petite backside from the sixty-something-year-old man sitting across from me. It should have weirded me out, but over the years, I had grown used to the countless women flirting with my uncle. He always winked, calling it an occupational hazard.

"Old Fashioned?" Uncle Monty eyed me, raising his glass to his mouth. "The Baylee I know usually stuck with beer."

"What can I say?" I leaned back into my chair. "LA has changed me."

"I hope for the better."

"I'll let you be the judge of that, but I think so."

"Good. Now, tell me what you've been doing since you came out here."

Hesitating, I contemplated how much I should tell him about what had been going on in my life over the past few months.

"Come on, Baylee. Let me hear it. Who is he?"

The waitress returned with our drinks, placing mine in front of me before doing the same with my uncle's scotch. When I noticed blue ink on the cocktail napkin she placed his drink on, I rolled my eyes. He simply smiled the boyish grin of his that shaved decades off his true age. He would never call her, but that didn't stop him from enjoying the attention.

"What makes you think—"

"I know you, Baylee, I can *always* tell."

Letting out a short breath, I took a sip of my drink and launched into everything that had happened since I arrived in California, repeating some things I had already shared with him. I told him about meeting a mysterious man when Sport tried to hump another dog; how he turned out to be my very successful, very handsome neighbor; how he had been helping me with Mom's bucket list, and that we had grown closer than I ever imagined; how I had a few dating disasters — first with a gay man, then with a man who turned out to be my gynecologist; how I had finally met someone who, for all intents and purposes, I should have been interested in, but I couldn't stop thinking about Sebby.

"Then what's the problem?" Uncle Monty asked after I finished. "It sounds like you're interested in each other. What's holding you back?"

I gave him a small smile. "He has a girlfriend, and after everything I've been through with Will, I just couldn't…"

He nodded in understanding, running his fingers against his chin. "I get it. You don't want to be the other woman."

"Exactly."

"Maybe you're looking at things the wrong way. Maybe you're *not* the other woman."

"Well, I'm not. We've kept our relationship strictly platonic."

"Apart from both of you being attracted to each

other."

"Sounds about right." I finished my drink. My uncle gestured to our server to bring another round. She was only too happy to oblige. I wondered what she would write on his cocktail napkin this time. Her bra size perhaps?

"Let me ask you this. Do you think he's happy with his girlfriend?"

I contemplated his question. "It's hard to say. She lives in New York, so they only see each other once a month at most. He says he loves the arrangement because it gives him space and time to devote to his career. He knows he'll eventually need to move to the East Coast if he wants their relationship to work, but he's not ready for that yet."

"Do you think that's because maybe, just maybe, he knows she's not the one for him?"

"He'd be crazy to think that," I scoffed. "You should see her. She's gorgeous, like she just stepped off the cover of a fashion magazine. She looks exactly like the type of women you date."

"Most men don't care about that," Uncle Monty responded quickly.

"What do you mean?"

"Trust me, Baylee. I've dated more women than I should probably admit. I've had a very successful career and plenty of women have been attracted to me…or my wallet. I never could tell which one." He winked. "I've dated my fair share of women who had more plastic and Botox injections than anyone should put their bodies through. Yes, I was initially attracted to their beauty, but there was no substance there. I know there's that old adage that opposites attract—"

"And Sebby says it's true of him and Mercedes."

He raised his eyebrows. "Her name's Mercedes?"

I nodded, stifling a laugh. If there ever were a more perfect name for a New York socialite, I didn't know what it was, except perhaps Muffy.

"Regardless," my uncle continued, "at some point, the excitement of being with someone completely different will fade. You're left with a tug of war, each person trying to pull the other to their side. Unless they're both willing to meet in the middle on some things, it's a losing game, especially when one person does all the tugging."

This was a side of my uncle I had never seen before. He had always been a big presence in my life, even more so after my father died. We were close, but more in a pseudo parental capacity. The way he spoke to me now, an unfocused gaze and a glimmer of unshed tears visible in the corner of his eyes, I couldn't help but think he was reminded of someone from his past.

"But wouldn't it be boring to be with someone who shared all the same interests as you?" I asked.

"I'm not saying you have to have all the same interests. Take your mother and father, for example. They were different enough. Your father was your typical southern good ol' boy, never wanting to leave his hometown. Your mother... God, she had so much life. She wanted to see the world, and she wanted the world to see her. And she did just that. But they worked because they loved each other enough to know when to tug and when to let go."

"But none of that matters," I said, shaking off the idea that Sebby and I had a remote chance of being together. "He's happy. I know how it feels to find out you've been cheated on. I couldn't do that to anyone, no matter what."

"And I'd never tell you to get involved with someone whose heart belonged to another. I haven't met this neighbor of yours so I can't speak too intelligently here, but if everything you've told me is any indication, I can't help but think his heart *doesn't* belong to someone else."

"Uncle Monty, how do you—"

"Trust me, Baylee Grace. I wasn't always the successful bachelor the entire family makes me out to be. There was a time when I didn't have a care in the world. I was fresh out of law school, had just taken a job as an associate at one of the biggest firms in Charlotte, and was on my own for the first time in my life." A sentimental look crossing his face, he smiled.

"Who was she?"

"Her name was Carmen and she was a file clerk at the firm. As you can imagine, there was a non-fraternization policy in place for all employees, particularly between associates and support staff. We became friendly, at first hanging out during office happy hour, then meeting to go to a museum, ball game, a concert here and there. I valued her company, and she enjoyed mine."

"But you couldn't take it any further because of your work," I said. He nodded. "What happened?"

"I started to hear whispers around the water cooler. People at the office noticed how I lingered at her desk when asking her to do something, how she joined me for lunch meetings in my office. Of course, no one believed we were just friends because how could a man and woman just be friends?" he asked sarcastically, rolling his eyes. "Since the entire firm was under the impression we had something going on and no disciplinary action had been taken, I decided I was going to tell her how I felt. It was a Friday evening and most of the office was at happy hour. I was working late since I had a trial starting the following Monday. I was having trouble focusing, so I decided to take a short break and head to our usual bar to see her."

He swallowed hard, his posture sinking. The confident and assured man I knew my entire life was nowhere to be found.

"I'll never forget the aching in my chest when I saw the flashing red and blue lights on the side of the road we all took to get to the bar. There was police tape roping off two mangled cars."

I gasped, bringing my hand to my mouth.

"They said she died on impact," he continued, his voice empty. "She didn't feel a thing. The drunk prick who killed her only got two years for vehicular manslaughter and driving under the influence, even though he was operating under a suspended license and had a previous DUI. I never got to tell her how I felt and I've regretted that every day since then. Please, Baylee." He clutched my hand. "Don't make the same mistake I did. Tomorrow isn't a guarantee. Reading your mother's journal should have taught you that. Put it all on the line. Take a risk."

His eyes met mine. For a brief instant, I believed I was speaking with my mother, staring into her eyes, as she gave me the motherly advice I had yearned for most of my life. Having spent the last several weeks channeling her spirit while I finished the list she was never able to made me feel closer to her than I imagined possible. Maybe my uncle was right. Maybe I needed to take a risk. It's what my mother would have done.

# CHAPTER TWENTY-THREE

"EASIER SAID THAN DONE," I whispered to myself. As I headed through the lobby of the hotel, I thought about my uncle's story. Sure, our situations were similar. We both had an obstacle preventing us from being with the person we wanted, but there was a huge difference between violating a non-fraternization clause in an employee handbook and asking Sebby to choose me over somebody he had been seeing for years. The devil on my shoulder told me to go for it. The angel kept whispering "The other woman" in my ear. I couldn't look beyond that.

I headed past the front desk and toward the entrance, stopping dead in my tracks when I saw Sebby walk through the revolving doors with Mercedes, cursing my horrible luck. Curious as to what they were doing here, I ducked behind a stone column in the lobby sitting area, trying to eavesdrop on their conversation.

As they approached the bank of elevators, I strained to hear what they were saying, but the sound of all the voices reverberating against the marble drowned them out. I knew I should take the opportunity to make my escape without Sebby spotting me. That doesn't mean I heeded my own advice, though. My curiosity got the better of me and, as stealthily as possible, I padded toward the bank of elevators, hiding behind a potted tree.

The irony was not lost on me.

"Are you sure you don't want to come up?" Mercedes asked, and I straightened my spine. This was unusual. Why wasn't she staying at Sebby's? He had inferred she wasn't a big fan of dogs. Maybe that was the reason she got a hotel room.

"I have an early day tomorrow."

"Okay." I could picture the pout on her face, although the tree branches blocked my view. "Think you can get away from all your responsibilities to meet me tomorrow for dinner? Even a late one?"

"I think I can do that," he replied after a short pause. There was a coyness in his tone I had never heard before. I slumped against the wall, consumed with the idea that the Sebby standing in the elevator vestibule was a different Sebby than the man I had fallen for over the past few months. When the dust settled, who was the real Sebby? "I'll just make sure Sophia's able to feed and walk Gidget."

"I don't even know why you have that dog," she scoffed. "You can't bring her to New York when you move."

My heart fell. *Sebby's moving?* I thought to myself. How could so much change in just twenty-four hours?

He ran his hand through his hair. "Mercedes..." I could hear his frustration and reluctance to discuss the topic further.

"You need to grow up and forget about your adolescent dream of producing for the NFL. That's a bit of a step down, don't you think?"

I wrinkled my nose and pinched my lips, scowling. I was starting to see a different side of Mercedes. This morning, she was friendly, but now that she thought they were alone, I saw the woman Sebby had described to me. After being in a relationship where my partner didn't support my dreams, I could sympathize with Sebby's situation. I was starting to like Mercedes less and less. She seemed to do all the tugging, and Sebby seemed to just give and give. I wondered how much longer it would be until he had nothing left to give and became a person I no longer recognized. A person *he* no longer recognized.

"I don't want to talk about this today."

"Fine," she huffed. "But Mitchell needs an answer from you by the end of the month on whether you're interested in the sitcom gig. He's doing this as a favor to me."

"I realize that." There was a pause as an elevator arrived. "There's just a few loose ends I need to tie up before I make my final decision."

"Good." Her voice was bright once more. "Pick me up at the gallery at eight." She spun on her heels and disappeared into the elevator.

Dissecting the conversation, I momentarily forgot where I was and what I was doing. Instead of taking Mercedes' departure as my cue to get out of there, I remained frozen in place, rooted to my perch. When Sebby started in my direction, I prayed to the gods of sleuthing that he wouldn't see me.

As if on cue, my phone began to ring and I hastily tried to silence the unmistakable voice of Kenny Loggins, drawing attention to myself as I clumsily reached for it, causing the branches of the tree to move with me.

Sebby looked in the direction of the tree, his torn expression turning into a genuine smile, the tension in his body melting off him. As he came closer to me, I squeezed my eyes shut and held my breath, as if that would prevent him from discovering me snooping on him and his girlfriend. There was nothing I could say that would explain my presence.

"Baylee?" I heard from behind as I kept my body turned in the direction of the elevators.

"Hmm? What?" I faced Sebby, making it appear as if he interrupted me doing something important.

Crossing his arms, he narrowed his eyes. "Do I even want to know what you're doing with that tree?"

"Just making sure it doesn't need any water."

"Mmm-hmm." He smirked, holding out his hand to help me up.

Grabbing onto it, I raised myself off the floor. "Well, this tree seems to be doing just fine." I wavered on my feet. The combination of the drinks I had consumed earlier and the sudden movement made me unbalanced.

"What are you doing here?" he asked, his brow furrowed.

"My uncle's in town and is staying here. We met up to have a few drinks."

"I see." He shuffled his feet, avoiding my eyes. A deafening silence settled between us, in stark contrast to the boisterous noise level in the lobby.

"Well, I should get going. Have a good night, Sebby." I turned from him and headed out the doors, smiling at the valet who had been waiting with my car for God knows how long at this point.

"I'm not going to New York!" Sebby declared loudly, following me outside.

I placed my hand on the roof of my car, hesitating briefly. Do I get into my car, leaving our conversation at that? Was it really any of my concern whether or not he was moving to New York? We were neighbors. Only neighbors.

"It's none of my business where you decide to live," I said, facing him. "But you need to really consider everything, Sebby. You can do your job from anywhere. You've said so yourself. Mercedes can't. If you really want things to work out between you two, don't you think you at least owe it to her to try?"

He approached me, the heat coming off his body warming me in the chilly night air. He looked at me in that way I often imagined a man would, the way Cary Grant looked at Deborah Kerr in *An Affair to Remember* when he found out the truth of what happened to prevent her from meeting him at the top of the Empire State Building. Time stood still and I wanted to stay in that moment. A moment where I forgot his heart belonged to someone else. A moment where we could finally act on the attraction that had grown stronger and more magnetic with each morning coffee, each crazy adventure. A moment where I could finally say to hell with just being friends and know what it felt like to be loved by someone.

"Maybe I *have* tried," he whispered. "Maybe I decided months ago that I didn't want it to work out anymore. Maybe I finally realized that I'd never be happy in New York, no matter what. Because..." He took a step closer, our bodies almost touching.

"Because...?" I swallowed hard.

"Because sometimes you need to fall in love with the wrong person. Sometimes you need to go through a failed relationship. If you know what it feels like to be with the wrong person, when the right person finally comes along, you can breathe again and say…"

He wrapped his arm around my waist and pulled me against him. This was so wrong. It went against everything I believed in, but all of my concerns had flitted away and were now strolling down Sunset Boulevard.

"Yes?" I whimpered, closing my eyes as I basked in Sebby's embrace. It felt as if I had finally found what I had been looking for my entire life.

"You can finally say, 'This is how it's supposed to feel'."

"How what's supposed to feel?" I craned my head back. Sebby's breath set fire to my lips, and every inch of me tingled with anticipation.

"Love," he murmured, his lips brushing mine. It was subtle, a ghost of a kiss.

"Sebby…," I exhaled, placing my hands on his firm chest.

"Yes?" He nuzzled my neck, making me want to drag him upstairs into one of the hotel's rooms. Returning from my trip to cloud nine, I pushed him away.

"Sometimes, Sebby…" I let out a breath. "Sometimes the grass may look greener on the other side, and maybe it is at first. Maybe it's something new and exciting, so it feels like you've finally found what you were missing for years. But then the novelty will wear off and you'll be left regretting everything."

"Are you really going to stand there and tell me you don't feel this?" His voice was powerful as he gestured between our bodies. "Tell me you feel nothing and I will happily return to just being friends…if that's even possible."

I wanted to say that I felt it, that I had never been so drawn to another man in my entire life, but I didn't. All I could think of was Mercedes and how she would react if Sebby left her for me. I couldn't turn her into me. Worse, I refused to let Sebby become a Will.

"I feel nothing," I uttered through a clenched jaw, spinning around.

"Bullshit," Sebby mumbled.

"What did you say?" I asked, facing him once more.

"You heard me." His eyes were narrowed and my heart raced at the fire and unyielding passion in his gaze. "I know you, Baylee, probably better than anyone else."

I scoffed, rolling my eyes.

"You can deny it all you want, but deep down, you know the truth. That you want this more than you've wanted anything. I get it. You're scared. So am I. I'm petrified of ruining one of the best friendships I've ever had because of the realization that, over the past few months, I've been unable to stop myself from falling in love with my best friend. But life is all about taking risks. I would think your mother's bucket list has taught you that. Think of all the experiences you would have missed out on if you didn't throw caution to the wind and live. And that's what I want to do. I want to show you how to live… How to laugh… How to love…and I'm not talking about what you've been led to *believe* love is. I'm talking about how to *really* love someone."

"You make it sound like you're so wise when it comes to this stuff, but you're just like everyone else…flirting with me even though you have a girlfriend! You don't know the first thing about love,

Sebby! If you did, you'd be up there with her, not out here with me!" I started to lower myself into my car. I wanted to rewind the clock to Saturday when I felt so free as I jumped from that plane, not a care in the world. Things were simpler twenty-four hours ago.

A hand grabbed my arm as I was about to get behind the wheel. Before I knew it, Sebby had me trapped against my car. "I know that I don't want to go another day without you next to me. I know that you fit in my arms better than anyone I've ever been with. I know that you make me happier than I've ever been in my life."

Before I could utter a word in protest, he crushed his lips against mine, his tongue invading my mouth. Fireworks erupted in my heart, in my veins, on my skin. His kiss was unlike anything I had ever experienced. It was electric. It was fulfilling. It was…magic. I wanted Sebby, but I was petrified I'd never find all the pieces that would be left if he broke my heart.

Just like he was breaking Mercedes' at this moment.

"We broke up," he murmured against my mouth.

My body stiffened and I flung my eyes open, unsure of whether I heard him correctly. "What?"

"I said," he began in a smooth voice, his arms still wrapped around me, "we broke up. We're not together. It's been over for weeks now."

I stared at him, shaking my head.

"That day you went to the farmer's market, then I came over and we cooked dinner together, you talked about how a relationship between two polar opposites is doomed to fail."

I swallowed hard.

"It made me think, Baylee. Before that, I was blind to all the tugging Mercedes was doing. I always thought if I didn't give her what she wanted, she'd think I didn't care about her like I did. But my happiness is just as important, so I ended things."

I gaped at him, incredulous at what he was telling me.

"I refused to stay in a relationship with her when my heart wanted someone else." He ran his fingers across my cheek, the contact welcome, albeit confusing.

Needing distance, I pushed away from him. "You haven't been together for weeks and didn't tell me? You watched me struggle with my guilt regarding my feelings toward you and didn't say anything?"

"I know it sounds stupid." He ran his hand through his hair. "At first, I didn't want you to know because I was worried things would change between us and get weird. After you found out I had a girlfriend, you were more carefree. I saw a side of you I hadn't been able to crack open during the previous weeks, and I tend to think it's because you thought you had to impress me."

I scoffed, crossing my arms in front of my chest. I refused to admit he was right.

"I knew I couldn't keep the truth from you forever. After a week, I decided to take a risk and see what happened. But you kept going on and on about how we were better as friends. And maybe you had a point. What if things didn't work out between us? I'd lose one of the best friendships I'd ever had. I wanted to take things to the next step with you, but I valued our friendship more. I regret not telling you from the start, but I'm rectifying that right now because I know what we have is unmatched anywhere. I know we're meant to be together."

I should have been thrilled with this news. It was exactly what I wanted. Instead, all I felt was betrayal all over again. My nostrils flaring, I spun from him, about to get into my car.

Sebby darted in front of me, stopping me. "I thought you'd be happy," he said. "I thought—"

"You lied to me!" I exclaimed.

"No!" he declared passionately. "I may have left out a few details because I didn't know how to tell you, but I never lied to you."

"A lie of omission is still a lie, Sebby," I murmured. After my last failed marriage, a marriage destroyed by a lie of omission, I couldn't put myself through that again, no matter what my heart thought it wanted.

"Baylee…" He wrapped his arm around my waist and pulled me close to him. I didn't fight it. After weeks of dreaming and fantasizing about what it would feel like to have his body pressed against mine, I couldn't resist him. "Don't you feel this, Baylee?" he asked, his voice husky as he ran his fingers down the contours of my abdomen, chills overtaking me. "It feels like…"

"Magic," I breathed, lost in the sensation of his lips whispering kisses down my neck. Closing my eyes, I flashed back to my life in North Carolina. After walking in on Will and my best friend banging on my kitchen island, I put on a front. I didn't want anyone to see how much his infidelity hurt. I had analyzed our marriage, trying to pinpoint where it all went wrong. As I did, I recalled some of our happier moments. They were all tainted by his lies, just as all my happy memories of my time with Sebby would be tainted with his dishonesty.

Letting out a long breath, I pressed my hands on

Sebby's chest, melting into him briefly. "But that's all it is… An illusion." I pushed him away and hopped into my car, peeling away from the hotel. As I looked in my rearview mirror, I saw him catch himself as he stumbled, confusion and heartbreak plastered on his face.

All the tears I had kept in streamed down my cheeks. Refusing to go home, where I'd only be faced with memories of Sebby, I drove around LA into the early hours of the morning, feeling as if my world were falling apart around me. When the sun came up and I was too exhausted to drive anymore, I finally returned to my condo. I half expected Sebby to bang on my door at some point during the day to confront me for my childish reaction. I didn't know what upset me more. That my stubbornness prevented me from admitting the truth, or that Sebby never showed up.

# CHAPTER TWENTY-FOUR

"WHAT'S UP WITH YOU, Baylee?" Uncle Monty asked as we sat at an upscale restaurant in Beverly Hills on Saturday, the last day of his visit. In a few hours, I'd be saying goodbye to him. I needed my life to return to some sort of normalcy, although I wasn't too sure what that was. The only normal I really had in my life in LA was Sebby. We hadn't spoken since he revealed the truth about his relationship with Mercedes. Every time I walked by his condo, I contemplated knocking on his door. I never did. My stubborn personality prevented it.

I had analyzed the situation with Sebby over and over throughout the past week. Maybe I was just overreacting. Maybe his failure to tell me the truth wasn't that big a deal in the grand scheme of things.

Then I remembered the guilt that consumed me whenever I tried to reconcile my feelings for him with the fact I was under the impression he had a girlfriend. He saw it plain as day, yet said nothing to assuage my feelings or remorse. I didn't know if I could ever forget that.

"Baylee. Earth to Baylee!"

I snapped out of my thoughts, returning to the present, only to be reminded of Sebby once more. Since the only exposure I had to the sites of LA was from hanging out with Sebby, the restaurant I was currently sitting in with my uncle was one I had been to with him.

"Hmm? What?" I stabbed my eggs benedict with my fork and knife. I didn't know how long I had been in a daze, but I had completely missed our server dropping off our meal.

Sighing, Uncle Monty threw his napkin on the table. "What's going on with you? You've been out of it all week. After our discussion at the hotel bar, I haven't been able to get you to talk about this neighbor of yours anymore."

"There's nothing to talk about," I shot back, shoveling a huge portion of egg, Canadian bacon, and English muffin into my mouth, as if it were the first time I had eaten in weeks.

"You can't pull the wool over my eyes," he said, his country accent coming through. "I've known you since you were in diapers. Hell, I changed quite a few of your shitty ones. Tell me what's *really* going on. It'll make you feel better."

"Doubtful," I mumbled.

"It's worth a shot. I'm not getting on that plane until you finally talk to me, even if it means delaying my flight this afternoon. It'll put me in a bit of a bind, considering I have a hearing scheduled for Monday morning, but family comes first."

I scowled. There was no arguing with my uncle. It was always a losing battle. Taking a long sip of my Bloody Mary, I swallowed the spicy drink, then wiped my mouth.

"Sebby and his girlfriend aren't together," I admitted softly.

"Really?" My uncle's eyes widened. "That's wonderful, Baylee!"

"Yeah. It's great." I rolled my eyes.

"It's what you wanted, isn't it?"

"Yes, but…" I slouched into my chair.

"But what?"

"He lied to me, Uncle Monty! They broke up weeks ago! Weeks! And he kept it from me, letting me believe they were still together. He saw me struggle with my guilt for how I felt about him and said nothing."

"And why's that?" he asked, resting his chin on his hands.

"He says it's because once I found out he was dating someone, I became more open and he didn't want to lose that side of me. Then he claims he was going to tell me but didn't because I kept going on and on about how we were better as friends and I wouldn't want to ruin our friendship. The only reason I kept saying that was for *my* benefit. I wanted to believe we were better off as just friends. It hurt knowing I had such strong feelings for this man and he couldn't be mine. Then I find out he could have been all along, but he never told me!"

My uncle considered my outburst for a moment. He was never a big talker. He always chose his words carefully, as if he only had a finite number he was permitted to use.

"And you think by him keeping this from you, he lied to you?"

I nodded.

He turned his head, watching people scurry up and down Rodeo Drive. It was the perfect late autumn day. The street lamps were decked out with garland and ribbons, signaling the start of the holiday shopping season. Returning his eyes to me, he grabbed my hand across the table.

"You know I love you, don't you?"

"Of course," I responded, shrinking into my chair. I had heard those words from him before, usually when he was about to berate me for being unreasonable, another trait he claimed I inherited from my mother.

"And you know I'll always support you, regardless of how asinine or impractical your decisions may be."

I nodded, swallowing hard.

"Then don't be upset when I tell you you're acting like a fucking child."

"What?" I straightened my spine, taken aback. I shouldn't have been surprised by his reaction, but his tone, almost a growl, was unexpected.

"Exactly what I said. Just a week ago, you were head over heels in love with this guy. You wanted to be with him and the only thing in your way was this girlfriend of his. And now that you've found that's no longer a problem, you've concocted some bullshit excuse."

"It's not bullshit!" I shot back, raising my voice slightly, but keeping it at a respectful level since we were in public. "It's the truth. He kept that information from me, just like Will kept his dick's propensity to fuck Julie from me. It's the same thing, and there's no way in hell I'm putting myself through that again!"

"It's not even *close* to being the same thing and you know it, Baylee Grace!" Uncle Monty exclaimed, his ears turning red, his nostrils flaring. Taking a breath to calm his Irish temper, he closed his eyes briefly before returning them to me. "I get it. You're scared."

"I'm not—"

He held his hand up, silencing me. "I've been where

you are. You feel such a strong connection to someone that you're worried you'll never survive if things don't work out, so you never take that leap. Regret can be a bitch, Baylee Grace. Believe me about that. Your mother wanted to live with no regrets. That's why she started that bucket list. Sure, she didn't get to check off everything, but at least she made the effort. She didn't let her fears stop her. You shouldn't, either," he finished, his voice low with a subtle tremble. His eyes glistened with unshed tears, and I couldn't help but think I was letting my mother down.

~~~~~~~~~~

AFTER I HAD SAID goodbye to my uncle and he left for the airport to catch his flight, his words still haunted me. Was I just blowing the situation out of proportion because of some subconscious fear? Was I willing to walk away from one of the best relationships I'd ever had because of what, according to my uncle, was an insignificant lie of omission? Would I be able to live with the regret of what could have been?

I knew the answer to all those questions. I needed to swallow my pride and talk to Sebby, apologize for overreacting, and beg for a second chance. I had already wasted so much time, I just hoped it wasn't too late.

Dashing through the lobby of my building, I pressed the elevator button, tapping my foot nervously as I waited for a car to arrive. Seconds seemed to stretch into hours, but no elevator came. I could feel my heart thumping in my chest. I had absolutely no idea what I was even going to say to Sebby. For someone who wanted to make a career out of words, I had writer's block when it came to my own life.

The elevator finally dinged and I rushed in, repeatedly hammering the button for the top floor. I bit my lower lip, watching the numbers above the elevator doors ascend higher and higher. Stopping on the top floor, the doors opened and I exited, rubbing my sweaty hands on my skirt. I paused in the vestibule, taking in my appearance in the large gold-framed mirror directly across from me. At least I looked somewhat presentable…the upside of having just gotten back from brunch in Beverly Hills. Smoothing the lines of my blouse, I reached into my purse and popped a mint in my mouth, trying to mask the smell of tomato juice, pepper, and Worcestershire sauce. Oh, and vodka.

Drawing in a long breath, I steeled myself for what I was about to do. It needed to happen now. If I walked past his condo and into mine, I didn't know if I'd ever have the nerve to knock on Sebby's door and confess my true feelings.

So, with determined but timid steps, I strode down the hallway and knocked on his door. I expected to hear Gidget barking. Instead, silence greeted me. When I didn't hear the drumming of his footsteps toward the door, I knocked again.

Still nothing.

I rang the doorbell.

At last, from somewhere within, light feet echoed, the sound growing louder as they approached the door. I rubbed my clammy hands on my skirt once more and braced myself for the conversation I was about to have. When the door opened, I started to speak, only to be dumbstruck by the tall blonde staring back at me, dressed in a Mets jersey and not much else. Her hair was disheveled, the complete opposite of her appearance during our previous encounters. She had that just rolled out of bed look, and my nostrils flared as I bit my lip.

"Oh, good morning, Becky," Mercedes said. "Hope you weren't waiting out here long. We were still sleeping. Late night last night." She smirked.

"My name is *Baylee*," I hissed through a clenched jaw. "And it's two in the afternoon."

"Right. So what can I do for you?"

"I came to see Sebby."

"I assumed as much. He's still asleep."

I paused, glaring. "Well, have him stop by my condo when he gets up." I gestured with my head to my door. "It's important."

"I will, but he has a meeting with the executive producers of a sitcom he'll be producing soon, then we have to catch the red-eye back to New York."

*We?* I thought. Did I miss my window of opportunity? When I told Sebby there would never be an "us", did he go running back to Mercedes the same night?

"When will he be back?"

"Oh, I'm sure he'll come back to finish packing up here."

"What do you mean?" I asked, my heart in my throat.

"You don't think he's going to live out here if he's producing that sitcom, do you? It's based out of New York. It's about time he smartened up." Her cell phone chimed in her hand and she peered down at the screen before returning her attention to me. "Busy day. I'll tell

Sebby you stopped by. Goodbye, Becky." She closed the door in my face, leaving me more confused than I was a week ago. I couldn't believe he was moving to New York without so much as a goodbye.

Tearing across the hall, I shoved my key into the door of my condo and flung it open. I paced the living room, Sport on my heels every step of the way, unable to shake the feeling that something didn't seem right, especially after our last conversation. I pulled my phone out of my purse and dialed Sebby's number, my heartbeat echoing in my ears as I listened to it ring once. Then twice. When the voicemail picked up, I knew he had sent my call there, not wanting to talk to me. In a last-ditch effort, I composed a short text.

*Sebby, I need to talk to you. Please call before you leave for New York. I still believe in magic.*

I slipped out of my shoes and flopped onto my couch, remaining there the rest of the day, staring at my phone, hoping Sebby would call. But he never did. As the clock neared nine in the evening, I tried to call him one more time, but it went straight to voicemail. I knew he was probably at 35,000 feet on his way to New York and his new life with Mercedes.

I stared at the television directly in front of me, trying to summon tears, but they wouldn't fall. I had done this to myself. It was times like these I wished my mother were alive so I could pick up the phone and ask for advice. My father had always insisted she was watching over me and all I had to do was look for a sign. Whenever he was at a crossroads in his life, he would look up at the sky and say, "Show me the way, Gracie May." Up until the day he died, he swore my mother never truly left him, that she was always looking down on us, guiding us.

Now, as I stared at the television in front of me, I started to think perhaps my father was onto something. Maybe there was such a thing as fate, as universal signs. Maybe my mother was sending me a sign that Sebby wasn't my someday. Maybe my someday was a tall, dark, handsome man with a sexy Irish brogue. I had never had one of those "a-ha" moments, but as I stared at a commercial promoting Irish tourism, the lush green hillsides of the Irish isles calming the heartache for a moment, I wondered whether this was one of those signs, too. Maybe my mom was trying to tell me I had it all wrong, that all my random chance encounters with Sebby were just that. Maybe fate had a different agenda.

Reaching for my cell and making a call that was out of pure desperation, as opposed to desire, I dialed Owen's number, remembering he had just returned from his trip overseas earlier in the day. I prayed he answered. I didn't know if I could handle yet another rejection today. I had never been one of those girls who needed to be in a relationship to know her self-worth, but at that moment, I needed *someone* to make me feel what I had been missing most of my life. I needed to feel magic.

~~~~~~~~~~

"OWEN." I STOOD UP from the stool in a trendy bar down the street from my condo. Thankfully, Owen had answered when I called, agreeing to meet me for a drink. I would have been lying if the thought of getting drunk enough to invite him back to my place didn't cross my mind. It felt wrong, so I prayed the numbing effect of the alcohol would work its magic.

"Hey, Baylee," he responded in that adorable Irish brogue that was like a key to a virgin's chastity belt. He leaned in toward me and I closed my eyes, expecting to feel his lips on mine. Instead, he turned at the last second, placing a friendly kiss on my cheek.

I stiffened at his brush-off, but hid my unease. Smiling, I retook my seat and signaled for the bartender, wanting to appear confident and fearless.

"How was your trip?" I asked after he took a sip of the dark ale he had ordered.

"Good, but it's always nice to be back home, especially after that long flight."

I nodded, taking a drink of my own beer. There was a stalemate between us that hadn't existed during our two previous dates. There was no chemistry. No spark.

No magic.

*This whole sign stuff is a bunch of shit.*

"I can imagine." I turned my eyes forward, watching some football game on the large overhead screen. I acted like I was invested in the outcome of the matchup when, in all reality, I didn't care who won. I couldn't even tell you which teams were playing. I just needed something to take my attention away from the heavy silence that settled between us.

"You got back in this morning, right?"

"Sure did. Still fighting jet-lag, but at least the beer will help me sleep tonight. It always takes me a few days to get set right again."

I laughed politely, glancing at him briefly before turning my eyes forward again. I ran my finger across the condensation on the pilsner glass, but it didn't take my mind off feeling as if there were an ocean between us.

"Thanks for meeting me tonight," I said finally. "I mean, with your jet-lag and everything, you could have just stayed home and slept it off—"

"And I thought about doing that," he interrupted. "Hell, when your number popped up on my caller ID, I almost didn't answer."

"But you did." My voice was steady with a twinge of hope. I met his eyes, trying to force my heart to beat a little faster, my lungs to breathe a little heavier, but I couldn't.

"I did."

"Why?" I wanted him to say how much he missed me, how he just couldn't stop thinking about me while he was gone.

"Did Cora tell you how old I am?" he asked. I shook my head. "Do you want to guess?"

"Not really. That's always a losing battle."

"Right you are." He trained his eyes on his half-full beer. "Well, I'm older than you by probably more than fifteen years, Baylee."

My eyes grew wide. I had estimated him to be in his thirties. He looked damn good for being in his forties.

"And when you reach a certain age, you stop wasting your time on relationships you know aren't going anywhere."

"What do you—?"

"I like you, Baylee." He grabbed my hand in his, his thumb caressing my knuckles. Our eyes met and we shared a look. In that instant, I knew he knew. "A lot, which is strange for me, considering we've only been out a few times. You're spunky, a breath of fresh air. I couldn't stop thinking about you when I was gone last week."

"I like you, too, Owen," I admitted, although I didn't mean it the way he probably did.

He held his hand up. "Do you?"

"What do you mean by that?" I scrunched my eyebrows.

"Like I've said, part of being a good photographer is seeing things most people can't. That's how you get those one-of-a-kind photographs no one else can come close to capturing. And I wish I had my camera during our last date so I could capture the look on your face when you left with me instead of your neighbor…"

I opened my mouth, trying to come up with a response, but I couldn't.

"It's okay, Baylee. I just don't think it's fair to either one of us to continue seeing each other when it's obvious you're not into me."

I tore my eyes from his. "I'm sorry. I guess I was hoping the more time I spent with you, the more I'd want to be with you, but—"

"It doesn't work that way," he interrupted.

"I know," I agreed. "I didn't mean to lead you on."

"You didn't." Throwing enough cash on the bar to cover our drinks, he stood up. "I wish you all the luck, no matter where life takes you." He planted a kiss on my forehead, then turned and left me.

*Alone again*, I thought to myself.

# CHAPTER TWENTY-FIVE

THE WEEKS LEADING UP to Christmas always seemed to fly by, but it was particularly true this year. It was my first Christmas in California and I thought how strange it was to see a palm tree decorated with hundreds of twinkling lights. It made me a little homesick.

After Sebby's unexpected departure from LA and Owen's rejection, I kept to myself, telling everyone who called or visited that I was on a deadline to finish writing my book. It wasn't true, but it gave me a plausible excuse to be alone. Every day, I would write several thousand words, then delete them that evening. My mood affected everything I did. What was once a light romance had taken on a dark and melancholy vibe. One of the most important elements of a romance novel was that there be a happily ever after. I didn't know how I could write about something I struggled to find myself.

One Friday afternoon a week before Christmas, my cell buzzed with a new text. Seeing it was from Marcel, I scowled, tossing my phone to the other side of the couch, ignoring his message. But something about that moment made me rethink my recent behavior. Maybe my mother's spirit was close by, finally slapping me upside the head and smacking some sense into me. Maybe I was tired of always feeling sorry for myself. Maybe it was from watching the Grinch's heart on my television grow three sizes. I didn't know precisely what caused it, but I suppressed the heartache I had allowed to consume me. I had moved out to California to finally live again. Remaining on my couch all day long wasn't living.

Grabbing my phone, I opened Marcel's text.

*Hey Dixie. I know you're upset about you know who and that's why you haven't been around. I don't believe your writing excuse for a second. We miss you. Don't celebrate Christmas alone. We're having our Christmas party tonight at Sophia's. We would all love to see you. Please think about it.*

I knew what I had to do. I had to bury my pride and go see my friends. And also come up with one hell of an apology.

~~~~~~~~~~

BOISTEROUS VOICES ECHOED IN the hallway as I approached Sophia's condo that evening. I could hear Christmas carols in the background, which were almost drowned out by Marcel's theatrical retelling of his latest drama-filled client. Drawing in a deep breath, I placed my hand on the doorknob and turned, pushing the door open and taking a few steps into the foyer. All the chatter stopped immediately and everyone turned their heads in my direction. The entire gang was there...Sophia, Darren, Cora, Lacey, Marcel, and even his new beau.

Seeing them all, compassion and understanding etched on their faces, I regretted my childish behavior of the past several weeks. True, things with Sebby hadn't ended the way I would have liked, but was it necessary to shut out the people who had become my family just because they all knew him? I knew it wasn't.

"I'm sorry I'm such a horrible friend," I blurted out.

Arms instantly wrapped around me from every direction, forgiveness filtering through the group embrace. This was what I needed weeks ago, but my thick-headedness got in the way.

"It's okay, Dixie." Marcel kissed the top of my head. "Real friends won't abandon you, even when you try to lie to us. You can't get rid of us that easily."

I nodded. "Next time I let a guy come between us, slap me." I grabbed the glass of wine Sophia handed me.

When the familiar sound of paws on hardwood echoed, I snapped my head in the direction of the hallway, my eyes growing wide when I saw Gidget running toward me. Her tail wagging, she jumped up on me and I hugged her, showering her with affection.

"What's she doing here?" I asked, scratching between her ears.

Sophia shrugged. "It's just temporary. Sebby didn't want to put her in cargo on the plane, so I agreed to keep her until he had time to drive her back to New York with him."

"That sounds like something Sebby would do," I added thoughtfully.

She nodded and I was lost in the crowd of my friends once more. I spent the next few hours catching up with all of them. We hadn't spent any time together since we all went skydiving, which seemed like ages ago instead of just weeks. Lacey showed me her latest tattoo and, after several glasses of wine, I agreed to get one. I had no idea what I wanted to brand onto my body for all eternity, but she assured me her "guy" was the best in LA and would work with me on whatever piece of art I wanted memorialized on my skin.

Marcel and his beau, Nicholas, had gotten pretty serious, even talking about possibly moving in together. My heart warmed when he shared this news. I hadn't known Marcel for long, but the night he met Nicholas, there was this lightness in him I hadn't seen before.

"Help me open some champagne, Baylee," Sophia called, interrupting another one of Darren's stories about some crazy assignment he was on. I glanced at her, the look on her face letting me know she wanted a moment alone with me. I kind of wanted a minute to talk to her, too. I wondered how much Sebby had told her about what happened. By the questioning, yet concerned look on her face as I approached, I figured not too much.

Clutching my arm, she pulled me into the corner of her kitchen where we both set to the task of filling the crystal flutes she had arranged on her poured cement countertops. I had a feeling Marcel did the remodel on her condo, too. He loved poured cement.

"Sebby refused to tell me what happened between the two of you. Technically, he's still my boss, so I couldn't beat it out of him. But you're not, so I *can* beat it out of you. What the hell happened?"

I shrugged, avoiding her eyes, focusing on pouring the champagne into each of the flutes. "Nothing. I found out he was lying to me about Mercedes this entire time."

Sophia nodded slowly, understanding washing over her expression. "No woman likes being lied to, even if it is just a lie of omission."

"That's exactly what I told him!" I exclaimed,

facing her. It was about time someone agreed with me. Smirking, she placed her hands on her hips. I let out a long breath. "You're fucking with me, aren't you?"

"For the record, I didn't find out about the breakup until Thanksgiving. None of us did. But if you're ready to throw away a friendship based on what you perceive to be a lie, be my guest. Remember, though. Regret is a bitch."

"My uncle told me the same thing."

"So why did you give Sebby the cold shoulder? You should have seen how heartbroken and dejected he was on the way to the airport. God, that was the longest drive ever, even though there was no traffic."

I furrowed my brow. "You drove him and Mercedes to the airport? I thought you couldn't stand her."

"Mercedes? Hell no. From my understanding, she and Sebby had a bit of a falling out."

I blinked repeatedly, trying to figure out what was going on. "It didn't look like that was the case when I went to apologize and she answered wearing one of his Mets jerseys that didn't leave a whole lot to the imagination."

"When was this?" Sophia asked, her voice rising.

"The Sunday after Thanksgiving. I had brunch with my uncle, who told me I was being thick-headed. So I went over to Sebby's to apologize and Mercedes was there. She said he agreed to produce a sitcom out in New York and they were leaving that night."

"Unbelievable," Sophia muttered. "He was over here the night before. Darren got him pretty hammered and we had to help him back to his condo. The following day, I went over there to check on him and take Gidget for a walk. When I got back, Mercedes was there, grabbing a few of her things that she had left there while they were together."

I swallowed hard, my heart falling into my stomach. "So he's not back with Mercedes?"

"No." She gave me a knowing look. "And he didn't go to New York to produce a sitcom. He's in talks with one of the networks to produce for the NFL."

My momentary flash of hope quickly deflated. "Then he *is* moving there. It's been his dream to produce for the NFL for years. I can't interfere with that."

"Baylee..." Sophia placed her hand on my shoulder. "I like you. I love Sebby, and I adore the idea of you guys together. It seems that, for the longest time, the universe has plotted against the two of you. Or maybe it was both of your own thick-headedness that did that. It doesn't matter. But I don't think Sebby moved to New York for the job. He could do that from anywhere. I think there was another reason he left, and I think you know what that was."

I nodded. I had barely left my condo the past month, everything about LA bringing forward another memory of my ruined friendship, but it still wasn't enough. He had invaded my life so fully and completely, it was impossible to find one part of my existence that didn't remind me of him...of us.

"So what are you going to do?" She crossed her arms in front of her chest, tilting her head.

I hesitated, unsure of what to do with all the new information I had. But did it change anything?

"Nothing." I sighed heavily. "After I went over to his place, I called and texted him, but he never answered. Maybe he's moving on. I can't fault him for that."

"Think about it, Baylee! Sebby was absolutely hammered that Saturday night. When I went to get Gidget, he was practically comatose. A magnitude eight earthquake couldn't have woken him up. And he was in the same shape when I dropped Gidget off a few hours later."

"You don't think…" I trailed off.

"I do. The Mercedes I had gotten to know whenever she came out here to visit Sebby, which wasn't often, always had to win at everything…including relationships. It must have killed her to know she lost to you, so when you appeared at Sebby's door, it gave her the perfect opportunity to gain the upper hand. I wouldn't put it past her to delete your voicemails and texts so Sebby would never get them."

"You don't know that for sure."

"No, I don't, but live a little. Haven't you learned that sometimes you have to take a risk and jump?"

She raised her eyebrows and I stared at her, considering her words. There was a chance Sebby wanted nothing to do with me after my reaction to his confession. *If you can't tell someone you love them, what's the point of everything?* I thought. With a spark in my eyes and a flutter in my chest, I spun from Sophia, heading toward the foyer.

"Where are you going?" she called out.

"To take a jump and live." Smiling, I placed my hand on the doorknob.

"Wait!" Sophia shouted and I stopped. She grabbed a piece of paper off her kitchen island and jotted something down on it. Approaching me, she placed it in my hand. "The address of the hotel Sebby's been staying at in Manhattan until he can find a place to live. It might come in handy." She winked. "And don't come back without him."

I smiled. "I don't plan on it."

# CHAPTER TWENTY-SIX

*I had my final appointment with my OB this morning. She said our daughter is progressing well, but because of my deteriorating health, it's best that I be induced while I still have a modicum of the strength that is necessary to go through labor. Of course, I've been warned things may not go according to plan. Nothing ever does, does it? I didn't plan to get cancer. I didn't plan to leave Perry to grow old without me. I didn't plan to never know my daughter.*

*Unfortunately, we're all dealt different cards in life. Nothing is certain. Tomorrow isn't guaranteed, especially mine, particularly based on how I've been feeling. I can barely get out of bed these days. Perry has to help me shower. I can see in his eyes how weak I've gotten. As I lay awake during the nights when the pain keeps me from slumber, I can hear his quiet sobs. I pretend I'm asleep so he doesn't know I can hear his prayers.*

*At this point, no amount of praying can stop the path I've chosen.*

*This past month, I've thought a lot about regret. A million what-ifs have floated through my mind. What if I never got pregnant? Would I have had a fighting chance with aggressive chemotherapy? What if I followed my doctor's advice and aborted the baby to potentially save my own life? Do I regret any of the decisions I've made?*

*The answer has been a resounding no, although there are times I do wish I wasn't pregnant so I could take medication to relieve the pain of the cancer eating away at my body. The only thing I do regret is the heartache I'm causing Perry but, in my heart, I know that will all become a distant memory when he holds our daughter for the first time. I'm sacrificing my own life to give him a legacy, a piece of both of us. Through her, I will live on.*

*So, my lovely Baylee Grace, if this journal finds its way to you one day, as I hope it will, here's what I wish for you...*

*May you find beauty in the world that surrounds you, even when things aren't going your way.*

*May you have a sense of adventure, whether it be dancing in the rain or bungee jumping. Experience everything the world has to offer.*

*May you find something you love doing and be able to make a life out of that passion because life without passion isn't a life worth living.*

*May you confront your fears head-on and not cower in the face of adversity.*

*Most importantly, may you love. Love hard and without abandon. Love with no regrets. Love like there's no tomorrow. For so many people, there isn't a tomorrow. Don't take it for granted.*

Swallowing hard, tears ran down my cheeks in the darkness of a Boeing 737 as I read my mother's final journal entry. I peered out the window as we flew across the country, nothing but emptiness below me. After leaving Sophia's, I had gone straight to my condo and threw some clothes into a small suitcase. I then booked the first flight to New York I could get, and four hours later, I was sitting in a first-class seat on a red-eye to JFK. Now, as the plane sped closer and closer to our destination, I wondered if I had been rash in dropping everything and going to find Sebby. Then I re-read my mother's final line...

*For so many people, there isn't a tomorrow. Don't take it for granted.*

That was exactly what I planned on doing. From this day forward, I would live with no regrets. I would face my fears head-on, regardless of the possible outcome. Sebby could very well slam the door in my face, but that was a risk I had to take. I refused to wonder "what if". I refused to question whether Sebby really was my someday. In my heart, I knew he was.

The wheels of the plane touched down just after sunrise. There was a pink glow to the sky, snow visible on the rooftops as we made our descent. The cold hit me like a stone wall when I disembarked. I had been so spoiled living in California, I forgot what a real winter felt like. It took my breath away. I pulled my jacket closer, rushing to get off the jet bridge as quickly as possible.

I exited into the busy terminal, surprised at how packed it was at just a little after seven in the morning. Every gate area I passed was swarming with travelers waiting to board their flights. The overhead speakers rattled with a different announcement every few seconds. It was a rude awakening after having spent the last five hours on board a peaceful flight wearing noise-canceling headphones.

This was only the start of the hustle and bustle because I was soon in the comfort of a chauffeured town car and on my way to the heart of Manhattan. Traffic was at a crawl as my driver navigated the streets of New York City. Horns honked all around me, making me think no one would even pay attention to hearing a car's horn, not with how liberally they were used out here.

I craned my head to look at the tall buildings surrounding me. They kept going up and up, almost disappearing into the clouds. I felt claustrophobic staring at these skyscrapers and enclosed city streets. I had no idea why anyone would want to live here. I needed space, air to breathe. People scurried along the sidewalks, covering almost every square inch of space. It was overwhelming and underwhelming at the same time. This was nowhere for Sebby to live. I was completely uninspired. For someone as creative and imaginative as Sebby, I was sure he felt it, too.

Deep in thought, I was in a world all my own when my driver came to a stop. At first, I simply thought it was more traffic. Then he got out and came around to the rear passenger side and opened my door, helping me out. I tilted my head back, soaking in the enormous building in front of me as snowflakes began to fall.

"Welcome to the Waldorf Astoria." A voice cut through my observations. I snapped back to reality and looked at the doorman in front of me.

"Thank you." I headed toward the front doors with slow steps. Golden light escaped through large windows and doors, illuminating the sidewalk and everything else around the magnificent building.

My eyes wide in awe, I walked into the hotel, trying to soak everything in. The lobby was pristine, that golden light even brighter inside. A lavish crystal chandelier was the centerpiece, successfully announcing to everyone who stepped foot in the hotel that this was *the* place to stay in New York City. I had never seen anything so grandiose.

Mesmerized by the chandelier, I forgot where I was and what I was doing...until I stumbled over the leg of a table, which probably cost more than my college education, and fell into a tall, dark suit. Thankfully, Mr. Tall Dark Suit was quick on his feet, wrapping his arms around my waist before I could break my own fall…and probably my ass, too.

"Whoa, there." He steadied me, helping me back on my feet.

Once I had my footing, I brushed myself off, trying to hide my embarrassment. "Thanks. I wasn't really paying atten—"

"Baylee?"

I shot my head up at the sound of that familiar voice.

"Sebby?" My eyes widened. I had come here to see him, but I didn't think I'd run into him in the lobby. I expected to have to sell my soul to bribe the front desk staff for his room number. Maybe this was a sign. Maybe I had just been ignoring all the signs for too long. Maybe all our random chance encounters throughout our friendship had happened for a reason.

It had been nearly a month since I had seen him. He looked the same, although his hair had grown out and he was sporting a bit more scruff than usual. He wore a dark suit that was perfectly tailored to his body. I had become so used to seeing him in his normal attire of a t-shirt and cargo shorts, I barely recognized him.

"How have you been?" he finally asked. His eyes were warm. The way he looked at me made me feel as if I were the only woman in the room. And I had a feeling I was in Sebby's eyes, even after everything that had transpired between us.

"Good," I replied. "You?"

"Good."

Another awkward silence passed.

"Listen, I—" I began.

"Baylee, I—" Sebby said at the same time. We both laughed nervously. "You go first."

I took a small breath, trying to sort through what I wanted to say. I had the perfect speech planned, but now that I was standing in front of him, I was tongue-tied. I envisioned doing this somewhere private, not in the lobby where anyone passing by could overhear.

"Sophia told me where you were staying while you looked for an apartment in the city."

Sebby looked down, avoiding my eyes.

"Congratulations on the NFL job. You must be thrilled."

"I am," he answered reluctantly, giving me a small, forced smile. He looked pained, not like someone who had just landed his dream job.

"Really looks like it." I rolled my eyes, laughing nervously.

Running his hand through his hair, he shifted from foot to foot. "I wanted to tell you about it, but..." He trailed off.

"I get it," I said. "I acted like a complete idiot, but you could have called, Sebby. I stopped by your condo the Sunday after Thanksgiving and Mercedes answered the door."

"She what?" His shoulders tensed.

"I thought you were back together. I texted and called that same day, but never got an answer. Sophia said you got pretty drunk the night before, so we just figured Mercedes deleted my text and voicemail."

He shook his head, his jaw clenching.

"But we can't change that," I said, not wanting to dwell on it. "The last time we spoke, we didn't exactly leave on the best of terms—"

"You could say that," he interrupted.

"And I realized I was just scared." I grabbed his hands in mine, pulling him close to me. "When I thought you were off limits, it was safer to love you because I knew we would only be friends, nothing more. Then when I found out the truth, it hurt…"

He stepped back, pulling his hands from my grasp. "Baylee, I'm—"

"Sorry. I know. But I get it now. We got to know each other as friends first, without bringing in all that relationship stuff. I fell in love with you as a friend, and then…" I looked away, swallowing hard.

"And then what?"

I drew a long breath. "And then I fell in love with you as more than a friend. You opened my eyes to so much that I had been happy to ignore for years. You showed me what real love should be like."

"And how's that?"

Smiling, I peered into his eyes. "Real love is jumping out of a plane when you're scared to death, but you do it anyway. Real love is spending time with that person and being happy in the silence. But mostly, real love is sharing parts of yourself with each other, pieces of you no one else gets to have. I always pushed to just stay friends, but I can't do that anymore, Sebby. I'm not happy with just being friends. I want more than that from you."

On edge, I gauged his reaction to my confession. I finally took a risk. I was ready to get my ass kicked by love. It was what my mother would have done.

"Baylee…" He let out a long sigh, running his hands through his hair. My heart dropped to my stomach. Sebby had the look that said "thanks for pouring your heart out to me, Baylee, but you should have just saved your breath". He had the look of someone who had fallen out of love, someone who had moved on. "After I told you everything and you shut me out, I didn't know what to do. I would walk around my condo and feel you everywhere. No matter what I did, no matter where I went, it brought back memories of time I spent with you. The way we left things, I just couldn't be around any of that, so I decided to finally listen to Mercedes and move back to New York."

My shoulders dropped at the mention of that name. I wondered if they were back together now that he was living here.

"I tried to forget about you. I tried to forget about dog walks, farmer's markets, and throwing pizza dough. Over the past month, I did everything I could to let go of those memories."

Nodding, I closed my eyes, fighting the urge to cry.

"But then I realized from the moment you gave me that bloody nose all those months ago, I gave you a piece of myself. I fought it at first, trying to convince myself that Mercedes was the perfect woman for me, but I knew I was wrong."

I opened my eyes, staring into his. He stepped toward me, pulling my body close to his. His musky aroma met my senses, transporting me back to that fateful day when I was the new girl in town and made a complete fool of myself in front of a handsome man with a dog named Gidget.

He cupped my face and brushed away the lone tear

that had escaped. "You're the first person I think of when I wake up. When I go about my day, I'm constantly wondering what you're doing at that precise moment. When I go to sleep, I can't help but hope that I'm one day closer to convincing you I'm worth the risk."

Raising my eyebrows, I smirked. "That *we're* worth the risk?"

A brilliant smile crossed his lips. "Yes, Baylee Grace," he crooned. "That we're worth the risk."

Tilting my head, I met his eyes. Time stood still as I lost myself in his arms, in his presence, in his everything. Licking his lips, he lowered his mouth to mine, and I finally felt what a real kiss should feel like. It was the perfect combination of forceful and reserved. In that one moment, his tongue exploring my mouth, I felt how much he needed and revered me. In that one kiss, I finally felt what I had been yearning to feel for years…

I felt magic.

# CHAPTER TWENTY-SEVEN

SUN STREAMING THROUGH LARGE windows woke me from the most wonderful dream I could remember. I had hopped on a plane to New York and confronted Sebby. I stopped being stubborn and told him my true feelings. I took a risk. Jumping out of a plane had nothing on traveling three thousand miles and pouring my heart out to the one person whom I couldn't imagine life without. So it was understandable how I would want to curse the sun for waking me up from that dream.

I stirred, knowing Sport would want to go out. When a strong arm wrapped around my stomach, I stilled. My eyes flung open and I rolled over, yelping when I saw Sebby lying next to me.

"Morning," he crooned lazily, running his fingers through my hair in an attempt to pull me back into his arms. The previous day came racing back to me. Coming to New York. Falling into Sebby when I tripped over my own feet in the lobby of the Waldorf. Kissing Sebby. Having pastrami on rye with Sebby. Skating in Rockefeller Center with Sebby. Then coming up to his suite and doing lots of other things with Sebby. I had the sore legs to prove it.

Smiling, I settled back into his arms, pulling the sheet up to cover my mouth. I wasn't sure if we were at that point in our relationship where it was appropriate for him to smell my morning breath. I didn't want to scare him off.

"Morning," I repeated.

He chuckled, the low rumble sexy and raspy. "Baylee, I love you, morning breath and all. Hell, if that snoring didn't scare me off, I don't think anything will."

I shot up from the bed, bringing the sheet with me to cover myself. "I was *snoring?*"

Grinning, he shook his head and pulled me back down beside him. "No. But even if you were, I'd still love you."

I sighed, melting into him. "Say it again."

"I love you, Baylee Grace Morgan."

"And I love you, Sebastian..." I scowled. "I don't even know your middle name."

He cringed. "That's not important."

"Tell me!" I pinched his sides and he struggled against me. I wasn't going to let this one go.

"Nope. Not going to happen."

A mischievous look crossing my face, I eyed the nightstand on his side of the bed...where his wallet was conveniently placed. With one quick motion, I rolled on top of him and reached for the wallet, flipping it open to reveal his driver's license before he could react.

"Bernard?!" I exclaimed, turning to him, beaming.

He shook his head, burying it in his hands. "I really didn't want you to find that out."

"I don't blame you, Bernard." I chuckled, falling back onto the bed beside him.

"You're never going to let me live this down, are you?"

I snuggled into his arms and hovered my lips over his. "Your name could be Asshole and I'd still love you."

His lips met mine for a quick exchange before I pulled back, furrowing my brow.

"You don't have another middle name I don't know about, do you? It's not Asshole, right?"

"Well, now that you bring it up…," he joked, his eyes bright.

Giggling, I returned to Sebby's arms, where I was meant to be. He brushed his hand through my hair, planting soft kisses on my head.

"Someday begins today."

# EPILOGUE

## One Year Later

SNOW FELL AROUND US as Sebby led me from our cab toward Bethesda Fountain in Central Park. The city was bustling with New Year's Eve festivities, but the park was calm, apart from the occasional tourist strolling through. It almost seemed fitting that this would be the last item I had to cross off my mother's bucket list.

The past year had been the happiest of my life. Sebby returned to California and started his job producing for the NFL. I had been in the control booth for a few games and finally understood why he loved doing this, as opposed to working on movies. It was heart-thumping to watch everything fall together during a live broadcast.

Earlier in the year, I finally finished my book. After a few offers from publishing houses, thanks to Sebby's contacts, I decided to self-publish instead. This story was the result of months and months of doubt and sleepless nights. I wanted to stay true to myself. While it wasn't an instant bestseller, I didn't care. I did something most people would never have the tenacity to do. Better yet, I finally had someone who supported me through it every step of the way, never uttering one discouraging word.

Unzipping the backpack he had slung over his shoulder, Sebby grabbed a large blanket and laid it on the ground. He helped lower me onto it and I stared at the fountain, the lights surrounding it bringing attention to the tiny snowflakes falling around us. Most people would want to watch the ball drop in Times Square to bring in the New Year. Not my mother. Now I understood why. There was something romantic about this setting and I hated that she never got to bring in the New Year this way. Still, I hoped she was watching over me and was able to experience it through me.

"Beautiful, isn't it?" Sebby commented, handing me a glass of champagne.

"It is," I responded, pulling my jacket tighter. He wrapped his arm around me as I continued to stare at the falling snow blanketing the ground with a soft cloak.

"Now what?" he asked after several comfortable moments passed.

"What do you mean?"

"Well, now that you're done with your mother's list, what are you going to do?"

I shrugged. The truth was, I had been thinking about that a lot lately. That list had been my compass the past year of my life. I worried I wouldn't know what to do with myself if I didn't have it guiding me toward my next adventure. But the more I thought about it, the more I knew that list was just a start. "I guess it's time for me to find my next big adventure."

"Any ideas what you think that may be?"

I shook my head. "No. But I'm sure it will come to me."

"I have an idea."

"And what's that?" I asked, eyeing him.

Turning from me, he grabbed the bag and rummaged through it, his back toward me.

"Me," he said, turning back around. My heart jumped into my throat when my eyes fell on a small velvet box containing a stunning round-cut diamond solitaire with diamonds embedded into the double band. "I want to be your next adventure. Together, we'll create our own new adventures. From the minute we met, I knew you were someone worth getting to know, and I'm sorry I was such a dumbass for the longest time."

I laughed, rolling my eyes. "You definitely were. I told you men and women couldn't just be friends."

"They can, but that's beside the point. I want to make up for all the time I lost with you because of our little misunderstanding. When I picture my future, I see you. And I know you see me. So please, Baylee Grace…" He grabbed my left hand and slid my glove off. Bringing the ring up to my finger, he said, "Marry me. Be my next adventure."

For the longest time, I had been hesitant to even consider marriage after my previous failed one. But as I sat there, staring at the pleading look on Sebby's face, I knew this time would be different. I thought about everything I had been through since leaving North Carolina and moving to California. I no longer recognized the girl I was back then and I knew I had Sebby to thank for that. He had opened my eyes and my heart to what could be. He did what he promised he would. He had shown me how to live.

My heart full of gratitude, I nodded. "Yes."

"Yes?"

"Of course! What did you think I'd say? Fuck off?" I flung my arms around him, clumsily hitting his nose in my excitement.

His hand covered it immediately as blood poured down his face. My jaw dropped in horror before we both burst out laughing.

"I love you, Dixie," he declared, clutching my cheeks in his blood-covered gloves.

"And I love you, Nosebleeder."

We sat and watched the snow fall, blood continuing to trickle from Sebby's nose, and talked about everything and nothing. It reminded me of the early days when I didn't even know he was my neighbor. Our love didn't happen overnight. It grew with each encounter, each joke, each smile. As the clock struck midnight and the year came to a close, I couldn't wait to see what the future held...now that I had found my other side of someday.

# The End

# Playlist

*Gonna Get Over You* - Sara Bareilles
*Blue Eyes* - Cary Brothers
*Mr. Night* - Kenny Loggins
*Backtrack* - Rebecca Ferguson
*Like A Virgin* - Madonna
*Don't You (Forget About Me)* - Simple Minds
*Red Headed Woman* - Bruce Springsteen
*Girls Chase Boys* - Ingrid Michaelson
*Time Warp* - Rocky Horror Picture Show
*Feel Again* - OneRepublic
*I Love L.A.* - Randy Newman
*Carolina* - Matt Wertz
*The Rebound* - Tristan Prettyman
*Forget About Joni* - Eric Hutchinson
*The Bitch Is Back* - Elton John
*Killer Queen* - Queen
*Keep It Gay* - The Producers
*Let's Get It On* - Marvin Gaye
*Fade Into You* - Mazzy Star
*Someone New* - Hozier
*El Camino* - Amos Lee
*Grey In L.A.* - Loudon Wainwright III
*Boys With Girlfriends* - Meiko
*Someday* - Alan Jackson
*Manhattan* - Sara Bareilles
*Sparks* - Coldplay
*I Hope You Dance* - Lee Ann Womack
*My California* - Beth Hart

*Manhattan* - Ella Fitzgerald
*Hello Sunshine* - MoZella
*I'm In Love Again* - MoZella

# Books By T.K. Leigh

## The Beautiful Mess Series
**A Beautiful Mess**
**A Tragic Wreck**
**Gorgeous Chaos**

## The Deception Duet
**Chasing The Dragon**
**Slaying The Dragon**

## Stand Alone Titles
**Heart Of Light**
**Heart Of Marley**
**The Other Side Of Someday**

For more information on any of these titles, please visit
T.K.'s website:
www.tkleighauthor.com

# Acknowledgements

I started writing this book back in Spring of 2014. My editor was working on *Gorgeous Chaos* and I was close to finishing my rough draft of *Heart of Light*. Up until that time, all I had written were emotionally heavy romantic suspense stories. I love suspense, don't get me wrong, but I wanted to be able to spread my wings and write more than just romantic suspense.

Of course, as happens, other books got in the way of my ability to work on this one. *Heart Of Light* spawned a companion novel, *Heart Of Marley*. Then I switched gears to write my Deception Duet. But this cute, fun, sweet romance about a girl who leaves home for the first time and enters the dating jungle of LA was in the back of my mind even when I was working on other projects. Finally, after publishing *Slaying The Dragon*, the second book in my Deception Duet, I was able to return to this story and give it the attention it needed.

This book was something completely different and new for me. Writing a romantic comedy is vastly different than writing a romantic suspense. Sure, I didn't have half a dozen white boards scattered around my office, making sure all the pieces connected to the big convoluted puzzle I had concocted to keep the reader on edge. Instead, I was charged with the daunting task of injecting humor into a story, something I had only had to do sporadically up until now.

The old adage that you write what you know is absolutely true. While this is certainly a piece of fiction, the humor is real. I pulled from conversations I've had with the people in my life, most notably my own North Carolina transplant husband. Since the idea for this book came into being, I had a readily accessible notebook on me at all times, ready to capture whatever snarky or country humor spilled out of his mouth. So Stan, thanks for your folksy sayings. You're the most amazing support system a girl could ever ask for. Thanks for everything you've done to support me in releasing these past eight books. And I'm sure you'll be there to support me for the next eight, and there after, good lord willing and the creek don't rise. (See what I did there?)

Next, I need to thank my fabulous group of beta readers for always dropping whatever they're currently reading to tackle my book and send me feedback pretty much overnight. Thanks for always being there for me... Lynne, Sylvia, Melissa, Karen, Stacy, Karen, Natalie, Victoria, and the other Stacy.

Also a big thanks to the only editor I'll ever allow to touch my babies, Kim Young. I'm so glad we share a brain and that you're able to figure out what I meant when my brain didn't. Your talent knows no bounds.

Thanks, as always, to my admins who help me manage my social media presence: Melissa, Victoria, Lea, and Joelle — you girls are my rockstars.

I wouldn't be where I am today without my ever growing group of women who volunteer their precious time to help spread the word about my books online and on the street. When I first started this book adventure, I had no idea what a street team was. I'm glad I found out. My angels aren't just my street team.

They're some of the best friends I have. My advisors. My shoulders to cry (bitch) on. My support group. Everyone needs a street team, even if they're not an author.

A special shout out to my #BurnhamBitches. You girls make me smile every day and I'm so glad to be able to call you all my friends.

Last but not least, thank you to YOU, my readers. Thank you for taking a risk on an indie author who, just three years ago, had absolutely no idea what she was doing. Thank you for picking up that first book of mine and joining me on this journey. And for those who are just finding me, welcome! Thanks for taking a risk on me. I hope you have all enjoyed this ride I took you on. I'm not done yet. I had so much fun writing this first romantic comedy, I'll be doing it again, say in 2018 perhaps?

To the moon and back, y'all…

~T.K.

# ABOUT THE AUTHOR

T.K. Leigh, otherwise known as Tracy Leigh Kellam, is a *USA Today* Bestselling author of the Beautiful Mess series, in addition to several other works. Originally from New England, she now resides in sunny Southern California with her husband, dog, and three cats, all of which she has rescued (including the husband). In late 2015, she gave birth to her first (and only) baby. When she's not planted in front of her computer, writing away, she can be found training for her next marathon (of which she has run over fifteen fulls and far too many halfs to recall) or humming *The Imperial March* from *Star Wars* to her daughter, who giggles every time she hears it.

T.K. Leigh is represented by Jane Dystel of Dystel & Goderich Literary Management. All publishing inquiries, including audio, foreign, and film rights, should be directed to her.

32490575R00211

Made in the USA
Middletown, DE
06 June 2016